The Secret Room

Walter Spence

Published by Full Moon Publications

PRINT VERSION
ISBN 13: 9780985483722
ISBN: 0985483725

Cover Photo: © Lario Tus

Walter's Photo: © Deborah M. Spence

For Debbie, who believed.

"In each of us there is another whom we do not know." *Carl Jung*

The first coffee of the day sits like hot mercury in my stomach long after I leave the Warming Hut, my head down, my shoulders hunched. It's cold. Or perhaps I should say colder than usual for San Francisco during this time of year.

A stiff wind blows my way from the nearby shoreline as I navigate the length of the Promenade. It whips my skirt against my bare thighs, a familiar sting. I keep walking.

In the distance I spy the length of the Golden Gate Bridge, rising from a sea of fog as it leaps across the bay. Its orange vermillion struts stand out in sharp contrast against the cloud it appears to rest on, as though the sky has fallen to Earth. I neither stop nor pause.

Shortly thereafter, I continue past the parking lot on my way to the east sidewalk. As I do, I look up into the face of Joseph Strauss's statue, posed atop its white circular pedestal as though the somber gentleman has been waiting for me.

Then, suddenly, I hear them again. Footsteps. Still some distance behind me, but just a bit louder, just a little closer.

My name is Marie Abigail St. Claire, and I have fifteen minutes to live.

I was born on a Sunday. I know this because my mother told me the story of how she, a long time Southern Baptist, had been occupying the rearmost pew during worship services when her water broke. I tease her here, because the real reason she'd been sitting in the back was because, at that point in Mother's pregnancy, I'd been putting so much pressure on her bladder that she didn't feel safe being more than half a dozen steps from the nearest restroom. According to her, my father—who normally did not attend church services, but had showed up that day— had slipped in the veritable pool of amniotic fluid puddled on the floor as he stood to help her up, consequently banging his head so hard on the back of the pew, he almost blacked out.

The date was December 7, 1975, a caboose panting at the rear end of a freight train's worth of female pulchritude who graced us with their presence that year: Drew Barrymore, Eva Longoria, Fergie, Christina Hendricks, Charlize Theron, and Kate Winslet, not to mention Milla Jovovich. Oh, and Angelina Jolie (can't forget her). Also one of the Spice Girls. I can never remember which one, though.

Not to minimize those future obsessions of TMZ fans everywhere, but a few other things did happen that year. Charlie Chaplin was knighted by Queen Elizabeth. Bill Gates founded Microsoft. The SS Edmund Fitzgerald sank (I'm fairly certain those last two were unrelated). John Wooden coached UCLA to its tenth national championship, and Muhammad Ali defeated Joe Frazier at the 'Thrilla in Manila'. The Rocky Horror Show opened on Broadway, followed later in the year by the cinematic release of the Rocky Horror Picture Show. George Carlin hosted the premiere of Saturday Night Live, and Peter Gabriel left Genesis, to be replaced by drummer Phil Collins. Then Thornton Wilder died, on the same day I was born. (Again, I believe, an unrelated event.)

Oh, and Saigon fell, ending the Vietnam War.

I take pains to mention that last item because my father served in Vietnam. Two tours, both as a volunteer. He once told me that he hadn't been particularly patriotic, he'd simply enjoyed eating regularly (my mother and father had been born on opposite sides of the tracks). When they shipped Dad out the second time from Fort Bragg, that same afternoon my mother loaded her suitcase and her infant daughter (my sister Bethany), into Dad's old Buick LeSabre with its stereo 8-track tape player to drive halfway across the state to Sneadsville, where her parents had been living since they were newborns themselves: my grandfather Roland Sneads and my grandmother Pearl, along with a wide assortment of aunts, uncles, and numerous cousins of varying degrees.

Then, about a year later as it was told to me, Dad showed up with no warning right out of the blue, knocking on our front door like a Jehovah's Witness. Bethany didn't recognize him of course, so when he reached down to pick her up, she screamed bloody murder and ran back inside the house just as Mother stepped out of the back bedroom, a loaded shotgun in her hands. To hear my father tell it, she didn't lower the barrel right away either. Eventually she did, though, and Dad moved back in, having been honorably discharged from the Army.

And according to the finger-counters in the family (which is to say, pretty much everyone) my conception probably occurred sometime during that week, maybe even that very same night.

A month or so later, Saigon fell.

Dad got a job about a week following his return, working as a deliveryman at the Sneadsville Fruit and Produce Company, which was just a short walk from our house at 362 Berry Street in East End. I hadn't realized, until I started going to school, that we had been living on 'the other side of the tracks'. But the rent was cheap (i.e., free), since the house we were living in belonged to Grandma Pearl. Which annoyed Grandpa Roland, as prior to that he'd been depending on that income to make the bank payments on his Ford F-150. But with Mother being the only girl out of Grandma's six children (not to mention the youngest), that was one argument Grandpa lost.

Mother made up a bit for that, staying at home to take care of us while doing cut rate bookkeeping for Grandpa's grocery store, with the promise of a larger paycheck once the economy improved.

This might put the old man in somewhat of a dim light, but he wasn't really a bad fellow. I was once told that it had been my Grandfather who got Daddy his job, due to Marvin Sneads (the owner of Sneadsville Fruit and Produce) being his first cousin. Those two had grown up together, hunting as children for tadpoles in Newcomb's Creek, a muddy rivulet feeding the infamous Snead's Pond, then later working side by side priming tobacco for old Henry Beaumont, who—according to local legend—was so tight with a dollar he never owned a tractor, instead using a mule to pull both his plow and his antique tobacco sled.

It will assist your understanding of our particular family dynamic to know that, unlike my sister (who trailed after Mother like the hem of a wedding gown from the day she learned to walk), I was a Daddy's girl from the beginning. This parsing of roles might have been due, at least in part, to my father's absence during Bethany's early formative years, though they always seemed to get along well enough.

One story my Poppa enjoyed sharing was how one night, while we were all sitting in the living room watching television, Bethany curled up next to Mother on the sofa and me perched as usual atop my father's lap, I suddenly made the announcement that Daddy and I were going to get married when I grew up.

After some chuckling from the adults, my father then asked what would become of my mother. According to him, I looked over at her and said in a voice redolent with compassion, "She can stay too, I guess."

I don't remember any of that. What I do remember is how Mother always seemed to prefer my sister's company over mine from my earliest memories, which led me to wonder whether that story might have been Dad's way of explaining an obvious favoritism. A favoritism which grew even more pronounced and exaggerated after my father disappeared.

But that was much later.

Truth is, like most folks, I have few memories of my toddler years. Though there is one which remains strong, even to this day, as if etched in metal.

It was a Saturday evening, and our parents had gone to the VFW Dance. Our grandparents must have been unavailable that night, because Mother had hired a neighborhood teenager to watch us, a girl who would babysit us if Grandpa and Grandma were busy, right up until she went away to college (at Duke University, no less). I have never forgotten her. Her name was Barbie Evans, and she truly could have doubled for one of those busty blonde icons from Mattel, being the kind of girl who, walking down a Main Street sidewalk in a tank top and cutoffs, could have slowed traffic to a crawl. I heard years later that she married into wealth (one of the Durham Prince family), returning afterwards to her hometown only rarely, like when one of her high school girlfriends got married or some such.

I could not have been much more than three when the following events occurred. About an hour after our parents left for the VFW dance a storm came up, accompanied by a wind strong enough to rip the eye screw latch out of the sill and bang the screen door nonstop against the outside wall. I had curled up with my sister in Dad's recliner while listening to the thunder rumble overhead in electric blue waves as flashes of lightning stung the air like ozone. Part of our terror we absorbed from Barb, who got more and more nervous as the storm grew worse, jerking upright in her seat whenever a particularly loud crash shook the house.

Then the lights went out.

Bethany and I screamed, and it took Barb several minutes to calm us down. As soon as she did, she got on the phone which, unlike the lights, was still working.

"Is the power out there, too?" I heard her say in a rush. "No? Well then, could you give me a hand with these kids and help bring them over? I can't carry both of them by myself, and I don't want to leave one behind." A pause. "I'll leave a note for their parents, okay?" Another pause. "All right. Please hurry."

She returned to the sofa, then waved us over. We scrambled out of the Lazy Boy and huddled on either side of her. Rain beat down on the roof like a flaming red drumroll as the wind roared like a train overhead. Finally someone started pounding on the front door and Barb flew to answer it.

"I'll take her," Barb said breathlessly as she came back into the room while pointing at my sister. "You get the other one."

"I can carry both," a male voice replied.

"Not while keeping the two of them under your umbrella and dry, you can't," Barb said. "Bethany's older, but she's a stick and her sister's still carrying a lot of baby fat, so get her if you would please."

I heard him grunt an acknowledgment as he walked in, his head barely clearing the top of the doorway. He reminded me of Daddy, a broad-shouldered man with a thick head of hair hanging down over his forehead, half covering his face. He reached down and hoisted me up with his left arm, the right holding an umbrella as it dripped water on the floor. I caught the strong bass note of a familiar scent. Old Spice.

"You go first," he told Barb. "That way if you have any problems getting back, I'll see."

She nodded, Bethany a slim bundle in her arms, the blanket from the couch covering both of their heads. "Cut through Margery Beaumont's backyard, it'll save time," she told him. He nodded while following her to the front door.

I remember the rain. It fell in thick grey sheets, pounding on the front porch's tin roof so loudly it hurt my ears.

The man carrying me squinted as he looked over my head. "Lights are still on," he said. "Get going. I'll be right behind you."

I watched with him as Barb made a sudden dash down the porch steps, running like a deer as her bare feet splashed through the innumerable puddles. "Where the hell are your goddamned shoes?" he yelled after her, then looked down at me. "Oops. Um, sorry."

I made no reply, instead burrowing my face into the hot moist space between his neck and shoulder.

"Don't worry," he said, patting my back with a hand as broad and flat as a frying pan. "I'll keep the umbrella over your head. Just close your eyes, and we'll be high and dry in no time."

He leaped down from the porch into the downpour and had time to take two steps.

Then the world exploded.

I screamed right into his ear. It seemed for all the world as if the biggest light bulb in the universe had blown up right in front of my face with a white flash redolent of burnt sugar, followed by a thunderclap so loud I must have gone deaf, because he was off like a racehorse yelling words I couldn't make out, the umbrella dangling broken and useless in his right hand. At some point he must have dropped it, because I remember the sensation of both of his arms around me. It felt as though I was standing under a lukewarm shower as the rain soaked me from head to toe. I never felt in danger of being dropped, though. He held me so tight I could hardly breathe, crushing me to his chest while he ran.

When we got to their house, Barb found some towels and something dry for us to wear. The man, whom she kept calling Damien, excused himself, red-faced, when she began stripping us out of our soaking wet pajamas. By that time I could hear again.

The storm finally passed, and Barb made us some soda crackers with peanut butter. Mother finally showed up with Dad around midnight or so, waking us as they carried Bethany and me to the car, and then home.

Even without the trauma, I could never have forgotten that night, since our front yard hosted a permanent reminder of it. Our enormous oak tree, with its spare tire swing standing less than ten feet from the front steps, had been literally split in half by the lightning bolt that had struck it.

Eight years later, Dad walked down those very same steps and never came back.

⁂

The wind picks up as I approach the entryway to the east sidewalk. I've been walking in a daze for what feels like hours, barely aware of my surroundings. It's been years since I last set foot on the Golden Gate Bridge, and never this early, which explains my surprise as a uniformed figure comes into focus near the gate. A Bridge Authority security guard, grizzled and grey, eyes fixated on me to the exclusion of all else, his arms folded in suspicion, or perhaps just against the cold. I approach him.

"Pardon me, sir," I say to him in one of my special voices, breathy and a bit husky, instinctively pitched to light up those particular neurons in the male brain activated by a (well, relatively) young female in need of assistance. "I can't be sure, but I think someone's following me."

His response is both immediate and predictable. The spine straightens, the chest puffs out, the belly is sucked in. "Really?" He looks over my head. I slump a bit to make it easier, since he's not very tall. "I don't see anybody," he says as he peers over my shoulder.

I shrug and try to make myself smaller still. "I heard the footsteps. They were quite a ways back, though. I *could* have been imagining it, I suppose . . ."

His jaw tightens, and I know I have him now. "Don't you worry. Go ahead, and if anyone who even thinks about looking suspicious comes along, I'll have a word with him."

I mouth a thank you as I go by. He nods and focuses his glare south, brow furrowed as he squints into the misty gloom.

Even this early on a Sunday, one would expect to be overwhelmed by the noise from passing traffic, but in my distracted state all I can hear is the slapping of my sandals on the concrete, no more mysterious footsteps.

As I make my way down the sidewalk, I allow my hand to slide along the handrail, the cold metal mottled with dew, on which someone has printed in large block letters the words 'BEST FRIENDS FOREVER', followed by a heart. Everything else, the canary yellow aura of traffic thrumming beside me, the distant steel beams and thick cables overhead, is muffled and obscured by a wall of white as thick as a Smoky Mountains blizzard.

The world is a snow globe, and I am alone.

My hidden misery, briefly squelched by the sight of the guard, rises in my belly once again. I pick up my pace.

Ten minutes later I reach the midpoint where the suspension cables droop to their nadir, and I turn to face San Francisco. Fog has settled over the distant shoreline like a snowdrift, and I cannot see the city. I position myself as best I can so that (in my mind's eye) I am facing my husband's beloved 'Painted Lady', before giving voice to the swollen ache filling my chest like an infection.

"YOU LIED TO ME!" I scream. My vocal cords protest against the unaccustomed strain as pain slices the inside of my throat, like a maniac's blade in a slasher flick.

"YOU LIED TO ME!" I cry, again and again, the words glowing with the bright crisp halo of a halogen bulb. Finally, exhausted, I choke out my last words in a hoarse beige whisper.

"You promised me I would die first."

Then, with a quick, sudden motion, I slip over the rail.

Before leaving home I had done some quick research. The deck is approximately two hundred and forty-five feet above the bay. It takes a falling body about four seconds to hit the water at a speed of around seventy-five miles an hour. Most jumpers die from impact trauma, though there are the rare few who survive the initial fall and subsequently drown, or die of hypothermia in the frigid waters.

The fog parts as I descend. I feel as though I am skydiving, dropping through a cloud. My skirt flaps in the rushing air like a sail as I plummet through the mist, feet first, and I suppress the absurd impulse to push it back down over my hips. Waves, white-capped and surging, rise rapidly to greet me.

I once read an article which claimed that many jumpers don't actually perish due to impact, dying instead from heart failure before they reach the ground. But either that is not the case, or a longer fall is required. Because, speaking from experience, I can tell you this isn't true.

You remain conscious.

All the way down . . .

⎯✠⎯

At first I didn't realize Daddy was gone. One would think that a seismic event such as the disappearance of a parent would leave its mark in the air, due to the sudden vacuum. But it didn't.

Our mother had dinner on the table at the usual time, a mix of my sister's and my favorites. When Mother started eating right after the two of us took our seats, and our father had yet to show up to take his usual place at the head of the table, Bethany and I looked at one another, eyebrows raised.

I should have known something was wrong right then. Mother always required that we say grace before we could eat. Occasionally she made me do it, or my sister would volunteer. But my stomach was growling like a cat warning that its hindquarters were not to be trifled with, so I followed Mother's example and dug in. It wouldn't have been the first time Dad had worked late and missed dinner, after all.

This all happened just after New Year's, 1986, halfway through my sixth grade year. With my birthday coming so late, I should have been a grade behind, but Mother must have pulled a few strings to get me into school early. Either that or she'd simply lied about my age in order to get me out of the house. I had turned eleven just the month before, with Dad making a big deal out of my birthday, just as he always did. I'd once heard him tell Mother that it wasn't fair to combine it and Christmas, the two being so close together and all, so he always went out of his way to make the anniversary of my arrival into the world special.

When it came time for *The A Team* and Dad still hadn't shown up, that's when I really started to worry. It was our favorite show. The two of us always sat together in front of the television, me burrowed into the warm place between his arm and his side while swapping taglines—either my favorite, "I pity da fool!", or my father's favorite, "I love it when a plan comes together!"—while my sister looked on; not scornfully but in utter

9

confusion, while Mother would occasionally mutter something like, "Tom and Jerry for boys acting like men."

But since it wasn't unknown for Dad to work the rare double shift, neither my sister nor I said anything, and instead of watching *The A Team* exchange endless rounds of automatic weapons fire with bullets that rarely hit anything, I pouted while Mother and Bethany watched a rerun of *Little House on the Prairie*. Afterwards, as I lay awake in bed listening for the rattle of the front door opening. I imagined my father at the warehouse, tied up by robbers in the back room, while I phoned Hannibal Smith, later meeting up with the team in the parking lot to accompany them on the rescue mission.

At some point, while bantering with Mr. T, I fell asleep.

When I woke up, I looked at my clock. Nine a.m. Good God, I had overslept and now I was late for school! I raced through my morning routine, flung on my clothes, and ran into a living room full of my mother's family.

I looked from one to the other. Bethany, a gawky thirteen, was still in her pajamas. Head lowered, she stared at me from underneath her mile-long bangs.

I marched up to her. Everyone stared at me, but no one spoke.

"What's wrong?" I demanded of my sister. To this day, I cannot tell you why she was the one I asked, the sole non-adult in the room. Bethany looked away from me and toward Mother.

I turned as well. A frozen panic had nailed me to the floor, and I couldn't move.

"Mom?" I asked. "Where's Dad?"

There were no tears, no displays of crying or misery. My mother stepped away from the fireplace mantle, crossed the room, then crouched down in front of me, meeting my eyes and holding my gaze.

"Your father has left us," she said.

Now not only could I not move, I couldn't breathe either. "What?"

"He has abandoned his family," she said, her voice as clipped and precise as a metronome. "He has abandoned Bethany. He has abandoned his wife." She leaned forwards, with a still unblinking stare. "He has abandoned *you*."

For what felt like an eternity, I could not speak. And when I did finally break the silence, it was to ask one simple question. "What did you do?"

My mother's face did not change, her expression remained stolid.

Then she slapped me. Hard.

"Go to your room," she said, her eyes still wide and fixed.

With throat clenched and my eyes burning, I did as I was told.

⚜

I lay back, eyes closed, held firmly in place by the smothering comfort of my husband's weight. His thrusts rocked me forward and back while I sighed, a prolonged expulsion of comfort while losing myself in the oh-so-familiar motions. A warm liquid rush, sweet as velveteen honey, spiraled upwards into and throughout the furthest reaches of my belly. I stretched like a tabby waking from its nap, then wrapped my limbs around him, my arms encircling his neck to pull him close as my legs coiled around his. Hooking my heels against the backs of his thighs, I hissed as I strained to pull him deeper inside me.

Then he screamed.

My eyes flew open and I stared, muscles frozen, into the pale watery eyes of a stranger.

Then *I* screamed.

He scuttled away from me like a crab, falling to the floor with a bone-cracking *thump*. I stared down at him from atop the cold metal table I was sprawled on, wearing not a stitch of clothing. I rolled away as well, but in the opposite direction, desperately—not to mention instinctively—trying to cover my nudity with my hands.

He was younger than Julius, a whip-thin ferret of a man. His trousers and briefs, puddled around his ankles, preventing him from standing. His eyes, wide and wild, rolled in his head as he sputtered. "You!—I—"

I backed away on my hands and knees, my only thought to get as far away from him as was humanly possible.

There, to my left, an open door. I rose to my feet, then circled, keeping the stranger in front of me as I retreated to what appeared to be the room's only exit. He stared at me, his face contorted with pure terror.

Then I bumped into something.

I looked over my shoulder, a second scream already working its way up my throat. Another man stood just behind me, blocking the doorway. He wore a

11

white lab coat, unbuttoned, over a blue chambray shirt and dust-colored khakis. His eyes flicked between me and the sputtering man on the floor.

"What the hell?" the newcomer asked, as if confused.

The first man let go of his trousers long enough to point a trembling finger in my direction. "Lester! She!—That is—"

'Lester' glared at each of us in turn, then shook his head as he regarded the partially-clad man. "Jesus Christ on a pogo stick, Sid! Seriously?!"

'Sid' scrambled to his feet, still struggling with his pants. "Lester, she was dead! She was fucking *dead*!"

Lester slid his arms around me, up high, avoiding my breasts, and—again, instinctively—I took half a step backwards into his protective embrace. "Sid, will you please calm the fuck down!" he said.

Then his left arm rose to clamp across my throat, shutting off my air flow. The rough cloth of his sleeve viciously pinched a fold of my skin, bring tears to my eyes. I tried to gasp, but nothing came out.

"She'll be dead for real soon enough," Lester said with a grunt, tightening his grip.

I clawed at him, searching for his eyes as I fought desperately to breathe. He clasped his hands together for increased leverage as I started kicking backwards, lifting me off my feet. I hung there, suspended by his left arm, as though dangling from a hangman's noose. He twisted sideways to protect his crotch. "Sid, would you pull your goddamned pants up and give me a hand?" he snapped.

Unable to reach his face, or land a solid blow with the heels of my feet, I kicked outwards, connecting with a nearby tray table covered by a white cloth. It flipped over, its contents exploding like a mirror on the floor. Bright winking implements, a surgeon's toolbox—some sleek as razors, others jagged as saws—rang like prismatic wind chimes as they bounced over the porcelain tiles.

Oh, my God, I thought with a liquid sense of horror while watching the bright turmeric flash of the blades scatter across the room, *Those were for me. Those were meant for* me!

Snatching at my ankles, Sid finally managed to grab hold of one, then the other, and held both tight. Little lights, sharp with a sulfurous bite, burned like Fourth of July sparklers in the growing black. Vision blurring, I saw Sid look over and past me. His eyes grew wide again. "Les!"

Then something hit me from behind.

Or rather, something hit Lester. Slamming through his body into mine, the impact propelled us both across the room. Flashbulbs like roman candles went off as my head banged against the opposite wall. Then a warm wet wave of something sticky splashed over me.

As it did, I heard Lester screaming. I forced my eyes shut, then blindfolded myself with my arms. A moment later his cries ceased, only to be replaced by Sid's as my erstwhile rapist screamed. "No, no, no, wait! WAIT!", followed by a choking sound, as though he was drowning.

Then there was no sound at all.

I huddled into a ball on the ice cold tiles, waiting for what must surely now be my turn. Soft footsteps padded closer, like shadows sliding down a wall, and a voice whispered, "Abby?"

I opened my eyes a slit. Blood. Oh, my God, so much blood. It covered me, as well as the floor in front of me. Some of it had soaked my hair. I looked up.

A man crouched down in front of me. Well, recently a man, not long since a boy. His jade green eyes peered at me through a shank of coal black hair as he regarded me with clinical detachment. He looked young enough to be rushing a fraternity, save for one vivid detail: a thin white line running down his left cheek like a dueling scar.

"Abby?" he repeated.

I stared at his outstretched hand, encased in a crimson glove almost to his elbow. "Yes?" I somehow managed.

Then he smiled, as if at some secret joke.

"Come with me if you want to live," he said.

⚞⚟

I could not move, could not think. Instead I stared dumbly at his fingers, still dripping blood. He sighed with impatience, then grasped me firmly by my upper arms and lifted me to my feet. Gooseflesh flowed in a wave over my bare skin. The air in the room was absolutely frigid, as were the ceramic tiles underfoot, a checkerboard series of black and white squares, except for the splashes of blood sprayed over the floor like a Jackson Pollock pastiche created by Jack the Ripper. In the far corner two familiar bodies lay, broken and mangled almost beyond recognition. I tried to breathe, but all I could manage were tiny puffs of air.

The man/boy released me, then paused, as if reassuring himself I could stand on my own. When I didn't immediately collapse, he stepped away. I watched as he washed his hands and arms in a metallic farmhouse sink before returning to me, a wet sponge in hand. He wiped at my face and hair, removing the worst of the blood, then ransacked through various drawers and cabinets, returning with a white lab coat similar to the now-deceased Lester's. I started when he tried to move behind me, retreating and pressing my back against the wall, limbs shaking as the adrenaline coursing through my veins wore thin.

He sighed through his nose, a brusque airstream of frustration. "I know you're frightened," he said, briefly acknowledging with his eyes the two corpses on the opposite end of the room. "I get that. But there may be more of them on the way, and while I doubt they'd pose much of a threat to me, I can't promise the same where you're concerned. And since I cannot risk anything happening to you," he said as he gestured with the coat, "take this and put it on." A pause. "Now."

I stared at the garment he waved in front of me like a bullfighter's *muleta*. He sighed yet again, then pulled me away from the wall before twisting my arms through the coat's sleeves. I resisted, though only for a moment. Then the shock settled in and I relaxed, unresisting and pliant in his hands, allowing him to take control.

There were no shoes (Where *were* my clothes?), so after covering my nakedness, he took me by the arm and escorted me out, half leading, half carrying me along a utilitarian hallway, then down a flight of concrete steps edged with yellow caution paint. A metal door, its sole window a small pane of glass reinforced with a wire grid, greeted us at the bottom of the stairwell. The young man shouldered his way through it, now almost completely supporting me. I felt the cold, salty bite of gritty concrete on the soles of my bare feet as he led me outside into the shadows between two distant streetlights. Nighttime. We had just emerged from an ancient brick building, its filthy outer walls a sharp contrast to its well-scrubbed interior. Dilapidated four and five story buildings lined the street in front of sidewalks crowded with the prone bodies of derelicts, the kind of people Warren often referred to as 'urban campers'. A small group of distant shadowy figures turned to stare in our direction. I looked up and saw a street sign. O'Farrell. We were in the Tenderloin.

The young gentleman/murderer led me down the steps. No one approached us, but still I kept my head down, resisting my guide only once in order to dodge a woman's blue pump, its heel broken, a crushed cigarette butt visible in the toe.

We walked alongside a brick wall, painted yellow and covered with graffiti in bright, primary colors, punctuated by the graphic form of a nude woman with a skull for a face and red flames for hair. A broken desk chair lay propped on two of its three remaining legs next to a barred doorway. A black Mercedes idled nearby. The man led me to it.

Next to the passenger's door leaned an attractive blonde woman, a vision out of a Raymond Chandler novel. A half-smoked cigarette rested in the V of her fingers. I stared at her, dumbfounded. From the neck down she reminded me of me, generous of bust and hip. But there the resemblance ended. I focused on what had to be one of the tiniest waists I'd ever seen on a fully-grown female. Twenty-one inches, if that. She could have been a body double for Anna Nicole Smith.

"I seem to recall saying that it would be best if you remained in the car, Constance," my walking crutch told the woman (His mother?), the formality of his diction out of place with his obvious youth.

To my surprise, she lowered her head submissively. "Yes, sir, you did. But you also told me not to smoke in it, and after your little chat with the neighbors," she said, indicating the shadowy figures with a toss of her head, "none of them seemed inclined to make a nuisance of themselves. So I figured it'd be okay." She dropped the cigarette butt, then ground it out with the toe of her stiletto before stepping forward. "This her?"

"Yes," he said, allowing 'Constance' to examine me while he glared at the distant forms, who muttered quietly to one another as they continued to withdraw.

The woman pulled the coat I wore open, then gasped. "She's naked. And—good Lord—her whole right side is black and blue." She looked at the man/boy. "Did you do that?"

What struck me about her question was the complete lack of shock in it, as though she had just asked her companion for the time. "She was like that when I found her," he said as he opened the car's right rear door. "Help her in."

As Constance took hold of my arm, I pulled back and turned to the man. "Who—who are you?" I finally managed to stammer.

He returned my gaze with a cool stare. "You can call me Mordant," he said. "Now, inside." A brief pause. "Please. Constance, get in with her."

"Not just yet," the woman, a teenager's fantasy MILF, said. She reached into her pocket to pull out an electronic car key, then thumbed it to open the trunk."

"I assume the blood isn't hers either?" she said as she circled back, a plastic blue tarp in her hand. She laid it over the backseat, then took my arm.

I thought again about resisting. After all, I didn't know either of them from Adam's house cat. What if they were taking me someplace worse?

But when I finally coaxed my lower half into motion, the pain hit, as though someone had drawn a hacksaw over my chest. Broken ribs, maybe?

Not going to get far on your own if that's the case. And even if you made a break for it, how far could you run? You can barely stand on your own two feet as it is.

As I bent my knees while trying to inch backwards into the Mercedes, I noticed the man who called himself Mordant stiffen, his head snapping from side to side, nostrils flaring as he stared into the dark spaces over the street lights.

Constance must have noticed as well, because I felt her turn away from me. "What is it, sir?"

The 'sir' again. And not just the word, but the inflection that came with it. A very familiar one, mixing the tones of an underling with another usage I was all too familiar with, where the word always came capitalized.

"Sir?!" A hint of panic now in her voice.

The man's teeth ground together. And I don't mean just the sight of his jaw muscles clenching. I could actually *hear* the molars grinding one against the other.

"Take her back to the house," he said as he swiveled in place, looking up as though tracking something.

But what could he possibly be looking up at? The rooftops?

Mordant reached past the blonde and pushed me into the Mercedes. I cried out, in fear as well as in pain, just as he slammed my door before taking Constance by the arm. He led her around the car, then opened the driver's door and shoved her behind the wheel. "We're splitting up?" she sputtered.

"Don't worry," he said. "No one will follow you. I'll see to it."

Constance gave a quick nod and started the car.

"Don't stop until you get there," he told her. "If there's any trouble on the way, just keep going. I'll be right with you all the while."

The absurdity of his remark struck me dumb as he shut the door and waved us forward. How in God's name was he going to keep up with us on foot?

Then Constance floored the gas pedal, flinging me from one side of the car to the other as she peeled rubber. I twisted to look back as we sped away.

But Mordant had disappeared.

⊣⊟⊢

Bethany and I never heard from our father again. Not so much as a phone call, not even a letter. Which in itself was odd enough. Certainly we weren't the only kids in our school whose parents had broken up, not even the only ones in our church. But this felt different. Other children, to hear them talk, knew (or at least suspected) why their folks split up, the typical culprits being money, infidelity, even violence. By contrast we never got a truly straight answer from anyone, friends and family alike, about what had driven our father away (my version) or caused him to leave (Bethany's). Mother's responses, whenever one of us broached the subject, typically varied from an icy stare without words (the usual) to the rare damp-eyed wince, like a paper cut to the heart. The rest of the family wouldn't even acknowledge our queries, instead simply playing deaf and/or dumb.

When the thing happened with my sister, Daddy had been gone for close to eleven months. After nearly a year of silence from our family, his continuing absence had worn us down (at least publicly) and we'd stopped asking questions, at least of the adults. In private, though, we continued to whisper and speculate, sometimes into the early morning hours, though less often the more time passed by.

The steadily yawning distance between my mother and me continued to grow, although never to the extent I lost all hope of one day winning back her affection. During the year following Dad's vanishing act, she started devoting more and more of her free time to church. We had always spent Sunday mornings there, Bethany and I taking the church bus to Sunday School while our parents joined us later for morning worship services. Now the three of us rode together, with Mother attending the adult classes. A few months later even this proved insufficient, and soon my sister and I found ourselves shifting restlessly in place during evening services amongst a congregation consisting primarily of the elderly membership, supervened in short order by Wednesday evening services attended only by the truly hardcore.

Mother's newborn pietistic fervor wasn't limited to the social. A crucifix, instead of a cross, hung now from her neck on a daily basis. Iconic paintings featuring Jesus in various biblical scenarios hung like tapestries from the walls. Even our entertainments were affected, with television strictly rationed, limited to an hour a night, which Mother rarely watched with us even then. Instead she would sit at the kitchen table with its red and white checked vinyl tablecloth, her Bible open, her lips moving as she read.

And as the year progressed, much to my surprise, Bethany began to mimic her. My sister's skirts—which prior to Daddy's disappearance she had tugged up high while waiting for the school bus, to show off her legs—now began migrating lower, finishing to just below her kneecaps, as previously snug T-shirts were slowly replaced by loose-fitting, high buttoned blouses with long sleeves. Mother noted this with approval, and on Bethany's fourteenth birthday she gave her a silver cross, which my sister put on and never afterwards took off, even after the 'Incident'.

Not that I put all of Bethany's diminished fashion sense down to our mother's pullulated interest in God, though. My sister had hit a prolonged growth spurt, causing her to tower over her classmates, boys and girls alike. At school I sometimes caught sight of her wandering the hallways like an embarrassed giraffe, her shoulders typically hunched and rounded, her waist-length hair hanging down either side of her face like blinders as she made her way from one class to another.

Not long after we became Wednesday night fixtures at Sneadsville First Baptist Church, Mother brought home two Bibles and wordlessly handed one to each of us. They were white, the covers made from something called 'leatherette', which, as far as I could tell, was just another word for 'fake leather'. I put mine in the bottom drawer of my nightstand, where over time it accumulated a respectable layer of dust. Bethany's, however, saw great use, so much so that after a while the pages began to fall out of the cheap binding.

So I was all the more surprised when I came home after visiting a friend one Saturday while Mother was attending some obscure church function and walked through the door of the bedroom I shared with my sister to find her sprawled on her bed making out like a teenager in the opening shot of a horror movie with her best friend, Karen.

I stood in the doorway, mouth agape, as I took in the squirming tangle of limbs. They didn't notice me (not at first), but when they did, they sprang apart like two positively-charged magnets.

Bethany yanked her blouse down where Karen's hand had been under it as her best friend flew out the door with neither word nor glance.

With the breeze of Karen's exit still savory and cool on my cheeks after I'd turned, gaping, to follow her exit, twin hands grabbed me by the arm and snatched me around. My sister stared at me, wild-eyed and terrified, her hair mussed, her nails digging into my flesh as she babbled, repeating herself like an echo, her face red and blotchy as tears flowed down her cheeks. "Please don't tell Momma, please don't tell Momma . . ."

And as I listened to her blubber, I felt an unfamiliar sensation. A sense of power.

"Please, Abby? Please?" Bethany pleaded, hyperventilating as though she was about to have a heart attack.

Don't misunderstand me. I loved my sister. But we were also rivals for our mother's attention and approval, with Bethany holding a comfortable lead. And I knew that what I had just witnessed could very well change that. And, for a moment, I considered telling.

But I couldn't betray my sister. Not like that.

So when I felt like I could think straight again, I nodded my head. "I won't say anything."

Her fingers tightened on my arm, as though trying to squeeze the blood out of my fingertips. "Promise!?"

I slashed my finger over my heart. "Cross my heart."

"And hope to die?"

I paused, then nodded solemnly. "And hope to die."

And I kept that promise.

Even to this day.

I couldn't help noticing later at school that Karen kept trying to get Bethany off alone to talk. My sister would listen, but always with her face turned away. And as the days went by, Karen started getting frustrated, then angry, then acted like she was begging. Not long after that, Bethany started avoiding her, instead hanging out more and more with her new friends from the Bible club, while her clothes became even more like our Mother's. But she was still such a pretty girl, if you could ever get her to stand up straight long enough to see past the veil of her hair. And God forbid a boy ever spoke to her. She would start, eyes wide and terrified, like a doe staring down a cougar, before muttering some unintelligible comment prior to fleeing.

Of course, as time went by, I turned out nothing like her.

⚓

Constance pushed the Mercedes, revving its engine as she ran traffic lights irrespective of color. Mordant hadn't buckled me in and—blindsided by pain at the time—it hadn't occurred to me either, which meant I now found myself being flung from one side of the enormous sedan to the other. Unable to secure myself, I considered rolling into the floorboard so I could at least brace myself between the front and rear seats. But my muscles had stiffened, and I could hardly move. With every breath I took, an invisible knife carved a chunk out of my ribcage. Eyes watering, I bit my lower lip to keep from moaning.

My chauffeur risked a quick glance back at me before spinning to face front just as a city utility truck, brakes screeching and tires squealing, swerved to avoid us as we flew through yet another intersection, like Luke Skywalker hunting womp rats in his T-16 back home.

"You okay?" she called back to me, thankfully still facing forward. "Do you need a doctor?"

No, I wanted to say, no more doctors. But when I opened my mouth to speak, a sharp pain slid into my side like a scalpel, just underneath my right breast, and I buried my face in the leather seat, biting it to muffle my cries.

"Fuck," Constance muttered, her head swiveling first to the left, then to the right, oddly repeating the sequence while bending forward and looking up through the windshield. "Once we get there, I'll have Arthur take a look at you."

A loud crash sparkled like fireworks on the roof, as though we'd been hit by a jumper. Glass shattered as an arm snaked in through the window beside me. Fingers locked on my upper arm as nails dug into my flesh, their touch burning like jalapeñoño peppers. Constance screamed, then whipped the car in a skating, ninety degree turn. A shadow dropped past the window down to the asphalt.

My driver glared into the rearview mirror. "Get him, sir," she hissed through clenched teeth. I forced my uncooperative body up far enough to allow a look out the rear window. There, underneath the sulfuric glare of a halogen street light, two bodies wrestled with one another, too far away to identify. Soon we left them behind.

"Hold on," Constance sputtered, now completely focused on her driving. She punched at the dashboard, and our hazard lights started flashing. We raced through one intersection after another, the car's horn blaring like a train engine's whistle as Constance pounded on it, and I silently prayed that—wherever we were going—Lombard Street wasn't part of the route.

"The police . . ." I began.

"Good!" she snapped. "The more attention, the better."

The decaying buildings and cheap neon of the Tenderloin had given way to residential streets lined with upscale homes. We'd reached Pacific Heights. Constance steered with her left hand while rummaging through a red Hermes handbag with her right, finally removing a cell phone. She thumbed the screen, then flung it into her lap.

"Hello?" a male voice said over the speakerphone.

"Arthur, we're headed your way like Thelma and Louise," Constance said. "And we won't be slowing down; if anything, we'll be speeding up. I need an open gate, along with an open garage door, or the front grill of this tank is going to be spitting out an engine in the next couple of minutes, followed by its two lovely passengers."

A pause. "Is he with you?"

"No, but she is," my driver replied, glancing back at me in the mirror. "Looking for all the world like she just spent the past hour in a steel cage match with Mick Foley. Even her bruises have bruises."

Another pause. "Gate will be open by the time you get here," the voice said.

Suddenly the car swerved hard to the left, flinging me against the door, the squeal of the tires an echo like burnt sienna. "Goddammit!" Constance growled as she fought to regain control of the skidding vehicle.

"Are you being followed?" the voice asked.

The hourglass blonde swore in a low voice. "Not by anything with wheels," she added.

Yet another pause. "Christ . . ."

Constance leaned forward. "I see you!" Without pausing for a reply, she floored it. A jaw-rattling bump flung me a foot above the rear seat as we somehow managed to avoid hitting either of the stone walls bracketing the wrought-iron gate.

"There you are!" the phone said. Then, less than a second later, "My God, woman, slow down!"

I saw an enormous house racing toward us as Constance literally stood on the brake, her arms locked tight on the steering wheel. We screeched down the length of the driveway into a wide garage, coming to a halt what must have been mere inches from the rear wall.

Two people stood just outside a doorway inside the large space, a man and a woman; middle-aged, attractive. The man standing watch held one of the largest rifles I'd ever seen, the stock nestled in his shoulder. Both looked back in the direction we had come from.

Constance didn't even pause long enough to turn the engine off, instead hopping out of the car and running around to my side. "Panic room!" she cried as she fumbled with the door handle.

The man handed his weapon to the woman beside him. "Take this, dear," he said. As she complied, he stepped toward the car, pushing his way past Constance. "Go!" he yelled at her. "You're the only one who knows the security code! I'll get her."

The blonde had reached into the car to drag me across the seat, none too gently. Unable to keep silent, I cried out. It felt as though she was ripping my arm out of its socket. "Okay then, you take her," she told the man. "Tracy, can you fire that bazooka?"

For an answer, the second woman thumbed back the hammer. "I'd rather have my grandfather's old elephant gun," she said as the man lifted me into a fireman's carry. "If it's one of Them, this air rifle won't be of much use."

I barely caught a glimpse of wide hallways and expensive wainscoting as we raced through the mansion. The man huffed and puffed while the women preceded him to what appeared to be a blank wall. Constance slid open a panel, unnoticeable until then, to reveal some sort of electronic keypad. "C'mon, c'mon," she whispered furiously as she punched the buttons. Then, with a hum, the walls parted to reveal a room, noticeably lacking an exit.

"Go!" Constance commanded as she waved us forward. The man— Arthur, I assumed—pushed forward while Tracy moved to a guard position just inside. As everyone struggled with the narrow entrance, I heard a rainbow explosion of shattering glass. Tracy's eyes widened. "Constance!" she warned, her voice struggling to conceal a growing panic.

"Close! Close, goddammit!" the blonde cried as she stabbed at another keypad just inside the room. The door, polished metal on this side, slid shut with a hiss, and I heard the clank of bolts sliding into place.

Then a crash shook the door.

"Oh Jesus," Constance murmured as she backed up to where Arthur now stood after lowering me to the floor. Tracy backed up as well, her rifle aimed forward.

Another crash. I tasted velvet dust in the air, stirred up from the shelving that lined the walls, and felt the sour vibration of the impact as glass bottles tinkled against one other.

"Please hold," Constance whispered in a voice white with fear. "Please hold."

A third crash, accompanied by a prolonged metallic squeal.

Then silence.

Despite a confusion bordering on shock, I couldn't help but share their fear. Whatever it was on the other side of that door, as thick and imposing as a bank vault, it had the three of them terrified. And I rode that fear with them, like a roller coaster nearing its apex.

Then was nothing left for us to do. So we watched. And waited.

High school drama. They should charge admission, with hot buttered popcorn served in the cafeteria alongside those undersized and overpriced boxes of Sugar Babies, Raisinets, and Peanut M&Ms. And a large Diet Coke to wash it all down with.

I was a freshly-minted sophomore who, not too many months prior, had been one of the ruling class, a freshman in junior high. Now I was a peon again. Bethany, by contrast, was a senior, and while nothing official had yet to be declared, everyone and his great aunt knew that she and Otis Sinclair had been 'promised' to one another.

It felt strange to me, their romance, as out of sync as one of those badly dubbed martial arts movies. Otis's father, old 'Fire and Brimstone' Hannibal Sinclair, was the pastor of the Sneadsville First Baptist Church, which the bulk of my mother's family has been attending since the days of the First Continental Congress. You hear a lot about preacher's kids, how they're such holy terrors, rebelling against their upbringing and all, but not Otis. He was just as religious as his father, being the President of the Sneadsville Senior High Bible Club. To his credit though, while he could sometimes come across as a bit holier-than-thou, he wasn't (at least, usually) obnoxious about it.

Ever since puberty had hit the poor guy, trumpeting its presence on a regular basis during choir practice, it had been the biggest open secret in school and church alike that Otis was hopelessly enamored of my sister. And it wasn't very hard to figure out what he saw in her, for while Bethany remained as shy as a hermit crab, she was well on her way to completing a prolonged and somewhat painful transformation into a real beauty, not unlike one of those anorexic teenaged models you see gracing the covers of women's fashion magazines (the kind of women my husband once referred to as "boobs on a stick'). You had to know Bethany and Otis, though, to be aware that they were a couple. They rarely held hands, and even I had never seen them kiss, except for that one time when the two of them got trapped under the mistletoe at the Young Adult Christmas party. Otis rode that pony for a solid week. But since he was never in any danger of making the cover of Tiger Beat, you could hardly blame him for grabbing whatever modest celebrity he could.

And it wasn't just us peers who were puzzled. Truth is, their relationship confused most of the adults as well, even the members of my own family. Bethany had been hit on by just about every popular boy at school at one time or another, but had shown no interest in any of them. And while Otis would on rare occasions experience the occasional green-eyed monster moment, he did (for the most part) a commendable job handling the male attention my sister typically drew like flies to honey.

(Though, to my ever increasingly sophisticated mind, it did occur to me that my sister's attraction to him might possibly have owed far more to his oft-declared and frequently emphasized prohibition regarding the moral turpitude of premarital sex than to any surplus of male confidence.)

Me? I was a different kettle of fish altogether.

Now, you shouldn't go reading too much into that. While it's true that I did have a bit of a reputation as a flirt, I was always smart enough to save my more outrageous comments for mixed crowds of three or better. And while I never was what one would call slender, I did have what some considered a striking figure, along with a bust that was the envy of more than a few of my classmates, since I'd never had to cheat by stuffing Kleenex into my bra from the tender age of eleven on. So I got my fair share of male attention as well and never—well, not overly much—resented my sister's head-turning profile. (Although I would have killed for those goddamned cheekbones).

One of the more splendid ironies I experienced during that time was that, unbeknownst to my mother, the numerous double-takes I was frequently rewarded with whilst trawling the school hallways was due in no small part to Mother's ingrained sense of thriftiness. While hand-me-downs are as Southern a staple as grits, my sister's nosebleed height combined with her broomstick figure meant that we shared little in the way of clothing, this due in no small part to my grandmother Pearl, who believed that the Sneads (as the founding family of our little shire) had a reputation to uphold. Grammy would dress my mother down in a heartbeat at even the suggestion of her granddaughters being seen in public wearing thrift market clothing like the poor white trash from Five Points, whom even the denizens of East End looked down upon.

Because of this, my wardrobe consisted primarily of items purchased from J.C. Penny's exclusively for my sole use. But you can't get blood out of a turnip, so as a rule, my wardrobe did not grow much except during birthdays, holidays, and other special occasions. For this reason, my dresses, blouses, sweaters, and skirts tended to fit a bit on the snug side as I slowly outgrew them, accentuating a set of curves two grades ahead of most of my peers. This, combined with an already precocious manner as regards the opposite sex, is what I attribute that one day's incident to.

It was the tail end of 1990, with autumn segueing towards winter. We girls had just finished our Phys Ed class, volleyball that day. Coach Rook—one of several teachers we girls took care not to be caught alone with, him being on the handsy side—had just sent everyone to the showers after ordering me to gather up the loose balls and put them away.

I collected them, then walked the length of the gym on my way to the storage room, passing by the boys' class, which was running the court at the time. Good peripheral vision is an asset to any female, and I noticed not a few glances cast in my direction as I walked by in my high-cut gym shorts with my nose in the air, pretending to ignore them all while (it must be said) putting into my hips what Grandma Pearl would have called "a bit of a hitch in the transmixer."

A good bit of fumbling was required to get the door to the storage room open, what with my arms being full, but somehow I managed (though I dropped one of the balls and had to kick it ahead of me). I had collected the loose one and flung it into the bin with a barely-recognizable-as-such jump shot when I heard the door open and close again.

I turned around to look, and there stood Reggie Pendergrass, all hot and sweaty from his running. He looked at me, glanced back at the door, then looked at me again, like he was trying to make up his mind about something.

Too young and stupid to be nervous, much less scared, I stared back at him, my left hand on my hip. "Can I help you, sir?" I drawled.

For an answer, he slipped his left thumb into the waistband of his shorts and then, with his right hand, pulled his thing out.

I could not help but stare. While I had participated in the occasional game of Doctor with one or two of the neighborhood boys back when I was a child, those diminutive objects—their 'pee-pees'—had been smaller than my little finger, and just as sexless.

Not this. It was heavy and thick, nestled in a mat of wiry black hair. Reggie stood there, rubbing his thumb over the head as he looked at me.

"You wanna suck it?" he said, as calmly as if he'd been asking for the time of day.

I stood there frozen, my heart beating so hard and fast I thought it would leap out of my chest, as if I'd just downed three cups of Grandpa Roland's 'smack-your-momma' coffee one right after the other. But there was something else too, though I couldn't admit it to myself until much later, a simultaneously fascinated/disgusted curiosity at the sight of the first truly male organ I had ever seen.

But mostly I was terrified.

He took a step forward, waving his penis at me like a dog treat. "I know you did it for Andy Macintosh," he said. Which puzzled the hell out of me, since I'd never seen anything more intimate of Andy than the pale white legs sticking out of his Bermuda shorts at our church's Labor Day cookout two months prior.

"C'mon," he said, taking another step forward.

I felt it building in my chest, a scream choking me. Because something ancient, wired into the female brain since the caveman days, was now flashing a klaxon call in my head, warning me that it had seen something ugly in Reggie's eyes, a look that said, "You better get yourself ready, because this is gonna happen, one way or the other . . ."

Then the door banged open and Jesse Collins strode in.

Jesse lived in Five Points. His family had had their own share of troubles, what with one brother dying in a car accident as a toddler and another disappearing years later, never to be found. Most everyone referred to him by his nickname, Freight Train. He played defensive end for the Sneadsville Vikings and reminded me of one. He weighed maybe two hundred and sixty-five pounds, had been shaving since the eighth grade, and was a holy terror on the football field. It had been claimed that offensive linemen from opposing teams would play Rock, Paper, Scissors to decide who had to play opposite him during a game.

He stared at Reggie, a dumbfounded look on his face. A look that turned mean real quick.

"Jesus fucking Christ," Jesse snarled. "Really?"

Reggie stuffed his thing back into his shorts and slid sideways toward the door. "Hey, man, *she's* the one who wanted it," he said.

"Really? What, you mean like the way Wayne Asycue's little sister wanted it? That pissant of a wimp might be too chickenshit yellow to kick your sorry ass, but I'll do it and give you ten minutes to draw a crowd! You hear me, asswipe?"

Without another word, Reggie slunk past Jesse, head low as he fled.

Deprived of one source of his wrath, Freight Train turned back to face me. "And you! What's your fucking problem?"

The pounding in my chest, a slow series of jabs that had all but paralyzed me moments earlier, had ratcheted into a hailstorm of body blows. "Huh?"

"HUH?" he repeated, mocking me with the cruelty of a six-year-old. "Are you retarded? Walking past a bunch of guys swinging your ass like that? You're lucky I couldn't find my cleats. Hey, maybe next time I walk in here on you and Needledick, I'll just excuse myself and lock the door on my way back out. How about that?"

The throbbing in my chest had accelerated into a jackhammer vibration, and I tasted salt in my mouth. Sweat poured over me as I slid down the back wall to the floor.

"Hey, you okay?" Jesse said, anger fading as he approached me. "Christ, I didn't mean nothing, not really. Hey! You okay?"

I looked up at him, towering over me, and somehow forced my mouth open.

"I think I'm dying," I said.

I split my attention between the security door and the three of them, huddled into a circle, studying each in turn from beneath my eyelids while curled up pretending to be asleep in the far left corner of what Constance had referred to earlier as the panic room. There hadn't been any more banging for some time, although since I wasn't wearing a watch (not to mention much in the way of clothing) I couldn't have said for how long.

Now that the immediate crisis appeared to be on standby, they pretty much ignored me, instead speaking quietly amongst themselves in voices pitched not to carry, but which I could just make out. (As a child, I'd had a reputation in my family as a champion eavesdropper.)

"Still no answer?" Tracy whispered to Constance, who was fiddling with an ancient phone in her lap, one of those heavy black ones made from Bakelite, the kind that the old AT&T monopoly used to rent to their customers back when I was a kid, with the stiff rotary dial which could so easily slip from your finger while you were dialing, forcing you to hang up and start the entire process all over again.

"Keeps going straight to voicemail," Constance said.

Arthur slid a protective arm around Tracy's waist. The intimacy of the gesture had 'wife' written all over it. "I'm sure he's fine," he said.

"Well now, don't I feel all better?" Constance replied, her tone a thick mixture of acid and cream. "Goddammit, he's so . . ." Then she paused.

"What?" Tracy said, a smile toying with the left corner of her mouth.

Constance sighed. "Look, don't get me wrong, okay, either of you. I'm loyal, and just as devoted to him as I was to Juliet." She glared at each of them in turn, as though daring either to contradict her. "Well, almost." She waved her hand, as if she had run out of words. "It's just . . ."

Arthur nodded. "I understand. Better than you might think."

She turned on him. "Do you? You two spend most of your time perched over Manhattan in that Central Park penthouse of yours, playing with options and deviates, while I—"

"Derivatives," Tracy corrected.

Constance frowned. "Don't patronize me. I'm a bottle blonde, I misspoke. I know what a derivative is. Which is why I keep all my money in REITs."

They were quiet for a few minutes.

"Constance, if it makes you feel any better, we worry too," Tracy finally said in a low voice. "We all know how young he is."

"Not to mention that we owe him our lives," Arthur said, his tone rigid and a bit defensive. "*All* of us."

It sounded like a familiar argument, one they had had before.

"Don't you miss Penelope?" Constance said, half to herself, after a brief silence. "I know I miss Juliet. No—no, *miss* is a poor pale shadow of a word. I ache for her, so goddamned much . . ." She sighed deeply with a catch in her throat, like a woman close to tears.

Another silence. "Of course we do," Tracy eventually said, a strain in her voice that hadn't been present a moment before. "Sometimes I see her in my dreams, smiling at me from across a crowded room, and I think, 'It's all right, it was just a nightmare.'" She swallowed, an audible sound. "Then I wake up."

Arthur cleared his throat loudly, as if to break the reverie. "He's special too, though. Surely both of you must realize that by now."

"So *you* say. So *they* seem to think," Constance muttered. "But we're the ones who are going to live or die over his inevitable mistakes." She chewed on a thumbnail as she stared down at the phone. "I've heard rumors that he's younger than me," she whispered, shooting Tracy a glance. "Younger even than *Moira*, for Christ's sake!"

No one spoke for quite some time afterwards.

Head aching from my effort to follow their bizarre conversation, I focused instead on the nightmare I had just escaped from. I'd no idea what the date was, but I had to assume it was the same day, now the same night. Which meant that Lester and Sid must have followed me to the bridge, then pulled me out of the water.

Lester, she was dead! She was fucking dead!

The cold, that had to be it. The frigid bay waters, followed soon after by the cold of the lab, so keen I had seen my own breath in the air. Frigid enough that, unconscious, I had appeared to be deceased.

She was fucking dead!

I shuddered.

"He does remind me of someone, though," Arthur said, breaking my reverie.

Tracy smiled, a full one this time that reached all the way to her eyes. "This again?"

"Who?" Constance finally asked, when no one seemed inclined to elaborate.

"Childhood hero of mine, lived a very long time ago," Arthur said. "Born in Macedonia."

Constance's brow wrinkled, then with a conscious effort she smoothed it. "Alexander the Great?"

The man nodded. "Ruler over virtually the entirety of the civilized world by the time he was thirty, then wept that he had no more worlds to conquer."

"And died two years later," Tracy replied, a bit petulantly. "Not to mention his most disturbing habit."

"Which was?" Arthur said.

Tracy gave her husband a thoughtful glance. "His dangerous, some might even call it suicidal, need to be at the forefront of every battle."

Their banter had the flavor of a long-running debate.

"Our House is going to fall, isn't it?" Constance finally said, her tone dark and bitter. "They're going to kill him. And once he's dead, they'll come for the rest of us, and finish what they started in Alaska."

Arthur and Tracy looked at one another, instead of contradicting her. In that moment, I could feel, like a tangible thing, the intensity of their shared bond with one another.

I knew what that felt like, once upon a time.

"I don't believe it will be quite that simple," Arthur finally replied. "He has powerful—if not friends—then parties with a common interest, who believe his ultimate fate to be tightly bound with their own."

"Is this your way of saying we have nothing to be afraid of?" Constance said with a sniff.

The man shook his head. "On the contrary," he murmured. "We have a great deal to fear."

The blonde blinked. "But you just said . . ."

"Constance, do you think his enemies—which makes them *our* ene-mies——cannot see what we see? What *I* see?" He snorted. "Of course they do. Which means that in order to seize the upper hand, or at least the ini-tiative, they must act quickly and with great haste. Because the more time they allow him to consolidate his position, the greater a danger he will become in the days ahead."

"In this, I'm inclined to agree with my husband," Tracy said as she reclined against Arthur. "The rumors were flying, thick and fast, through all the *hashnas* in Andole." She closed her eyes, as if ruminating. "They all spoke of prophecies."

Constance appeared to consider this. "So if that's all true," she finally said, "then tell me something."

"What?" Arthur replied.

Constance twisted to face me, her face an impenetrable mask. "What's so important about *her*?" she asked, voice raised to ensure I heard her question.

Now all of them stared at me.

I shook my head, wishing I had a hole into which I could crawl and hide. "I don't know you're talking about. I don't know any of you. I don't know why those people wanted me, why they wanted to do . . . whatever it was they were going to do to me!" I heard my voice rising to a hysterical level, so I forced myself to take a few calming breaths. "I don't even know why I'm still alive."

Constance's brow furrowed. "You don't remember him dragging you out of that building?"

I opened my mouth, then shut it again. I hadn't been talking about the horror show in the laboratory (or whatever that place was) but rather my plunge into the San Francisco Bay.

But perhaps they knew nothing about that.

As I tried to think of a reply, the panic room's metal door shook from a sudden impact as though it had been struck with a sledgehammer. *Boom!*

I screamed, as did one of the other women. Constance, I think.

We focused on the door as a second, and then a third blow, rattled it in its frame.

Then a familiar voice.

"Little pig, little pig, let me in," Mordant said.

⚏

He led us into what appeared to be a small library, or possibly a large study. Heavy curtains of hunter green, accented with gold-colored thread, had been ripped down from their bronze mounting rods and flung across the room. Multi-colored fragments glittered in front of a gaping hole in a six-foot window frame, the shards spraying out fan-like from the stained glass panes. I looked everywhere for blood, but didn't see any, not even on Mordant. The crimson-splattered shirt from earlier had been replaced by a white button-down and a faded a pair of Levis.

The Three hung nearby, as though looking to him for protection, and the incongruity of this struck me. Who was this young man? Some billionaire's pampered offspring?

Then I remembered the two dead men, their blood soaking Mordant's sleeves halfway up his arms. (What had he cut them with, anyway? One of the surgical knives?)

No. Whatever descriptive might have applied to him (Psychopath? Sociopath?), 'pampered' wasn't one of them.

What, then? He was a killer, I had seen that for myself. Could he be the child of some Mafia-style syndicate boss, out to prove himself? But if so, then why bother to save the life of a complete stranger, now a potential witness?

My muscles began trembling uncontrollably, and I hugged myself in an unsuccessful attempt to still them.

Maybe he was the lone, eccentric heir to some fabulous fortune. That made the most sense, given the conversation I'd overheard earlier. Some great tragedy had occurred, leaving this young man as the sole successor to a Bruce Wayne-style conglomerate, and these three were his employees. Given the deference they showed him that made the most sense, since I couldn't imagine family members acting quite so servile.

But why was *I* here?

Oh, I imagine you'll learn that soon enough. Though if I were you, I wouldn't be rushing the revelations.

"You're certain he's gone, sir?" Constance asked, her head swiveling in all directions. "Or was it a she?"

The young man grunted. "He," Mordant said. "And as sure as I can be. I've searched everywhere for him, inside the house as well as out, before I came for you. No sign of him; or anyone else for that matter. He gave me one hell of a fight in the city, though. I was concerned he might have friends on the way, so I yanked him down to street level to force him into the public eye. That's when he landed on your car. I caught up with him, pulled him off. Then he ran. He was wearing a mask of some kind, like one of those *luchador* wrestlers, so I have no idea what he looked like. I worried he might beat me here, so I used my cell phone to call 911 and report a burglary in progress at the house down the street. I figured the lights and the sirens might chase him away if he got here first." He smiled, a feral grin. "Seems I was right."

I caught Arthur smiling in Constance's direction, as if to say *You see?* The 'bottle-blonde' ignored him, instead giving her full attention to Mordant as she lifted her hand, tracing his hairline with her fingers. "You're bleeding, sir."

He started at her touch, then brushed her hand away. "It's nothing," he said, glancing in my direction. "It'll heal."

Constance nodded, then stepped back. "What now, sir?"

Mordant looked around the room, as if challenging us to comment further on the torn flesh just above his ear, or the thin line of blood now staining his collar.

"No clear idea yet," the young man finally said. "But we're definitely relocating. That barred window didn't slow him down at all," he finished, half to himself.

The older man stepped forward. It was such an odd sight. Arthur looked like the CEO of a Fortune 500 company, or maybe a vice-presidential candidate. But he stood deferentially, head lowered just so, in front of a young man barely out of his teens, if that. "Sir?"

The boy looked up from his reverie. "Yes?"

Arthur looked in my direction. "What about her?"

An unpleasant salty tightness squeezed my chest, and I flinched as Mordant focused now on me, his green eyes edged with an orange glow like a flame.

"No more talk until we're someplace secure," he said. "We'll take two cars. Put her in the trunk, so there'll be no way to know which vehicle she's in. Constance and I will take that one, you and Tracy the other. Two different directions as well. I only saw the one following us, but there could be reinforcements by now." He switched his gaze to Tracy. "Is our backup plan in place?"

Tracy nodded. "I reserved the Presidential Suite at the Fairmont well before we left New York. Expensive, and they're probably wondering why someone is paying fifteen thousand dollars a night not to sleep there, but it's ready and waiting. I'll phone, let them know to expect us. By the way, what do you want me to do about the staff?"

"Tell management we want any butlers and maids kept at arm's length," Mordant said. "Volunteer nothing, but if you think that might create more problems than it solves, tell them it's a security issue."

Tracy nodded again. "Understood."

"Constance," Mordant said, "She needs something else to wear. Naked except for a lab coat might draw a stare or two. You have anything appropriate?"

"In her size?" the blonde said incredulously, while studying me. "Top, sure, but that waist . . ."

"Make it happen," he said.

Constance made a noise, the sigh of the long-suffering and much put upon. "Let's go," she said, leading me away by the hand as she muttered *soto voce*, "thank God for Spanx."

Arthur followed Constance and me into the bedroom, a black leather bag in his hand. I flinched, despite myself, as he opened it. Noticing my reaction, he worked hard to put me at ease, his voice a soothing navy blue as he poked and prodded at my injuries. Despite the clinical appraisal as his fingers slid over my skin, I could not help but flush.

"No broken bones, thank goodness," he reassured me. "Looks much worse than it actually is."

He whispered something into my companion's ear, then smiled at me before taking his leave, black bag in hand.

Then came a bath, as I was far too weak and shaky for a shower. Constance helped me into the tub, then used a shower attachment to hose the blood off. I sat in a puddle of near-scalding water, watching as the runnels started out a dark red, eventually dissolving into a nasty bubblegum pink before fading altogether. She then filled the tub and bathed me, as if I were a child, then made me stand so she could dry me off, rubbing at my skin so hard it hurt.

After evaluating and then discarding a number of clothing items drawn from a large portmanteau, Constance finally managed to squeeze me into a blouse and skirt combination, both designer label, followed by a pair of 'come fuck me' pumps. The Spanx bit at my injuries like a living thing, and I couldn't keep the tears from flowing. She noticed, reached into her purse, found a bottle, then shook out a pill.

"Percocet." She reassured me when I hesitated, "Trust me."

She handed it over, then fetched me a glass of water to chase it down with. After giving me a studied look, she slipped the bottle into one of my skirt's pockets. "Keep it," she said. "I have CVS on speed dial."

I hadn't taken any pain medication stronger than Tylenol for almost two decades. Not to mention I was the cheapest of drunks; a single glass of wine had me snoring in no time. But my ribs hurt so much I overcame my suspicions and popped the tablet down. And despite my concerns, this turned out to be a good thing, because when it came time to lock me in the boot, I was long past any fears of being confined, instead crawling into the narrow dark space like a toddler being put to bed. I even slept part of the way.

We arrived without incident. Eschewing the revolving door, Arthur and Constance guided me in through one of the side entrances instead, avoiding the front desk while Tracy checked us in. Mordant kept up the rear like a border collie, herding us to the elevators where we waited for Tracy, who rejoined our party in short order. I'd heard stories of the Fairmont, but had never so much as set foot in the lobby, much less their Presidential Suite. A brief elevator ride later and we were inside, the Three surrounding me while Mordant prowled through the suite, checking the rooms. Once I could have sworn I saw him sniff the air.

Once he finally seemed satisfied, the Three left me in a wing chair and moved forward to confront their young CEO (or whatever the hell he was).

"Sir?" Arthur said.

Mordant faced them, brow lowered. "Yes?"

The older man expelled a nervous sigh. "We've never done anything like this before," he said, including the two women, "but frankly, we—that is, all of us—would be derelict in our responsibilities by remaining silent."

Mordant smiled. "'First there was the strawberry incident',," he mumbled in a passable Humphrey Bogart impression, "'and then they all turned against me.'"

"What?!" Arthur said. "No! No, you misunderstand!"

"Then this isn't a mutiny?" Mordant said.

Tracy lowered her eyes, a thin smile barely visible. "More like an intervention, sir," she said.

Mordant nodded. "Very well. Take a seat and I'll hear you out," he said, following his own command by sprawling over a nearby chair.

The three sat on a sofa opposite him. "We understand your wish to take point in this situation, sir," Arthur said. "But we must speak our minds and warn you, such a thing is not only unprecedented, it is dangerous."

"For whom?" Mordant said, smiling.

"For you!" Tracy said in a distressed tone out of sorts with her previous aplomb. "I plead your indulgence, sir, but we all served our respective Ladies for many years, and never at any time did any of them take such an active and—if you will pardon me for saying so—impetuous role. Such risks were reserved for us. As they should be," she said, including her husband and Constance with a gesture as those two nodded their agreement.

Mordant appeared thoughtful. "I understand what you're saying. But isn't it true that during such times, you were never expected to deal with," and here he shot me a glance, "um, those like myself?"

Arthur shrugged. He looked tired. Exhausted, even. "The situation is unprecedented, I'll grant you."

"To say the least," the young man said. "In fact," and here he stood, "if there is anyone critical to the well-being of this household who is at risk under these circumstances, it's not me," he said as he pointed in their direction. "It's you." Then he frowned. "Which is why it may be best to send all of you home."

They gaped at him incredulously. "You can't be serious!" Constance blurted.

"Very," Mordant said.

"But sir!" Tracy interjected. "How will you . . . ?" She then looked in my direction. "I mean . . ."

The young man gave her a half smile. "I think I could manage."

"But . . . !" Constance said.

"You have two options," he told them. "Either I expect the three of you on an outbound plane first thing in the morning, or . . ." He paused.

"Or what?" Tracy finally said, filling the now yawning silence.

Mordant sighed. "Option two, you remain in this suite, never leaving it without permission, after getting on the phone to the local stores and obtaining suitable—supplies."

They sat, staring at him with blindsided confusion. "But how . . . ?" Arthur finally ventured.

Mordant scanned the suite. "Create a safe room. Order anything you might need. And afterwards not one of you is to set foot outside of it once preparations have been made, unless or until I say otherwise. Do you understand? I can't risk losing any of you. Not at this time."

Constance folded her arms, her jaw clenched tight. "But you force us to risk losing you," she mumbled bitterly.

Mordant looked thoughtful. "I hadn't wanted to say anything before now," he said after a time, his voice soft and low. "But I've made preparations in the event of my sudden absence. If anything happens to me, you will email an address I'll give you with the message, 'Initiate Plan B'. You should hear back promptly. Follow any directions you receive."

All three looked stunned. "You want us to switch Houses?" Arthur finally said.

Mordant shrugged. "Or go your own way. The choice is yours."

Tracy slid her hand into her husband's, then took Constance's as well.

"We honor our duty," Arthur said, after a low exchange with the two women. "But only because we are being given no option to do otherwise."

"Understood," Mordant said.

Arthur sighed. "Very well. We'll remain here, under the conditions you've outlined." Then he looked at me. "But what about her?"

All of them stared in my direction.

My head spun. I had no idea what was going on, or what any of these people were talking about. All I knew was that someone wanted me dead. Or dissected. Which amounted to the same thing, when it came down to it. And I still hadn't the slightest notion as to the who, or the why, or anything.

"I'll wait until you've made preparations," Mordant told them. "Then, after sundown, I'll take her with me. I will either call or text you every hour, on the hour. If I'm more than ten minutes late, assume the worst and proceed accordingly."

The three nodded, as if defeated.

I don't know where the words came from, but somehow—despite everything that had happened—I found the courage to speak. "Where are we going?" I asked, addressing Mordant.

He smiled, as if at yet another secret joke.

"We're going to solve a mystery," he said.

⚜

Just as the morning sun began peeking between the clouds and the horizon, Mordant led me into one of the suite's bedrooms. He followed me inside, then shut the door and ordered me into bed. My heart jumped like a frog into my throat, but there was no reason for concern; whatever interest he had in me, it wasn't sexual. Instead of approaching me, he pulled up a chair and sat with his back against the now-closed door, his focus on the windows, their curtains closed so tight not even a stray sunbeam could have found its way in. He glanced at me while I stood next to the bed, my fingers toying with the buttons of Constance's silk blouse, my face flushed. He smiled, a sarcastic grimace, then leaned his head back against the door while closing his eyes. Relieved, I stripped down to my undies, my muscles and bones toothache sore, before sliding in between the elegant sheets with their four digit thread counts. Shivering like a newly shorn lamb, I listened to the comings and goings in the next room, to voices identifying themselves as deliveries were made. At some point I fell asleep.

When I woke, I saw that Mordant had moved to the window, its curtains now open to reveal the night sky. The tales I'd heard of the Fairmont's gorgeous views had not been exaggerated. The city lights burned in a peppermint river, like the Milky Way on a clear country night. Mordant stood there, looking out, as if searching for something. Then he turned in my direction.

"You snore like my sister," he said with a weary smile.

I stiffened. Some of my earlier shock had faded, replaced now with a faint but growing anger. "What's going on?" I asked. "Who the hell *are* you? Why are you here? Why am *I* here?"

He stepped away from the glass and moved toward me. There was a beauty in his movements, a liquid grace all but distracting me from my burgeoning hissy fit. Black hair and eyes that all but glowed completed the feline image. A sudden motion placed him on the bed, so near my breath caught in my throat. I heard his nails scrape against the comforter as he leaned forward, his mint green eyes locked on my own.

"Tell me something," he said.

More than anything, I wanted to look away. But I couldn't. "What?" I finally asked.

His gaze flickered over my face, as if searching for something. "How did your husband die?"

I choked down a moan of despair and pulled away, retreating to the headboard where I curled up, shaking.

He leaned back, giving me space, though less than I would have liked. "How did he die?" he repeated.

I grabbed at the sheets, covering my exposed legs. "I—that is, he was at the Metro station. He, he—"

Was pushed?

Jumped?

"He fell in front of the train," I finished lamely.

The day after the appointment with the oncologist.

Mordant looked thoughtful. "The local news speculated it might have been a suicide?"

I pulled the sheets up to my neck. "I don't know anything about that," I said in a tone as stiff and rigid as my spine.

Mordant nodded, then reached into his back pocket. "I want to show you something," he said.

I followed his every motion, my muscles so taut from fear and tension I could feel them burning. His hand reappeared, holding not the knife or razor blade my paranoia had envisioned with crisp detail, but rather a worn sheet of paper. He unfolded it and held it out to me.

"Do you recognize any of the names on that list?" he asked.

I reached out with nerveless fingers. Torn from a yellow legal pad, its folds worn and creased, I focused on the handwritten words. Two columns. Names on the left, the first third or so paired with a date on the right. Some recent, others much older. I scanned down from the top to the first one I recognized. Theodore Kasparov.

Hendrick's lover.

And as I recognized the name, I recognized the date as well.

December 15, 2009.

The day Theo died.

Remember the pictures? His head all but floating in a pool of blood?

I forced the image away and continued reading the list. None of the names following Theo's had a date. I didn't recognize all of them, but those I did—I realized with a numbing terror—all belonged to our group. Our little family of preverts, as Warren frequently referred to us. Hendrick's name was there. So was Warren's, even Miss Sunny's. And when I got to the end of the column, a wet chill slid down the length of my spine like melting ice.

Julius Percival St. Claire.

My husband. My dead husband.

Then another name, just below his.

Marie Abigail St. Claire.

My name.

I looked up. Mordant stared into my eyes, his glare like an auger boring into my brain.

"Do you know," he began, a terrible intensity in his voice, "a man by the name of Charles Jefferson?"

Tension constricted my throat to the point I couldn't reply, so I shook my head instead.

He got up and began pacing the room. I dropped the list and wrapped my arms around my knees.

After a minute or so Mordant came back to the bed and retrieved the sheet. "Other than your name, and that of your husband," he said in a soft, low voice, "do you recognize any of the others?"

I forced myself to take deep, long breaths, trying to think clearly while staring at Mordant. Could this be the man who had stabbed Theo to death in a bathroom stall, the wounds so deep and wide, it had (according to the investigating detective) looked as though Theo had been operated on with a machete?

And everyone had assumed it was just another hate crime.

What's really going on? Did he murder Theo? Or is he a relative, or maybe an old friend, looking for the killer? What's he really doing here?

Finally I blurted out, "Theo."

"And he is . . . ?"

I swept the bangs from my damp forehead. "He is—was—a member of our munch group."

Mordant frowned, not in judgment, but in confusion. "Munch group?"

I flushed. "Just a bunch of friends who get together for dinner. We meet over at Carlyle's on the third Tuesday of every month."

I didn't elaborate, reluctant to share the private elements of my social life with a complete stranger, despite the fact that he had saved my life.

After you tried to take it.

Poor Theo. We had been so tight, he and I. Not my closest friend in our little circle. That would be Warren, with Nancy a close second. But I had always found comfort in Theo's gentleness, his dedication to Hendrick mirroring mine to Julius's as closely as Theo's eyes matched my own, the soft pungent gray of antique pearls.

I pointed at the list. "What is that? Where did it come from?"

Mordant refolded the paper with slow, careful movements, lost in thought. Finally he looked up.

"It belonged to someone I know. I mean, knew. A man by the name of Charles Jefferson. We found it mixed in with his possessions," Mordant said. "He used to work for me."

I shivered. "Is he dead, too?"

The corner of Mordant's mouth twisted. "Not so far as I know," he said reflectively, before returning his full attention to me. "But most of the people whose names are on this list, they *are* dead."

I felt dizzy. "Most?"

He lifted a shoulder. "Some are simply—gone."

I stared at his fingers, watching as they slid over the paper he held, at the oddly shaped nails which had been sculpted to subtle points. Such an odd affectation from a young man who, in terms of attire, gave every appearance of being quite conservative, as though he'd just stepped out of a Ralph Lauren ad. A secret part of me, unasked and unbidden, wondered how those nails would feel, what lines they might make, down the length of my exposed back. I felt my cheeks flare with a wintergreen heat at my body's coarse betrayal of my marriage vows.

You're not a wife. You're a widow.

"This Charles Jefferson," I said, tilting my chin at the list. "You say he was an employee of yours?"

Mordant's jaw clenched so tightly it popped. "Yes."

I retreated from the naked rage in his eyes. "He was a—bad person?" I finished lamely.

"Yes," he said, as though the word was a tooth being extracted. "And very dangerous. Not only that, he wasn't working alone. Whatever he was involved with, he had company. Friends, associates." He slid closer. "Do you recognize any of these names, other than the ones from your group?"

I swallowed. "Let me look again."

He gave the list back to me, and I studied it. The letters were block-printed, almost childishly so.

I tried to speak, to say no, I didn't recognize the others, but the words caught in my throat. I knew nothing of this man. Well, I did know one thing. He was a killer. Maybe even a murderer.

So why the hell was I cooperating with him?

As if he'd read my mind, he reached out and placed his hand over mine, swallowing it. His palm was cold, in sharp contrast to the blazing heat radiating from him the previous night as he'd held me up while navigating the stairway at the laboratory.

"This—Charles Jefferson," I husked. "How does he know Theo? Know me and my husband? You said he has friends. Who are they?" I heard my octaves rising, a hot pink vibrato. "Did he know those two men in that room? Why do they care about me? About *my* friends? For fuck's sake, why do we even *matter* to them?"

Mordant shrugged. "I don't know."

I shifted my gaze to the far wall. "So tell me something you do know."

"If I can," he replied.

I faced him again. "What's your part in all this?"

Now he looked down. I could see the muscles in his neck, taut as wires.

"If I hesitate to share what I know with you," he finally said, "it's only because I don't want to involve you any more than you already have been."

I couldn't believe what I'd just heard. "Are you serious?" I asked, stupefied. "Two men tried to vivisect me less than twenty-four hours ago! I'm *already* involved!"

He didn't speak.

"Mordant?" I asked. Hesitantly, because all of the possible answers terrified me. "Why were you there?"

He shifted, as if embarrassed. "I've been, ah, watching you."

My body clenched fist-tight. "And how long have you been watching me?" I said carefully.

He met my gaze, unapologetic. "Ever since your husband's funeral."

Oh God. "How did you know?" I whispered.

He drew himself straight. "The obituary came up while I was doing a Google search on this list," he said. "We flew out that night."

I remember once, as a child, going on a camping trip with my parents. Bethany and I had had a tent to ourselves. I remember the noises throughout the night, some just outside the tent walls. Unidentifiable sounds, terrifying because we had no idea what was making them.

This felt like that. But worse. Much worse.

Mordant clamped down on my fingers when I tried to pull away. "Abby," he said, "I know you're scared. You do not know, *cannot* know, how deeply I understand what it is you're feeling. But I believe something bad, very bad, is happening. I need to know more. And this?" He shook the sheet of paper in front of my face. "This is all I have to go on." He was silent for a moment, then spoke again. "I need your help."

I wanted to maintain eye contact, but I was too much of a coward. "What happens if I say no?" I whispered.

Silence. Then I heard him sigh.

"If you don't help me," he said in a cold, deliberate tone, "then you remain here with us. And every day I'm going to bring in the local newspaper, so I can read to you from the obituary section. Because everything I know tells me that the lives of the people on this list, the ones with no date next to their names, are at risk. I don't know why, but I'm convinced of it. Then we'll see how many of them have to die before you decide you can trust me.

"So, that being said, what's it going to be?"

❊

ASD.

Atrial Septal Defect.

They told me later Jesse had burst through the doorway of the high school infirmary as though it were an offensive line, knocking Mr. Wu the chemistry teacher (who had been reaching for the doorknob) flat on his ass before grabbing the nurse by the arm and babbling that a girl (me) was dying over in the gymnasium. Ms. Iglesias was an elderly woman with a strong Spanish accent who, it was said, had been a doctor in Cuba before the Revolution, after which she—as a member of the moneyed class—had to flee for her life. Ms. Iglesias called 911, then made her way to the gym where she found me shivering on the storage room floor in a puddle of my own sweat.

Someone found Bethany and brought her so I didn't have to ride alone in the ambulance. Someone else must have called my mother, because she was waiting in the emergency room when they wheeled me in.

ASD. That was the eventual diagnosis. A hole between the chambers of my upper heart. Might not be too serious, the surgeon told my mother. Could, with time, close on its own, assuming it wasn't too large. Or it might be small enough that I could live with it, if we wanted to take that risk.

The alternative was surgery. Cut my chest open, seal the breach.

Mother said we would think about it.

After the surgeon left, she had paced the room. Usually the most serious surgery the Willard P. Jessup Memorial Hospital saw for people my age was a tonsillectomy. Particularly when the holidays were coming up, Mother had once acerbically noted.

After a day to think about it, she gave her approval.

I remember standing in front of my bedroom mirror much later, tracing the length of the thick, ugly scar running across my chest, tears sliding down my cheeks as I realized I could never wear a bikini in public again without drawing at best disgusted, at worst horrified, stares. Which disturbed my mother not at all, since she made no secret of her belief that two-piece bathing suits were created to separate tramps from decent girls with good Christian values.

And not only swimsuits. Also gone were halter tops. And sundresses, and tube tops, anything that might have given some extra confidence to a young girl carrying just a few extra pounds.

Which grew to more than just a few, as time went by.

⚜

"What were they going to do to me?" I said, palming another of Constance's Percocets before popping it down.

Mordant spared me a glance, then faced front again. The heavy traffic appeared to make him nervous. His head swiveled constantly, and I got the feeling he did very little of his own driving. "You don't know?"

I recalled the metallic clang of something resembling a rib spreader as it bounced across the lab's tile floor, and folded my arms protectively over my stomach. "How would I?"

"So you didn't know either of those men?"

I shook my head as I stared out of the passenger window, people watching as we navigated the hilly streets. "Never saw them before last night."

For a while we rode in a silence broken only by the calm and steadying voice of the Mercedes's built-in navigator, announcing the distance to the next turn.

Then, after a throat-clearing cough, Mordant spoke again. "You and your, ah, mulch group . . ."

Despite everything, I could not help but smile. The pain meds had kicked in, and now I felt a bit floaty. "Munch group," I corrected.

"Oh, right. Tell me, have you ever noticed anything strange about any of them?"

A crazed laugh bubbled inside my chest, and I fought to hold it down. "Umm . . . Such as?"

He shrugged. Whatever was on his mind, he clearly felt uncomfortable talking about it. Pure vanilla, I decided. Not even a dash of cinnamon for flavor. "Like, um—just as an example—people pretending to be vampires?" he asked.

I smirked. "Vampires are passé, or haven't you heard?" I said. "Everyone's into zombies nowadays."

He turned to stare at me, as if confused.

"You've never watched *The Walking Dead?*" I said, unable to believe this even as the words came out of my mouth. He was, after all, part of their prime-time demographic.

"What do you mean? Like, the Terminator?"

The Terminator? Seriously? Didn't this kid get cable? Or was he one of those new 'unplugged' types, with broadband and a Netflix subscription? "The Terminator isn't a zombie, he's a cyborg."

Mordant frowned. "I knew that," he muttered.

I leaned back and closed my eyes. "When vampires hit the Young Adult Best Seller lists, that's when they died as a genre. So to speak," I said with a giggle that refused to be suppressed.

Careful, Abby. You're starting to lose it. Again.

He was quiet for a moment. "I see," he finally said.

I could feel the oncoming wave of hysteria as it approached, like that tsunami in *The Impossible,* threatening to suck my sanity out to sea. I began running off at the mouth to stave it off.

"I mean, really," I babbled. "It's not as though I don't understand the appeal, the evolutionary imperative, as it were. Dominant male, and all that. Mating with someone who's not only the strongest, but who has no compunctions whatsoever about killing to secure his place in the world. What did the female sloth say in *Ice Age?* 'All the sensitive ones get eaten'."

Mordant cleared his throat. "Something to that, I suppose," he mumbled.

"Yes, but what would be the reality?" I said, unable to stop venting. "What about a normal life? Christ, what about children? Schtupping the undead might be good for a fling, but that sort of thing would get old after a while, don't you think? A human relationship can only go so far on chemistry and adrenaline, after all. And vampires are supposed to be immortal, right? Wouldn't you think that after a hundred years or so, they'd be at each other's throats? Literally? Like the elderly couple from that old TV series, *In Living Color?*

"Of course," I continued, not allowing him time for a reply, "It can't be any fun for the vampire either. I mean, watching the love of your life turn into your mother? Followed by your grandmother? Until you get to the point she looks like that old lady in the Playboy cartoons, running around in Victoria's Secret lingerie? Which I imagine is what Hugh Hefner must look like to his paramours nowadays."

The laughter forced its way up my windpipe, clawing at my throat like a trapped animal. Mordant spared me a single look, his glance cool and distant, before returning his attention to the busy streets.

I wrestled with my growing panic attack and finally forced it down. Neither of us said anything for some time.

"This place we're going," he said after a while. "A lot of communists live there?"

I turned to look at him. "Pardon me?"

His shoulders visibly tightened. "Isn't that why they call it the Castro district?"

I almost mocked his ignorance before realizing that, despite having lived in San Francisco for over a decade, I had no idea why they called it that either.

Finally we arrived, much to my relief, and no doubt Mordant's as well.

"Park in front of the carport," I told him. "Hendrick hates to have his gate blocked."

As we slowed to a stop I practically leaped out of the vehicle, and—while waiting for Mordant to join me—wondered for a brief moment if I should say *screw this and* make a run for it.

But if someone really was trying to murder my friends . . .

"Here's something I haven't seen much of since I got here," Mordant said as he exited the vehicle. "Your friend has a side yard. And even trees." He looked over the hood of the car at me. "Do you have trees at your house?"

"We have a bush," I said with a shrug. "And even a side yard. All three inches of it."

"Your husband was a land baron?" he replied sarcastically.

"Have you priced real estate in this city? No, wait," I told him as he headed for the gate. "I know you can't see it from here, but there's a front door." I waved my hand. "This way."

He paused, then followed me, his head twisting in all directions as he scanned the shadow-strewn trees like a soldier on point.

I thumbed the doorbell and waited for Mordant to join me. Just as he did, the door opened.

Hendrick looked out at the two of us, his expression mild and a bit puzzled. I was no midget, having inherited—as had my sister—my father's height. But Hendrick towered over me, the old scarecrow. Not a man who had aged well, the years had worn lines, thick and prominent, into a face now resembling a skull. I teased him once that he looked just like the monster in that ancient horror film, Nosferatu. Except for the tan, that is. (I sometimes kidded him that if he didn't stay out of the sun he was going to turn into an alligator handbag.) Hendrick opened both the door and his arms, welcoming me.

"I wondered when you were going to come around," he droned. I rested my head against his narrow chest, the steady *thump-thump* of his sluggish heart a comfort to my ears. He was an exercise junkie, despite his age, just as Julius had been. *Only way to keep pace with the twinks*, Hendrick had once told me. "Haven't heard one word from you since the funeral," he mumbled.

"I'm sorry," I whispered into his bat wing of an ear.

"No need," he murmured before stepping back. "Are you ill, dear?" He ran a long, bony finger along the length of my jaw. "You look as though you've lost weight."

Everyone had been saying that, ever since the funeral, on the assumption that I had shed a few pounds due to a reduced appetite; rooted in depression, no doubt.

But then, I knew why.

I moved my chin away. "It's the Spanx."

"They make those for cheekbones nowadays?" He looked past me at Mordant, and for a moment I saw the old Hendrick, taking in the beauty of my companion. "And I see you come bearing gifts."

Mordant looked confused. Christ, I wondered, Hendrick couldn't possibly be the first gay man he'd ever met. Could he?

"He's not a friend," I corrected, and saw Hendrick do a double-take. "I mean, we haven't known one another for very long."

Hendrick eyed Mordant, then me. "I judge not," he said, waving us inside.

I felt my cheeks flame. "It's not like that!"

"Please, sit down," the old rake said in that monotonous, almost tone-less voice of his, the kind that could have whispered on a Shakespearean stage and been heard all the way back to the cheap seats. After we sat, he sprawled opposite us and said, "So tell me then, what *is* it like?"

I gaped like a fish, then turned to my companion, since I hadn't the slightest idea what to say next.

Mordant cleared his throat. "Mr. Hendrick—"

"Einhorn."

"Pardon me?"

"Hendrick is my Christian name. My surname is Einhorn."

"I see. Well, Mr. Einhorn—"

"Hendrick, please. Mr. Einhorn was my father."

Mordant, for the first time during out brief acquaintance, looked un-sure of himself. Not surprising. The old goat loved to keep people, particu-larly new acquaintances, off balance.

"Sir," I broke in, "Mr. Ember here . . ."

"Ember, you say?" Hendrick said. "Are you affiliated with that selfsame musical group?"

Mordant shook his head. "No."

"Pity, that. There can never be too much beach music, you know," Hendrick mused, his eyes half-lidded.

I cleared my throat. "Sir, it's about Theo."

The eyes snapped open again, their soft butterscotch glow now a harsh glare. "I beg your pardon?"

My fingers knotted at the pain in his voice, still fresh even now. "Show him," I encouraged Mordant, who removed the legal paper from the pocket of his jacket.

"This was found among the possessions of a person who, I have reason to believe, may have been involved in at least one murder," the young man said as he handed it over.

Hendrick frowned as he took the folded sheet. "You don't seriously expect me to believe you are an agent of John Law, do you?" he said as he unfolded the list.

Mordant shook his head again. "This is a—family matter."

Hendrick stared long and hard at him before turning his attention to the list. I watched as his eyes widened.

"Do you recognize any of those names?" Mordant asked. "The first twenty or so, I mean. Ms. St. Claire told me about the others."

"Did she now?" Hendrick murmured as he studied the paper in his hands.

I leaned forward. "Sir, this is very serious. You see—" and here I had to swallow before the words would come, "I was, um, kidnapped last night."

"I never knew you to have a predilection for abduction scenes," he said in a low, distracted tone, his eyes still on the list.

I clenched my fists. "Goddammit, Hendrick!"

Now he did look up, eyes wide with surprise. I tried to speak, but couldn't, instead huddling back in my chair, arms crossed to suppress their trembling.

"You're serious," he whispered, looking from me to Mordant.

I nodded. "This was no game, Hendrick, no 'scene'," I forced myself to say. "I woke up yesterday evening in some kind of medical lab in the Tenderloin. I was being raped by one man, then, when I fought him off, his partner tried to kill me." I began shaking uncontrollably. "There was a table, with scalpels and bone saws and . . ."

"How did you get away?" Hendrick said, real emotion coloring his voice with a harsh fluorescent glare. "What about the police? Have they apprehended them yet?"

I struggled to find words to answer him with. "I don't—That is . . ."

Mordant leaned forward and took control. "Mr., I mean, Hendrick, you know very well why the police haven't been contacted."

My friend returned the young man's stare with unfeigned astonishment. "And why is that?" Hendrick finally managed.

For answer, Mordant reached over and tapped the top of the sheet. "Because those first two names belonged to law enforcement officers," Mordant said. "Officers who vanished without a trace."

I looked from him to Hendrick, who leaned back in his seat, deflated.

"Do they?" I asked.

Hendrick bowed his head. "It was a very long time ago."

The sorrow in his voice throbbed like a toothache. "Who were they?" I asked.

A pause. "Old Guard," he eventually replied. "The blue boys, like the military, have always been a conservative culture. Being gay was bad enough. But practicing masochists with a predilection for Bear Daddies?"

He shook his head. "You kept your mouth shut, or else things happened to you others pretended not to see."

I thought for a moment, then shook my head. "This can't be about gay hate crimes. You know me, Hendrick. I'm so straight the light from Lesbos won't reach me for another twelve parsecs."

"Don't confuse time with distance, my dear," Hendrick said. "Han Solo could get away with it. You can't." He chewed the edge of one thumb as he continued to study the names in front of him.

Mordant cleared his throat. "Mr. Einhorn, can you tell me anything, anything at all, about the names on that list?"

Hendrick looked off to one side, as if lost in memory. Then he stood. "We are done here."

"Excuse me?" I said.

"My dear, I love you like a daughter," he said. "But you and your friend here have no business acting out . . . well, whatever police drama is currently in vogue. I watch very little television, as a rule."

"But I was *kidnapped*!" I yelped.

"I believe you," he said mildly. "And it is for precisely this reason I recommend that the two of you hie thee immediately to the closest bobby and tell him or her, in excruciating detail, what happened to you."

I froze. Go to the police? And tell them what? That I had watched Mordant practically (no, literally) disembowel two men? And that I hadn't reported it because I was terrified there were others waiting in the wings to finish what they'd started?

Sid and Lester hadn't been serial killers, I felt certain of this. That laboratory had been crammed from floor to ceiling with a combination of very expensive-looking medical equipment, computers, and Christ only knew what else.

Whatever they'd been doing, whatever they had been about to do, looked as though it had been seriously bankrolled. Venture capital level stuff.

People like that had friends. Important friends. Like with the police. Maybe even in the government.

Something told me Mordant knew this.

My friend walked to the door and placed his hand on the knob. "It is my considered opinion as one of this city's finest legal minds that the two of you should climb right back into the Mystery Machine and drive directly to the nearest police station," he said. "And I hope you will give my suggestion serious merit. This isn't a Nancy Drew novel, my dear. People could get hurt."

People have already been hurt, I almost replied, but didn't. Nor did the petulant child within make mention of her annoyance over an archaic Nancy Drew reference being directed at me, a longtime Marshmallow.

I looked over at Mordant and saw it again in his eyes. That orange flare edging his irises, his pupils as large and distended as bullet holes. I reached over and took his hand, squeezing it as tightly as I could manage. Eventually I got his attention.

"Of course you're right, Hendrick," I said, while tugging Mordant upright. "I know you only have my best interests at heart."

"I do have a few friends on the force, people I trust, if that's a concern," my friend said. "I could make some calls . . . ?"

Calls, eh? And what kind of calls *might those be?*

I shook my head. "Don't go blowing your hard-earned favors on us," I said, forcing a smile to mask my newborn paranoia. "But we appreciate the offer. Don't we?" I asked Mordant.

Much to my surprise, though slow to do so, he nodded in agreement.

There didn't seem to be anything else to say. So we left.

⚓

As we waited for the traffic light to turn red, my stomach grumbled, and I realized how long it had been since I'd last eaten. And on the heels of that thought came a stabbing pain in my side that took my breath away. Jaw tight, I searched the pocket of my skirt for the Percocet, then shook two of them into my palm and swallowed them dry.

"Is there anyone else we can talk to?" Mordant said, his sentinel gaze still scanning the streets and sidewalks.

I thought about it. "There's Mistress Sunshine."

He spared me a glance. "Mistress who?"

A nervous giggle forced its way past the knife in my ribs. "Most folks call her Sunny." I checked the street signs as I waited for the painkillers to kick in. "She and Hendrick have run our munch group for as long as I've known them, benevolent dictators that they are." I looked at Mordant and, like the Cowardly Lion, found a spark of courage. "Speaking of Hendrick, what about what he said?"

He wouldn't look at me. "About going to the police?"

I forced myself not to cringe at the frustration in his voice. "Doesn't that make the most sense?" I asked in the most diplomatic tone I could manage.

"On the surface, yes," he conceded.

I sighed. "But we're not going to do it, are we?"

Mordant frowned. "Here's what *I* believe," he said. "I believe there are people, very powerful people, with access to the kind of wealth that could finance a small country, who have a secret agenda of their own. People who want you dead. Who want *me* dead." He glanced in my direction. "And not only us, but others. Everyone on that list, for example. And not just them."

"Who else?" I asked.

The lines of his mouth grew even tighter, if that were possible. "Acquaintances of mine."

I felt the Percocet seep through my body, while simultaneously fogging my brain. "But why?"

"I'm not sure," he said, his voice low and dangerous. "That is, I think I know why they might want to kill *me*." His large hands wrenched a groan from the steering wheel. "What I don't have is the first idea why they would want to kill *you*."

I shrank back against the car door. "Me either."

He grunted an affirmation. "So until we know more about the why, I believe we'll be safer keeping to ourselves. Based on what little I know, it's not a question of whether or not they *do* control people in positions of power within the government and law enforcement." He spared me another side glance. "It's a question of how many."

I found myself scanning the faces along the sidewalk as he had been. "*They* say a lot, don't they?" I mused, as the drugs pulled me down into a soft, fluffy mattress. "For example, 'they' say, 'You can't have your cake and eat it too.' To which I say, what's the point of having cake you can't eat? What else are you going to do? Make a centerpiece out of it?"

Mordant did a bit of a double take. "Are you all right?"

Two more of these Percocet, I thought, *and I'll be more than all right*. I hadn't been this stoned since sorority rush week as an incoming freshman. "C'mon," I wheedled. "Tell me who 'they' are."

He took his time answering. "Abby, believe me when I tell you it's better if you don't know."

I tried to wrap my steadily-softening brain around that statement, but couldn't. Two men had tried to perform an improvisational autopsy on me, and this snotty, stuck-up (but—it had to be admitted—ridiculously hot) frat boy thought there was something worse than that?

Which made me wonder, sweet Christ, what if he's right?

Mordant cleared his throat, apparently to get my attention. Either that or he'd already been speaking to me and I was so high I hadn't heard him. "Tell me, where can we find this 'Mistress Sunshine' of yours?"

It took me a moment to collect my thoughts. "She lives on Nob Hill, about half a block from the Sunken Mansion."

"Sunken Mansion?"

I smiled. *I know something you don't know*, I almost sang. "Famous landmark. Some merchant built it, fellow who got rich selling picks and shovels to the gold miners back in the day. One of the few structures in that part of town that didn't collapse during the Great Earthquake of '06. That's 1906, by the way. Now that we've burst out the starting gate of a brand new century, these distinctions are *not* unimportant. Anywho, instead of falling down like a house of cards, as did so many other buildings that day, or burning up (most probably because of the copper roof), it sank down a couple of stories. Very loose soil in that part of the city. Lots of sand. Not to mention landfill from way back. Still three stories above ground level, though. First week I spent here, my husband—my fee-yon-say at the time—took me there one night and showed it to me. From outside the eight foot fence, that is. Privately owned, 'No Trespassing' signs everywhere. Julius promised me that one day we would live in a house *just* as magnificent."

"But you went in anyway, didn't you?" Mordant said, the ghost of a smile on his lips.

"Christ, no! Are you kidding? Everyone's heard the stories, how people have been killed in there, falling through the upper floors while rummaging around on a dare. Place is a death trap."

I would have said more, but it all happened so fast.

We were at a stoplight, one car in front, another to the rear. I heard doors opening behind us, then caught a flicker of motion just outside the passenger window and had half a second to flinch away before the hammer swung at me.

Safety glass shattered, spraying over my face. The hand holding the hammer dropped it into my lap before reaching for the latch and opening the door. As he did this, a second man's arm slid in. There was a flash of winking metal, and I felt the seatbelt go loose as the first man reached past the second to grab me, yanking me out of the car.

As he pulled me out, I turned instinctively toward Mordant. He was struggling with his own seatbelt, and I opened my mouth to warn him as a third man stepped up to the driver's window, a pistol in his hand.

It sounded like a string of firecrackers, the quick, repeating shots being fired. I watched as one of the bullets punched through Mordant's head, slamming him back against the seat. Blood and other substances sprayed throughout the Mercedes, splashing off the burgundy leather, coating the interior. Mordant's dead eyes stared blankly at his assailant as I was yanked away.

I struggled to escape, to run, then felt the razor's edge of a blade at my neck and froze.

"Not here, not here!" the first man hissed. He looked like a street bum, almost disappearing into the old camouflage army jacket he wore. "This way! Go! Go!"

Army Guy had grabbed my free arm, and between him and Knife Man they rushed me down a dark and narrow alleyway. I heard someone behind us, and turned to look. It was the shooter, swaying as he worked to conceal his weapon inside his coat.

A small part of me mourned the now-deceased Mordant, but the rest could only think of the knife or razor or whatever it was, the steel cold against my skin. That kept me upright and struggling to keep up, the terrifying certainty that were I to slow down, or inconvenience any of them in any way, Knife Man would not hesitate to use it.

We exited the side street, and I saw a van, its door open. "Get her in," Army Guy said.

I felt my legs turn to water, and despite my fear I collapsed, almost dragging my captors down with me. "Get her in there, goddammit!" Army Guy cried.

I twisted and fought, no longer afraid of the blade, since I was convinced that, if they got me inside that van, I was dead anyway. I struggled to break loose, to flee back into the shadows of the alley they had dragged me down.

Then Mordant stepped out of the darkness, and I screamed.

There was blood all over him. Crimson streaks trailed down his face like tears, and through the blood I saw the white of his teeth.

Oh my fucking god, his *teeth* . . .

Something wiggled in a hole just above his left eye. It squirmed like a maggot, until finally it fell to the asphalt with a single metallic *click*.

A bullet.

"Now," the creature coughed from a throat so clotted with fluids he sounded as though he was drowning, "Where were we, exactly?"

Then he was on us.

He swiped at Army Guy's face, a lazy gesture. Blood sprayed like spittle over my face as the grizzled bum's eyes vanished in a sheet of red. He screamed, a womanish, high-pitched screech as he fell. I twisted, babbling insanely, desperately trying to escape.

Knife Man swung his blade. He was dressed in some sort of uniform, like you'd see in a fast food restaurant. A ridiculous sight, or would have been were it not for his weapon. It looked like a straight razor, one of those old-timey ones you might see in an upper class barber shop. I watched as he cut a deep gash in Mordant's neck.

But the—*thing*—still kept coming.

He yanked the blade away from Knife Man and flung it away. Blood that had sprayed out from Army Guy dripped down Mordant's chin. I watched him lick the droplets from his upper lip. He was so close I could see his eyes. The irises were gone, completely consumed by the pupils.

Then his jaw dropped, impossibly low.

"No," I breathed.

He ripped out Knife Man's throat. But even then, that wasn't what almost made me almost lose control of my bladder. It was the *moans*.

Not Knife Man's. *Mordant's*.

I watched him slam his victim against the van. Metal crumpled. Bones crunched like peanut shells. I saw the terrified gunman standing nearby, pistol in hand. He looked down at his weapon, as though seeing it for the first time.

Then he dropped it and ran.

Mordant paid him no mind, instead giving Knife Man his full and undivided attention. I covered my ears with my hands, but couldn't shut out the sounds.

Until, finally, there were no sounds at all.

I heard crying. Sobbing. It took a moment to realize it was coming from me.

"Abby?"

I shook my head. "No. No, no, no . . ."

Silence.

"Abby?" Mordant repeated.

I looked up.

He crouched over me. I tried to scream, but all that came out was a faint squeak. Even his teeth were red.

"It's so unfortunate you had to see that," he whispered.

Then he reached for me, and I fainted.

⊰⊱

I was a senior in college when I first realized there was something different about me.

Not physically. Or perhaps I should say, not *medically*.

That day in school, when Reggie had 'shown me his thing', as Bethany would most likely have put it, I had felt the first touch of it, bubbling up from some hidden spot deep in my gut, a confusing cinnamon heat like an atomic fireball that had frightened the living hell out of me.

I took a page from my sister's playbook and started avoiding boys after that.

Going away to college helped, at least as far as the opposite sex was concerned. My freshman fifteen, combined the thick, lumpy scar on my chest, made me self-consciousness enough in the beginning to keep things with boys from getting too . . . complicated.

So it came as a surprise to both of us, the guy and me, when it did finally happen. I'd spent the early part of the evening sipping on a beer, but not so much that I was seriously impaired, so I can't blame it entirely on the booze. I had simply come to think of my virginity as if it were an appendix, an integral part of myself that no doubt performed some useful function, but I'd be damned if I could figure out what that might be, especially with birth control readily available.

So when I was approached at a frat party my roommate had dragged me to so she wouldn't show up alone, I let him think *he* was talking *me* into going upstairs. I clearly remember thinking at the time, *Finally! Now I'll learn what all the fuss is about.*

But I didn't.

He was remarkably cool about it all, particularly the blood, though there wasn't much of it. And I do remember reaching a climax, albeit a small one, so it's not like the experience was a total waste.

I just remembered feeling somehow . . . unsatisfied.

He said he'd call. A white lie, to my great relief. Once in a while afterwards I ran into him around campus. At first he looked embarrassed and found someplace else to be, this going on for a longer period of time than even I thought healthy. Eventually we both got over it.

After that, every few months or so, I would put myself into the position of allowing a boy to 'seduce' me. It took that long to forget my disappointment from the previous time, allowing optimism to raise its febrile head. I would let myself be (at least partially) undressed, with all the hope and anticipation of a child on Christmas morning, only to open that elegantly-wrapped package and, instead of a delightful toy, find myself staring at a pair of granny panties. And so it continued.

Until my senior year.

Grandpa Snead had bought me a present for my birthday. A brand new computer with a one gigabyte hard drive, sixteen megabytes of RAM, even a jaunty CD-ROM drive. And, in addition to that, America Online, pre-installed.

I'd missed the 'Eternal September', when AOL had added USENET (to hear the pissing and moaning on the message boards, you'd think the world had come to an end), but made it just inside the window when AOL, instead of charging by the hour, went to a 'flat fee' of $19.95 a month. That I had to pay for myself.

Still, I never spent much time on it, not early on. As I said, this was my senior year, and I'd quickly recognized the addictive potential of it all.

So I budgeted myself to a strict hour a day and two on the weekends, and somehow managed to make it stick. For the most part.

Until the day I went to the nurse's office.

I'd become a bit of a hypochondriac (having a heart attack at fifteen does strange things to the psyche), so I spent more than the usual amount of time in the infirmary. The nurse was busy with someone else when I arrived, so while I was waiting, I pulled a magazine out of a nearby pile.

Even now, I don't recall the name of that particular periodical, or even the title of the article. Something salacious, I believe. What I do remember was the interview. Or rather, the interviewee, who described an encounter with someone she had first encountered in an AOL chat room. They'd met at a coffee shop, talked for a while, then went from there to a local motel where . . .

Well, he *did* things to her. Things which, at first take, shocked and confused me.

And she liked it.

I cannot explain, in a fully satisfactory way any normal human being could possibly understand, what I felt going through me as I read her descriptions of what took place that evening, what he did to her. My damaged heart was beating a mile a minute while my skin flushed with a peppermint heat. And even though I couldn't lift my eyes from the pages, my conscious mind screamed at me, *What the hell is* wrong *with you?*

I still hear that question at times, bouncing around inside my head like a phosphorescent echo.

And there it was, at the end of the article, the name of the AOL chat room, located in a separate area from the heavily-moderated public ones, a Wild West where one could find places catering to practically every desire known to mankind. *La Chateau.* Which, the article had carefully pointed out, came from a classic novel I'd never heard of. *The Story of O.*

Despite being an English major, this was my first encounter with a reference to that tale told by the French author Anne Desclos, under the pen name Pauline Réage, written originally (or so Desclos claimed) as a series of love letters to the publisher Jean Paulhan, an admirer of the writings of the Marquis de Sade.

I left the nurse's office after a few minutes of being poked and prodded, then made my way to the library where I searched the stacks until I found a copy of Réage's work, its salty bindings ancient and worn. I curled up in an isolated chair among the stacks, hiding the book so no one could see the title, and read until the lights flashed to warn that the library was closing. By that time I was halfway through the slim volume, which I rushed to check out before closing.

And though I resisted the knowledge, not only during my final year of college, but for years after returning to my hometown to teach high school English Literature, something within me knew the truth of it even then.

I was lost.

⊹

The first thing I noticed was the wind.

The second thing? The cold.

I rolled over, wincing as my elbow rubbed up against the small stones and grit of whatever it was I lay on. Staring up, I saw clouds scuttling past the moon. Outside. I was outside.

"Are you all right?"

I snapped into a sitting position, head twisting, posed for fight or flight. Mordant, eyes fixed on me to the exclusion of all else, stood next to a low wall. He'd gotten clothing from somewhere, though it didn't fit very well, being snug to a fault. Behind him the windows of a nearby building glowed with a savory fluorescent gleam. We were on a rooftop.

"Abby?"

He struggled a bit with my name and I wondered what they had done to him, those bullets, punching through his brain like flechettes. After all, he should be dead.

But he wasn't dead.

I stared at him with the fascination of a mouse waiting for the snake to strike.

Insane. That's the only possible explanation. You're insane. Either that or you were hallucinating. You had to have been, probably due to the Percocet. Because what you saw, what you think you saw, did not happen. Could not have happened. It's . . . impossible.

"Are you going to kill me?" I somehow managed to husk out.

Mordant kept staring, his face tombstone pale. The blood mask had been washed away, leaving his hair slick and dark against his scalp, and I knew I hadn't imagined what I'd seen. What he was. What I now knew him to be.

God, he was so beautiful. Just like in all the novels I downloaded onto the Kindle Julius had bought me for Christmas to consume like popcorn.

As I gazed wordlessly at him, I remembered something my deceased husband had once told me, about a trip he'd taken to Africa long before we met, the story of a group lecture from their guide on what to do in case of an encounter with dangerous animals in the wild, such as lions or hyenas.

"What about leopards?" one woman asked.

"You don't have to worry about them," the guide said.

"Really?" the woman replied, obviously relieved.

"Oh yes," the man said with a smile, "Because if you see a leopard, it's already too late."

"Are you going to kill me?" I repeated.

He sighed. "I don't know yet."

It was only when my chest started burning that I realized I had forgotten to breathe.

"Might be the kindest thing," he mused. "At least from me it would be quick. And more or less painless. In fact . . ." And here he smiled a rictus smile. "I could make sure you enjoyed it." He turned back to look out over the cityscape. "Down to your very last breath."

I shifted, looking instinctively for whatever doorway he had carried me through. Nothing. Not so much as a fire escape.

How did he bring me up here? Oh Christ, don't tell me he can fly too!

"Or I could just put off the inevitable," Mordant continued, half to himself. "Delay the decision while lying to myself that 'they' wouldn't find out, right up to the moment the choice would be taken out of my hands." He sighed. "God only knows what they might do then. Will do," he amended.

I struggled against the panic screaming at me to flee, even if it meant leaping off the building, consequences be damned.

"But why the interest in you?" he continued, his brow furrowed and suspicious. "Have you ever met anyone else like . . . um, me?"

I shook my head. "You're the first. So far as I know," I amended.

He nodded. "And what are we going to do about that?" he asked, as if of himself, his voice low and thoughtful.

For some reason I can't explain, I became very much aware of my wedding ring. A week had passed since my husband's death, and I still hadn't been able to take it off. "Are you going to turn me into, ah, one of you?"

Now he laughed. "It doesn't work that way."

It doesn't? How does it work then, Mr. Ember? Exactly how did you become what you are? Were you born this way?

"So what are my options?" I asked with forced levity; wondering, all things considered, why I even cared what the answer might be.

You know why.

He was quiet for a moment. "You have to understand something," he said slowly. "Me, what I am, I wasn't—I wasn't brought up in the culture."

"What were you?" I asked, filling in the silence that followed.

Another pause. "An accident," he said, frowning. "An anomaly. An outsider, then and now. Currently on probation, you might say." He took another step toward me. I forced myself not to run. After all, what good would it do?

"The others," I said. "Constance and the rest. They . . ."

"What?"

How to say it? "See to your needs?"

He nodded in reply.

Take your time. You have to phrase this very carefully. "Any chance maybe that I . . . ?"

The cold look he gave me was all the answer I needed. "Having not been brought up *topovar*, none of them would accept you," he said. "Much less my own kind. You would be considered untrustworthy, a bomb in danger of going off at the worst possible time. Unintentionally, perhaps, but that wouldn't matter." He closed his eyes. "And even if I were to press the issue, something might—happen. Perhaps not directly; I doubt any of my own people would run the risk of offending, much less angering, me. But a few words, dropped into certain ears, could very easily lead to an unfortunate 'accident'." He pursed his lips. "They are, each and every one, secretive to the point of fanaticism."

I swallowed. Oh well, it had been worth a shot. "So I guess that's it, then."

Mordant nodded in agreement. "Yes."

Then he came for me.

I closed my eyes. After all, if I couldn't see it coming, maybe we could skip the terrifying prelude and go straight to the (or so he had claimed) pleasurable final act.

I felt him take me by the wrist. "I'm so sorry," he said.

Then he pulled me to my feet.

"This makes me a selfish bastard," he said. "But I have too many unanswered questions. Questions which, for whatever reason, keep leading back to you. So I'm afraid I can't let you die. At least, not yet. But I will make you this promise. If it looks as though they've learned about you, if they find out you know about them—about us—then I swear that I will do everything in my power to end your life before they can get to you."

For the life of me, I couldn't think of anything to say to that. "Thanks," I finally muttered.

And with a complete lack of irony in his voice, which frightened me more than anything else he had said, he replied, "You're welcome," as he led me away.

⬚

I closed my eyes as I tightened my hold around Mordant's neck, waiting for the inevitable slip, soon to be followed by the familiar sensation of falling. There was one anxious moment, swiftly corrected. Finally he paused.

"You can let go," he said. "We're down."

I didn't, opening my eyes instead to stare over Mordant's shoulder at the brick wall of the building he had just climbed down, the rough umami surface less than a foot from my nose.

Eventually I managed to relax sufficiently to release my grip. "What now?" I asked.

He looked at the van. "Can't take their vehicle," he decided. "They might be able to track it. And mine is sure to be a crime scene by now."

I found myself plotting alternatives, then the absurdity of my situation struck me. *This man has all but said he's going to kill you, and you're still trying to help him?*

63

Well, so what? Nothing is going to change, after all, I reminded myself. No matter how many different ways this story is told, it's still going to end the same way.

Of course, Mordant had no way of knowing that. And I still had my friends' welfare to concern myself with.

"This—Mistress of yours," he said. "Where did you say she lives?"

"Sunny's not my Mistress," I told him. "And she lives on Nob Hill. No, wait . . ."

He gave me a suspicious glance. "She doesn't live on Nob Hill?"

"Yes, she does. That is . . ." I took a deep breath. "Give me a moment, you're confusing me. What's today?"

He looked at his watch. "Tuesday."

I nodded. "Okay. Yes, she lives on Nob Hill, but if this is Tuesday, she won't be there. She'll be at Warren's."

"Who's Warren?"

I opened my mouth to explain, then gave up. He had no reason to know or care anyway. "He's a friend," I summarized. "She always spends Tuesday evenings at his house. He lives over in Liberty Hill."

Mordant looked around. "Is that far from here?"

I checked the street signs. "Not very." I made some mental calculations. "What about your other car?"

"My people have that one," he said. "But we'd have to make our way back to the Fairmont to get it, because I don't want any of them sticking their noses outside of that hotel until daylight, and that's a good distance from here." He frowned. "You say your friend's house is reasonably close by?"

"Yes," I replied. "There are buses. Or we could take a cab. Either that or walk," I finished, the arches of my feet grumbling in protest.

"Walk?" I watched him mull. "Walking might be safer," he decided, "since the people after you don't seem to be terribly concerned about vehicles. Not to mention witnesses." He grimaced. "I'd like a reasonable chance to see them coming, and the more people there are around, the more difficult that becomes. How hard will it be to dodge the crowds?"

I thought about it. "Won't be easy," I said. "But if we stick to the side streets whenever possible, we should be able to avoid the more heavily trafficked areas."

He stepped back with a wave of his hand. "Then lead on."

I remembered the last time I had seen Miss Sunny, only a couple of months earlier. Also at Warren's, who'd been hosting that month's play party. Sunny had been scening with Nancy, the diminutive girl hanging from the X-shaped timbers of a St. Andrew's cross as Sunny worked her exposed back over with a bull hide flogger. I'd cringed with every stroke, knowing from personal experience just how hard that thing could hit, the impact alone sufficient to take one's breath away, discounting the stinging—yet contradictorily delicious—pain.

By that point it had become a contest. Miss Sunny's face shined from her exertions as she worked to do what no one else had yet managed, to wrest from that delicate frame what Nancy—a longtime Jacqueline Carey fan like myself—referred to as her *signale*, her safeword.

"You're-mak-ing-me-look-weak!" Miss Sunny huffed, grunting with each stroke as Nancy hung from her bonds, her face glowing with a jasmine rapture.

Finally the dark-skinned dominatrix did what every other Top before her had done at one time or another. "Okay, I give." She tossed her flogger to the floor and rubbed her upper arm. "Warren, take the little brat down and lead her to the sofa. No need to carry her, she'll probably just float there on her own. And wrap her in a blanket so she stays warm."

Everyone chuckled as Warren escorted Nancy to the couch, the tiny bottom's eyes unfocused, her face wreathed with an ecstatic smile, her dainty feet barely appearing to make contact with the floor.

As I watched Miss Sunny pour herself a cup of punch from a sideboard, heavily laden with a variety of party foods and beverages, I felt a bit of the devil surface in me as well. As soon as she lifted the cup to her lips, Sunny saw me coming. "Oh, God," she murmured.

I skipped over to her, a series of movements designed to show my breasts off to their best advantage. "Good evening, Miss Sunny!" I chirped, bouncing in place on the balls of my feet.

She sighed. "And what in the name of all that's holy do *you* want? In case it's escaped your notice, my right arm is cramping something fierce. And I'm not ambidextrous, which means my left is worthless too. If that husband of yours forgot his toy bag, tell him he can borrow my flogger," she said, gesturing at the discarded item in question. "In fact, if he wants it, he can have it. Otherwise I'm going to take it back to Lolly's and trade it in for one made of rubber." She stared at Nancy, a small, flannel-covered bundle on the sofa. "And thick rubber at that."

"Oh no, we're not playing tonight," I said with what I hoped was a wicked smile. "I just wanted to tell you the good news!"

"Oh, dear God," Miss Sunny said in the tones of the long suffering and much put upon. "What now?"

I noticed my husband approaching, so I ramped up the exuberance. "We talked just before we left the house, and it's official!" I said as I continued to bounce. "We've redone the will, and guess what? If anything happens to Sir, *you* inherit me!"

She stared at me for a moment, mouth slightly agape, before turning to rest her hand on Julius's arm. "A lung, a kidney, half a liver," she said in a low voice. "Anything you need. All you have to do is ask."

⚏

Oddly enough, I had been the one responsible for introducing Warren to Mistress Sunshine. Like so many of the people who became an important part of my life during those years, we had met online. He had messaged me privately on AOL when he saw me in *La Chateau*, addressing me as 'Ma'am'.

After a brief interlude of uproarious laughter—and a recommendation by me that he learn how to read profiles—I informed him that the students I taught English Lit to at the local high school were the only people who ever referred to me as 'Ma'am' (and not that many of them). He apologized for the error, after which I apologized for making him feel the need to apologize. Following this display of table tennis regret, we both relaxed and, over the ensuing months, became regular BFFs. He had long entertained submissive fantasies but, like me, had not yet taken them 'real time'. After an hour or so spent getting to know one another, he told me that, unable to find a partner he felt he could trust, he'd been mulling over the pros and cons of employing a professional dominatrix, a concept so alien to my psyche it fascinated me. I had a made a few casual friends within *La Chateau,* but never before had I ever experienced such a genuine chemistry with another like-minded individual as I did with Warren. We sometimes talked into the early morning hours about our dreams and our desires, as well as our needs. And as the months passed, I found myself soaking up his educated and perceptive insights like a sponge on the seemingly un-likely chance I might one day grow a backbone and do more than indulge in 'wham-bam-thank-you-ma'am' cybering under temporary screen names, which I would always delete immediately afterwards, unlike my primary screen name, PhedreFan. That one I saved for chatting with friends and socializing within *La Chateau.*

And even though Warren didn't share much personal about himself during the early days of our friendship, I could tell the man had an IQ high enough to fry eggs with. I only learned later that he was fifteen years older than I and held a tenured faculty position at UCSF as a professor of cognitive neuroscience. Impressed by his intellect, I would occasion-ally tease him, encouraging him to give the dark side a try and cyber-dominate me. Though he never felt comfortable doing so, once in a very rare while I'd catch him in an experimental mood and he would make a plausible effort, only to collapse midway amidst a fit of the silly giggles, which I'd exacerbate by returning the favor with even less competent attempts:

PhedreFan: On your knees!
Severin: ::woof::
PhedreFan: Now take that flogger and give me a good whack on the rear, worm!
Severin: Which end do I use?
PhedreFan: The stiff end, pond scum!
Severin: Are we still talking about the flogger?

As the weeks passed, and our trust levels grew, we segued from online texting to the occasional phone call. It must be said, though, that I found it hard to reconcile Warren's deep bass voice with the submissive masoch-ist I had come to know, who craved humiliation the way Paula Poundstone craved Pop Tarts. But then, that went both ways:

Severin: I must confess I'm having a bit of trouble nowadays reading your Instant Messages without that Scarlett O'Hara accent of yours echoing throughout my head.

PhedreFan: What accent?

Over the ensuing months we grew even closer. I would call him to whine over abandonment issues with my father, or to share my concerns about my sister's now-troubled marriage, as well as the gossip raging at church over Bethany's friendship with her oldest boy's Sunday School teacher, Hannah Campbell. Not to be outdone, Warren frequently returned the favor, typically calling late at night (for such a brilliant man, the three hour time difference between North Carolina and California continually escaped him), sharing his guilt over his parents' disappointment with his perennial bachelor status and the accompanying lack of offspring.

Once, after a particularly disturbing online experience, I logged on to AOL, found him there, then wheedled a phone call out of him.

"What's wrong with me?" I asked, my voice barely audible even in my own ears.

He expelled a commiserative sigh. "What's the problem now, dear lady?"

It took me a while to work up the courage to share my latest cybering episode with him. It had been the most extreme one thus far, and I found myself obeying commands and doing things that both thrilled and horrified me. Then, after it was over and we'd both logged off, and I'd once again deleted the temporary screen name, a bout of depression had settled over me like a hot, wet blanket. Not an unfamiliar scenario, but this had been one of the worst.

I curled around my body pillow and held the phone close. "What sane person wants these things? *Needs* these things?" I whispered, my throat vinegar tight.

Warren clucked his tongue. "'In an insane society, the sane man must appear insane.'"

Despite my need to wallow in a cocoon of narcissistic melancholy, I couldn't help but smile. "Doctor Who, right?"

"Star Trek. And conversely," he continued, "in a sane society, the insane man must *appear* sane. Survival traits perpetuated via natural selection. You see?"

I pulled the covers over my head like a five-year old. "Well, I do remember that one episode with Kirk and Spock getting flogged . . ."

He sighed. "We are what we are, my dear. I say this not only as a friend, but as an accredited expert whose musings on this subject have polluted any number of periodicals both academic and populist. The average human being has no idea how much of his or her behavior, laboring under the commonplace casuistry of 'free will', is predicated by the collective hardwiring of our biology, determined itself by hundreds of thousands of years of evolutionary development. It's not what one *feels*, but rather what one *does* with those feelings, which draws the line between the rational and the delusional."

"'Love as thou wilt'," I said, repeating the quote like the mantra it had become for me.

Warren was quiet for a time. "My dear, when all is said and done, our particular aberrations are not uncommon. And fairly benign, all things considered. Trust me, there are far darker fantasies in the world. At least we can rationalize ours through the evolutionary imperative. And as a woman, you more so than myself."

"Chauvinist." I squeezed my eyes shut at the thought of what one of my fellow instructors, a hardcore feminist by the name of Tina Brown, would say about my secret proclivities. "And don't be so quick to make unwarranted assumptions."

"Humanity's origins lie in a cruel and violent past, my dear," Warren replied. "The consensual and negotiated sharing of power between men and women is a recent conceit, still struggling to be incorporated into modern society, and for a sizable part of the world it remains an alien concept still."

My cat, a Maine Coon I'd named Sir Stephen, burrowed under the sheets to butt at my hand with his grapefruit-sized head, demanding to be rubbed. "Gloria Steinem would spit on my shadow as I walked by," I mumbled miserably, scratching a nearby feline ear.

"Just remember this: feminism is supposed to be about the right to make choices. So long as it's *you* making the choices, even if said choice is to abrogate them, then it is a lifestyle, not a pathology."

I pulled Sir Stephen close, his rumbling purr a much needed comfort. "How many times have you given yourself that same speech?" I whispered.

"Made completely off the cuff," Warren said with a sniff, deftly avoiding my question. "Didn't have to call 'Line!' even once."

"Christ, I'm such a cliché," I pouted. "And a bad one at that."

"M'Love, we can be as vain as we please, but in the end, there is nothing new under the sun. Every uncertainty you have, every mulling hour spent questioning your innate nature, any number of others once did so long ago. And much more eloquently, I might add."

"Bite me."

"Only if you bite me harder."

So when the opportunity came, and Warren finally (albeit reluctantly) agreed to it, I created a private chat room on AOL and invited my friend in so I could introduce him to Mistress Sunshine. Since both lived in San Francisco, it had felt like a natural fit.

Miss Sunny had been a regular in *La Chateau* for years, though only rarely gracing us with her presence, and she and I had been online acquaintances for quite some time prior to my meeting Warren. The rumor was, in fact, that it had been she who had originally created *La Chateau*, though the lady herself neither confirmed nor denied this. And while I had long been convinced that the vast majority of the 'Doms' I occasionally cybered with had (if possible) even less real time experience than myself—and almost certainly spouses or girlfriends as well—it hadn't taken long for me to see the difference between them and her. Sunny exuded an unpretentious authority, which I could not help but respond to, and I quickly found myself going to her for information, advice, and even comfort on occasion when the more brutal regulars in the chat room (such as Bluebeard) routinely castigated me for a NeverWannaBe. Bluebeard was particularly cruel, attacking me on multiple fronts, including his exaggerated estimation of my weight, based on an unguarded comment I'd once made:

Bluebeard: Well, well, look who just popped in! Evening, Blimpy!

The saddest thing about those encounters was the sense of shame and self-recrimination overwhelming me when and after they occurred, because I *was* heavier than I'd have liked to have been, though nowhere near the gargantuan proportions Bluebeard cheerfully speculated upon. Like a carnivore parsing a herd for the easiest prey, he seemed to intuitively know when and how to pounce on my insecurities, like a jackal on a wounded lamb.

Why I even cared what he thought is something I cannot explain. Like the unwanted and undesired physical climax which on rare occasions can accompany a rape, my body insisted on betraying me during the infrequent visits Bluebeard (and others like him) paid our little group, though he was by far the worst of the lot. No matter how much I legitimately despised him, there existed within me an innate element of my psyche which not only couldn't help but physically respond to his humiliation, it even (goddamn it) sussed out within me the desire, the fucking *need*, to please him, with me realizing all the while how cheerfully and cruelly he would exploit this weakness on my part, were I to ever give him an opportunity to do so. Which made me despise myself even more, contributing to what became over time a hatefully vicious cycle.

Thankfully Bluebeard's appearances were infrequent, if not rare, and for the most part my evenings within those virtual walls kept me sane inside my lie of a life. I happily, if sometimes a bit wearily, listened to Warren as he shared the details of his newfound happiness after his 'collaring' by Mistress Sunshine, not to mention his euphoria at being included in their very exclusive (and very private) BDSM group. After so many years of ascetic loneliness my friend had finally found not only the satisfaction of his needs, but a sense of belonging as well, and I did my level best not to allow my unspoken, and unwarranted, resentment to fester over what a wonderful turn his life had taken, as compared with my own.

Then, several months later, Sunny introduced me to Julius.

⚜

Mordant and I navigated the darkened and, at this time of night, somewhat intimidating streets of the Mission District, taking care to avoid the crowds piled like autumn leaves in the doorways of various and sundry bars and restaurants. And while I would have felt far more comfortable trawling in his wake, Mordant would have none of that, insisting instead that I precede him. After two successive kidnapping attempts, my guess was he wanted to keep me in sight at all times. As we turned a corner we passed a particularly raucous band of celebrants who, upon catching a glimpse of my companion, started hooting and whistling, men and women alike. He ignored both.

"Not as cool here," he said in a preoccupied tone, eyes flicking from one miniature bacchanalia to the other.

"It's the microclimates," I said.

"The what?"

Constance's Percocet had begun to wear off, and I felt the bite of her Spanx, circling my waist like an irritable boa constrictor. "The temperature sometimes changes with the neighborhood. Not so much during the winter, though. When I first got here, my husband told me on more than one occasion, 'If you don't like the weather, take a long walk.'"

Mordant grunted a surly acknowledgment. "How much further?"

"Just a few blocks more."

A slim hand, nails painted a tangerine orange and belonging to an inebriated young man dressed as colorfully as a tropical bird, reached out to touch my arm. "Hey, why don't you and your friend join us?" he said, exhaling a cloud of alcohol like the hissing of sleet on pane glass.

I heard a noise behind me, and before I could draw enough breath to warn the little fairy creature away, Mordant stepped forward.

"Back the fuck off," he growled. And I mean, literally, just that. Growled, like a territorial animal warning a trespasser away from its kill. I looked down and noted with a sudden terror that the nails on Mordant's hand had extended out maybe half an inch or so, and for a moment all I could see was this rainbow attired man-child sprawled on the sidewalk screaming, his belly sliced open like a dumpling.

The boy (and that's really all he was, just a boy) lifted both hands as he stepped back, his falsetto voice cracking like a thirteen-year-old shaking hands with puberty for the first time. "Hey, man, we're all cool, right?" No bravado, no token attempt to salvage a challenged masculinity. Instead he back-pedaled to his friends, who looked at Mordant as if he were a Rottweiler who had appeared out of nowhere, mouth foaming rabidly. No aggrieved comebacks ("What's your problem?"), no awkward attempts to make light of the situation. Instead they huddled together, the boy and his friends alike, like rabbits seeking safety in numbers against the cold predatory glare of a circling hawk moments away from diving into their midst.

I took Mordant by the hand and led him away. "Correct me if I'm wrong," I whispered, "but wasn't the idea *not* to be noticed?"

Mordant shrugged, allowing me to guide him. He actually looked uncomfortable. "It happens sometimes, like that."

"What does?"

He frowned, not saying anything. We walked in joint silence for a couple of blocks, and I had almost forgotten my question when he spoke again.

"When—*it*—first happened to me," he said, his words as clipped and precise as the strokes of a chef's knife, "and I became what I am now, I . . . changed." Then he laughed, a short bark, like that of a bitter old man full of regrets. "How ridiculous does that sound? 'Changed'? Like someone who gets religion just before the trial starts."

I've always believed I have good intuition, at least where men are concerned, and mine was now elbowing me in the side and whispering that if I broke precedent and kept my mouth shut for once, I might learn something useful.

"We think we know who we are," he continued in a tone as dark as his mood. "Even when we're under pressure to take advantage of something, or someone, for our own benefit. Situational morality or whatnot. Or when we just give in to . . . whatever; anger, lust, fear. But even when we fall short of whatever image we have of ourselves, we still believe we know who we are. Right?"

I maintained my silence, watching the fingers of his right hand clench and knot, the knuckles crackling with a strobe-light intensity.

Finally he let out an exasperated sigh. "You know how it is when you see things?" he continued. "And smell things? Especially that, the way the mind associates emotions with odors?"

I nodded, wondering where this train was headed.

"It's like . . . you feel yourself reacting—emotionally, that is—to familiar things, but not in a familiar way," Mordant said. "You smell bread baking, but instead of making you feel hungry, it makes you feel irritable. You hear a song on the radio you loved once, but now you're confused, because you can't remember *why* it made you feel good. You see a pretty girl walk by, but instead of wanting to see a smile that lights up her face, you want . . ."

"You want what?" I finally asked, regretting the question the moment it left my mouth.

He didn't respond right away. "Nothing," he finally grumbled, in lieu of elaborating, much to my relief. "Never mind."

A conversational lull followed, which continued for some time before Mordant spoke again, his voice even colder than before. "Then, as time goes on, it gets worse. You—who you were, the person you remember being— keeps shrinking, down to a dot, like the picture on one of those old cathode ray TV sets after it's been turned off. Then one day you find yourself in front of a mirror, staring at a complete stranger while asking, 'When did I lose myself?'."

Then he turned, and the strange smile that suddenly lit his face un- nerved me; an unfamiliar distortion, like a reflection in a funhouse mirror. It reminded me how some cultures consider the showing of teeth while smiling to be an act of aggression. "But then, isn't it all up to us in the end? Who and/or what we chose to be?" he said.

My swollen feet hurt from all the walking I'd been doing in Constance's elegant stilettos, not to mention that each breath I took now came with a stitch in my side. "Not according to Warren," I said as I shook two more Percocet into my palm.

Mordant stared down at the sidewalk. "Your friend the college professor?"

What was that in his voice? Irritation? Insecurity? "He's a scientist who also lectures. Specializes in cognitive neurology." I filled my mouth with saliva, then popped both the tablets and swallowed. "According to him, there is no such thing as free will, it's just an illusion. He told me once we're all just bags of chemicals, programmed through the process of natural selection and conditioned by our environment to think however we think, feel however we feel."

Mordant frowned. "Do you believe that?"

One of the pills tried to stick in my throat, and I swallowed repeatedly to clear it. "He makes a strong argument," I said when I could speak again. "He's written multiple papers on stuff like that, as well as evolutionary psychology, how as human beings our behavior is basically hardwired. Like being gay, for example."

Mordant shook his head. "I don't understand how that would work. If a man is really a homo—um, homo*sexual*, how does a trait like that get passed down from one generation to another?"

I took slow deep breaths to stave off the blade in my side till the meds could kick in. "I'll explain it to you the way Warren explained it to me. Answer me this: As a father, what is a gay man less likely to do than a straight man?"

Mordant's brow knitted. He now seemed to be enjoying our little back and forth. "Get married?" he said, smiling.

"Not a fan of the afternoon talk show circus, are you?" I replied, returning the smile. "I majored in English Literature, but I minored in History. Trust me, I could give you a list as long as your arm of the reasons why gay men throughout antiquity, who weren't even physically attracted to women, procreated, starting with the lion's share of ancient civilizations who believed that the primary purpose of women was to continue the male line. Which is why so many modern cultures, even today, do their level best to isolate women from other men, whether it's the beekeeper suits in the conservative Islamic countries or the polygamists in Utah kicking boys out of their communities once they start to become men. Things like culture, religion, you name it, dress this sort of thing up in rhetoric, but according to Warren it all boils down to the same thing: the continuous transmission of one person's genes as opposed to someone else's. Traits that are successfully passed along predominate over time. Those that aren't, don't.

"Which, again, according to Warren, is why rape has always been so prevalent throughout human history. Not the most efficient way to pass along one's genes, but what it lacks in terms of boosting individual survival odds is made up for via sheer force of numbers as regards potential offspring. Easier than having to woo a choosy woman, particularly for those men who don't have much to recommend them in the first place." A faint, but pleasurable, buzz from the Percocet had begun to work its way throughout my head. "Which, at least for me, has always explained the antipathy of a certain kind of male toward birth control."

Mordant looked confused. "I thought we were talking about gay fathers."

I smiled while floating down the sidewalk. "We were. Sorry, playing mental hopscotch is one of my favorite pastimes."

He nodded. "Okay, So, back to your previous statement, and assuming what you just said is true, what is it then that—if he becomes a father—a gay man is less likely to do than one who's straight, thereby boosting the chances of his genes being passed along to the next generation?"

I leaned towards Mordant, speaking in a stage whisper that must have been audible twenty feet away. "Molest his daughters." I swayed a bit, then righted myself. The drugs had now officially kicked in. (We have liftoff!)

"Or do I have to explain why young girls who were the victims of such, particularly in ancient times, were far less likely to bring to term healthy carriers of genes—sorry, I mean children—who would then survive to adulthood and become parents themselves?"

Mordant frowned. "Not really," he said. "I saw stuff like that, growing up where I did."

"Really?" Chemical bravery surged through me like a double scotch. "Such as?"

To my surprise, he smiled. "When my sister was young, my mother had this boyfriend."

I tried to imagine someone stupid enough to do to this man's sister what it sounded like he was suggesting. "And you were how old?"

"Thirteen."

"And how old was she?"

"Eleven going on sixteen," he said, still smiling. "Not that she encouraged the bastard in any way. And he really didn't do anything . . . physical. But several times I caught him trying to sneak a peek through her bedroom door, or staring out the kitchen window while she was in the backyard sunbathing. Etcetera, etcetera. But then he stopped coming around, so that was the end of that."

"He and your mom break up?" I asked.

Now he was actually grinning. "Something along those lines," Mordant said. "Got expensive to come around our way."

"Oh? What, your mother was high maintenance?"

"Nope. Car trouble, whenever he came by."

"Ah."

"But back to free will. Your friend doesn't believe in it?"

I took my first painless breath in a while, sighing with relief. "Warren participated in an experiment once where they hooked some people up to a series of electrodes, so that their brains could be monitored. Scientists know in which part of the brain conscious decisions are made. They asked the test subjects to make a choice about something, and discovered that signals were being sent from that area well before the test subjects consciously made their choices. That is, if I remember correctly." I dodged a crack in the sidewalk. "Warren tends to blur the narrative when astride one of his favorite hobby horses."

Mordant pursed his lips. "And what about you?"

"Do *I* believe there's no such thing as free will?" The murmurs of passersby now floated about me like the glow of fireflies. "I'd like to think there is such a thing. Even if it *is* just an illusion." Off balance, I reached out to take Mordant's hand. He started, but allowed me to intertwine my fingers with his. "My favorite college professor once told me that we can go days without water and weeks without food, but how long can any of us live without a good rationalization?"

Mordant looked ahead, a sour grin on his face. "And if good rationalizations are all we have?"

I had no idea what to say to that, so I didn't respond, and we continued our walk in silence.

After a while Mordant looked up. "It's different," he said.

Master of the understatement, my friendly gentleman monster from Hell. I allowed myself a moment of gratitude that we'd managed to successfully bypass the less savory areas of the Mission District. Things in that neighborhood had improved since I first moved to San Francisco, but some of those streets were still pretty dicey at night, and the last thing I'd wanted to watch was Mordant ripping some gangbanger's arm off and then beating him to death with it. Literally.

"Here we are," I said when we arrived at Warren's Queen Anne. Its pastel blue walls and lemon trim lit the dark with a fresh licorice glow. A gable with a stained glass porthole topped its three stories, while three bay windows punctuated the facade on the second floor. Twin garage doors, a sybaritic luxury in this town, fronted the structure at ground level.

Mordant released my hand and, once again, made me take the lead to the front porch. I used the heavy knocker, eschewing the brightly-lit doorbell, an old code to let Warren know there was a friend outside and not some random solicitor.

I was about to try the knocker again when the door opened a crack and my friend peered out. His face morphed from surprise to sympathy in a moment's time. "Sweetheart," he said, his soft, deep voice floating in the air like a golden mist, countering the baritone scent of the Grey Flannel cologne he practically bathed in. "Please come in. Who's your friend?"

"This is Mordant," I said, feeling awkward as I made the introduction.

"My, what an interesting name," Warren said as he stepped back, allowing us inside.

"We didn't come at a bad time, did we?" I asked. True, he wasn't in scene garb, but Sunny had never been much for that sort of thing.

"Oh no, we were about to sit down for some coffee in the living room," he said, escorting us in. "It's funny, but we were just talking about you, and how no one had seen hide nor hair of you since the funeral. Oh, and do give Nancy a call, she's been worried sick. Or so she says," he sniffed.

The muscles in my shoulders clenched so tight, I knew I was moments away from a painful cramp. "I just needed some time to myself."

"Please, sit," Warren said, indicating the sofa. "Mist- Miss Sunny's freshening up, she shouldn't be but a moment. Can I get you something to eat? You look positively malnourished."

Give it some time, I almost said. "You're sure we're not intruding?" I asked, taking a seat on the couch. Mordant waited until I settled myself before joining me, a strange bit of courtesy that felt both odd and familiar at the same time.

Warren shook his head. "We were just commiserating over Julius. Still doesn't feel real, you know?"

I swallowed. "Yes."

"Need a tissue?" Warren said. "Fresh box in the kitchen. Wouldn't take more than a moment to break it out."

I gave him my best attempt at a smile. "I'll be fine."

He nodded, then sat facing us. "I thought I knew everything there was to know about you," he said, looking from me to Mordant, then back to me again. "Or is this a new friend?"

"We met only yesterday," Mordant said. His stiff tone and carriage filled the air between the two of them like an uncomfortable silence. "Ms. St. Clair found herself in a bit of trouble, and I happened along at just the right time."

"Excuse me, what?" Warren sputtered before turning in my direction. "Trouble?"

I took a deep breath, trying to think of some sane way to explain the events of the previous night, then gave it up. "Some people kidnapped me," I blurted out.

"Are you serious? You must be joking." Warren turned to Mordant. "Tell me she's joking."

Mordant frowned. "Why? Are you waiting for a punchline?"

Warren did a double take, which I couldn't blame him for. Being talked down to by someone who looked young enough to be carded wasn't something my friend, who struck terror into the hearts of grad students, was accustomed to. A fact now evident in his suspicious tone. "And your part in all this is . . . ?" he asked Mordant.

I interceded before things could get ugly. "He saved my life, Warren."

My friend blinked incredulously. "Why, for Christ's sake?"

"Well, you know how it is," Mordant said. "Slow evening, everything on the tube's a rerun—"

"That is *not* what I meant! Goodness!" Warren said, before refocusing on me. "My dear, why would anyone want to kidnap *you*? Julius wasn't what anyone would call a man of modest means, to be sure, but he wasn't Daddy Warbucks either. Not to mention the fact he's deceased, which would make collecting a ransom just a wee bit problematic."

The memory of Sid's weight as he lay on top of me robbed me of my breath, as did the recollection of my neck in the crook of Lester's elbow as he locked down on my windpipe. "I don't think they wanted money," I replied, once I could breathe again.

Warren lifted his hands skyward. "Well what, then?"

"Indeed," drawled a familiar throaty voice. "What, then?"

My eyes, and those of the two men, turned to the doorway as Miss Sunny stepped into the room.

She glanced over each of us in turn, her blue-black skin glowing like Chanel No. 5 in the ambient lamplight, her dress a simple white sheath which, as with everything she wore, enhanced a regal bearing as pungent as musk.

She lifted her arms and crossed the floor toward me. "Child."

Throat closing, I rose to greet her. Tears I'd been suppressing for days overflowed, and as she folded me into her arms I wept silently. She held me close, murmuring soft, unintelligible comforts. I bent down so the tiny woman could switch her embrace to my neck, allowing me to bury my face in the thick caramel mane of her hair.

"There, there," she whispered, stroking my back as though I were a rescue kitten. "You be still. I don't know what the problem is, but rest assured we will resolve it." She tilted her head toward Mordant. "And who might this be?"

I stepped out of Miss Sunny's arms as my companion rose. "My name is Mordant, ma'am," he said.

"Are you from Indonesia?" Sunny asked.

Mordant looked puzzled. "No, ma'am."

"I only ask because that is the sole country I am aware of in which the average citizen has just the one name," Sunny said.

"I beg your pardon," Mordant apologized solemnly. "Ember. My name is Mordant Ember."

"Not much of an improvement," she said, frowning, before leading me back to the sofa, taking Mordant's former seat as she drew me down next to her.

The flustered look Mordant gave her surprised me. I hadn't seen him quite so nonplussed, even at Hendrick's. "My, ah, family came from Europe. Originally," Mordant added.

"Whereabouts?" Miss Sunny asked as she placed her warm arm over my shoulders, pulling me close into a protective and exclusionary embrace. It was all I could do not to simply melt into it.

Now Mordant truly appeared uncomfortable. "All over, as I understand it, but originally from a place called Livoire se Andole."

"Hmm. Never heard of it. But then, geography was never my forte," she droned. "And I'm thinking I've missed a good bit of the conversation thus far. So," she said, turning to me, "catch me up, little one."

I skipped what had happened at the Golden Gate Bridge and began afterwards, explaining how I had woke up in some sort of medical lab in the Tenderloin. I told her about the attack, and about Mordant's intervention, leaving out the incidental disemboweling.

"Gracious," Miss Sunny said, almost mockingly. "And how fortunate you were when this stranger appeared out of nowhere to rescue you."

I shook my head. "I know how crazy it all sounds . . ."

"Child, you have a profound talent for understatement," she said. "Would you care to try again?"

"It's the truth!" I said, aware of the petulance in my voice, not to mention how disrespectful I must have sounded, but I couldn't restrain myself. "I don't know who they were, or why they wanted me, or—well, anything," I finished lamely.

"And what about you, sir?" Sunny said as she turned back to Mordant. "Do you always appear in the nick of time to rescue the fair damsel, like the hero in one of those cheap thrillers on basic cable?"

I could see the darkness rising behind Mordant's eyes, the initial flickering of orange around his irises. "A very dangerous man possessed a list of names, which included Abby's. And others," he said.

Miss Sunny lifted a skeptical eyebrow. "A man, eh? And who is this man to you?"

"He once worked for me," Mordant said, brow furrowing in thought. "He wasn't what he seemed." Mordant removed the paper from his hip pocket. "Here's the list."

Sunny took the proffered legal sheet, then studied it. "Some of these are our people," she said, sounding both surprised and suspicious at the same time.

"Do you recognize any of those names? Other than those belonging, or once belonging, to your group, I mean," Mordant asked.

Miss Sunny shook her head without lifting her gaze. "No."

Warren got up from his seat and peered over her shoulder. His eyebrows rose almost to mid-forehead. "I do," he whispered.

We all stared at him. Flustered, he took the paper from Sunny's outstretched hand. "And you would too," Warren told me, "if you had known their real names, as opposed to their User IDs."

I wet my lips. "Bloodlines?"

Mordant shifted his focus from Miss Sunny back to me. "Are you saying you're related to these people?" he asked me, gesturing at the list.

I shook my head. "No. At least, I don't think so." I returned Mordant's gaze. "You've never heard of Bloodlines?"

"No."

"It's a social media website for people trying to reconnect with their family tree," I said in reply to his bemused look. "Julius actually created it, one of those dorm room entrepreneurial projects like Facebook. Though not nearly so successful," I added before turning back to Warren. "You know who these other people are?"

He nodded. "David Collins here," he said, pointing near the top of the list. "That's BigBadWolf."

I jumped up from my seat and stepped behind him. "Where?"

"Right here," he said, pointing.

I squinted. "Archibald Collins?"

"Archibald is his first name, which he never uses," Warren said, a smile twisting the left corner of his mouth. "I'm sure you can understand why."

I felt my jaw drop. "BigBadWolf is David Collins? Jesus."

"Who is David Collins?" Sunny asked, bemused and a bit annoyed, perhaps at her own ignorance.

To my surprise, it was Mordant who answered her question. "He's a billionaire, originally from Sneadsville, North Carolina. He's created and then sold several Internet businesses over the past twenty years. As I understand it, he now owns and operates one of those venture companies trying to privatize space travel."

"Sneadsville?" Miss Sunny said, looking in my direction. "That's where you're from, isn't it dear? Do you know the gentleman?"

I saw Mordant's eyes widen suddenly, his gaze snapping in my direction. I shook my head. "He kicked the dust of our small town off his shoes a good many years ago," I told Miss Sunny. "I did go to school with his little brother Jesse, though."

"Jesse Collins," Warren mused. "The football player? The one they call Freight Train? Played defensive end for the Panthers?"

I nodded. "Another Collins who left town and never came back."

"How interesting," Miss Sunny said, her voice a violet drawl. "Are there any other billionaires or sports stars on that list?"

"Not that I know of, Ma'am," Warren said.

"And you are familiar with these names how?" she asked.

Warren and I exchanged glances. "Well, we were both members of Bloodlines long before I first met you, Ma'am," Warren told Sunny. "Very popular site for folks trying to climb their family trees, though I never did understand the .us extension."

"I seem to recall Julius saying that the dot com domain had been taken," I said.

Warren shrugged. "Neither of us had any idea the other was a member when we first met," he said, including me with a gesture. "No reason we should have, really. We haunted completely different forums."

Miss Sunny nodded. "I know you were adopted," she said, placing her hand over Warren's before shifting her attention back to me. "So I can understand you searching for your ancestors. But unless I am mistaken Abby, you told me you are very well acquainted with your family history."

"Only on my mother's side, the Sneads. I know next to nothing about my father's family, the MacAlisters." *Not to mention my father's current location,* I thought. *Or whether he's alive or dead.*

Miss Sunny switched her attention back to Warren. "You have yet to explain how you know these names."

"Mr. St. Claire asked for my help with a project," Warren replied. "As a consultant. There had been a volunteer medical survey."

"I remember taking that," I mused. "A long time ago, before I met Julius."

"As did I," Warren added. "Your husband had accumulated an enormous amount of data from those questionnaires. He and his chief programmer were working on some sort of algorithm he had hoped to monetize by helping people connect with previously unknown family members where there were no written genealogical records, or where questions of paternity existed. He hired me as an advisor." The paper rustled in his nervous fingers. "Julius had hopes that a successful algorithm would have increased site traffic exponentially, back before the site was hacked."

"Hacked?" Mordant interjected. "By whom?"

"We never found out," I said. "There were a few scattered posts over the Internet from people claiming responsibility for Anonymous, but we didn't take them seriously, especially after a lot of others popped up denying Anonymous had had anything to do with it."

"All that data, lost," Warren murmured sorrowfully.

"The hackers wiped out everything," I told Mordant and Miss Sunny. "They even—don't ask me how—found the cloud backups and trashed those, too."

"When did this happen?" Mordant asked.

Warren and I exchanged glances. "Maybe a month ago?" I offered.

Two weeks before the oncologist's appointment.

"I'm surprised Julius never mentioned this to me," Miss Sunny mused.

"You know how private he was about anything having to do with business," I said.

"I do indeed," she replied, half to herself. Then she straightened. "So, what now?"

"We've already spoken with Hendrick," I said.

"And?" she asked, retrieving the list from Warren and handing it back to Mordant.

"He thinks we should go to the police."

"A sensible suggestion," Sunny responded. "So why haven't you?"

"Because I have reason to believe there are law enforcement officers involved in this," Mordant said.

Sunny looked at him, then back at me. "Child, can you hear yourself?"

I folded my arms stubbornly. "I know what happened to me."

She shook her head. "This is positively insane. Not to mention dangerous. You claim that at this very moment there are psychopaths out there searching for you. And yet here you are, avoiding those persons best equipped to protect you."

I bit my lip. Everything she said made perfect sense, and it was getting harder and harder to justify my actions. "I'd be dead if it weren't for him," I stubbornly insisted. "Or worse."

"Assuming of course that your friend here hasn't been a part of this ridiculous conspiracy from the beginning," she said, looking at Mordant.

I froze. I had seen Miss Sunny stare people down before. She was fearless when her ire was up. But I had also seen the individual she was glaring at rip a man apart with his bare hands. More than once. And here she was confronting him. Worse, accusing him. She had no idea how dangerous Mordant could be, perhaps thinking that between her, Warren, and myself it was three against one. Safety in numbers.

How could I possibly explain? What if Mordant suddenly lost his temper? I found myself imagining the scene, a literal bloodbath, Sunny's dress soaked bright red, Warren a heap of torn body parts. I remembered the look in Mordant's eyes as he had shredded human flesh with his bare hands, the hot prickly blood spraying everywhere, like the fountains outside the Bellagio.

He returned her stare. "You're suspicious of me?"

She nodded. "Goddamned right I am."

Then Mordant smiled.

"Finally, someone with an ounce of common sense in this city," he said. "I was beginning to wonder."

"We only come out during the full moon," she said, folding her arms beneath her considerable bosom. Miss Sunny was quite well endowed, for such a small woman.

Mordant took a seat in a nearby empty chair. "May we start over, ma'am?"

"I'll consider it," she said.

He nodded. "As you wish."

Then he got up, retrieved a nearby phone from its base on an antique telephone table and handed it to Miss Sunny. "Is it still 911 even here?"

She looked at the phone without taking it. "It is."

"Then dial it," he said, placing the handset in her lap before sitting once again.

She looked at the phone. "So now the onus is on me. The question being, are you bluffing?"

"I've no reason to bluff," Mordant said.

"But you said there are police officers who cannot be trusted . . . ?"

"As you pointed out just a moment ago, you have no reason to trust me either," Mordant said. "But here's the thing. I did not come to this city with the intention of harming any of you, least of all Abby. To the best of my knowledge at the time, you were all potential victims. But then, I have no way of knowing that either, not for certain. So, there you are," he gestured at the phone. "Your call."

Miss Sunny picked up the handset. "If nothing else, you should be arrested for that atrocious pun," she said. "Warren?"

I recognized the shift in her voice. 'Mistress Sunshine' had taken the stage. "Yes, Ma'am?" Warren said deferentially.

"Return to the kitchen and bring us that coffee." She handed Warren the phone, then turned back to Mordant. "How do you take yours, Mr. Ember?"

I saw the orange flicker behind his eyes. "I don't drink coffee, ma'am. Nor tea, nor soft drinks of any kind."

"You must have blood like pure spring water," she murmured, before waving Warren away.

I covered my mouth to stifle the hysterical burst of laughter that threatened to overwhelm me. Sunny looked in my direction, frowning, as Warren quickly returned with a tray, balancing three brimming coffee mugs and a small pot.

"I put sugar in your special mug already," he told me with a smile, placing the tray on the table. I nodded my thanks and reached for it, relishing the warmth as I cuddled it in my hands.

Mordant looked at me, then at the tray. "How did you know?" he asked.

"Pardon me?" I said, the cup halfway to my lips.

He leaned forward. "How did you know which one was yours? The one with the sugar in it?"

I shrugged self-consciously. "It was the white one."

Mordant studied the cups. "They're all white."

"Not exactly," I said, feeling defensive and off balance, as I always did when this happened.

Mordant's hands gripped the arms of his chair. I could hear the wood groan. "I have excellent eyesight," he said. "Better than—most," he finished, glancing at Miss Sunny and Warren. "And I can assure you that those three cups are the same exact shade of white, with no chips or cracks to distinguish them." He stared round at us suspiciously. "What's going on here?"

"He doesn't know?" Miss Sunny asked me.

I shrugged, now embarrassed. "It's not the sort of thing that comes up in casual conversation."

"Know what?" Mordant said in a calm, rigid tone that terrified me, having last heard it from him as he stood over me soaked in two men's blood.

I looked to Sunny and Warren for help, then sighed when none appeared forthcoming. "I'm a tetrachromatic synesthete," I mumbled.

Mordant stared at me without expression, then turned back to Miss Sunny. "Does the lady come with footnotes?"

"I'd settle for subtitles," she drawled.

Mordant turned back to me. "What exactly is a, ah . . ."

I looked over at Warren, begging with my eyes. "Would you? Please?"

Warren snorted. "As if I don't do enough lecturing in the classroom," he grumbled. "Oh, very well."

He turned back to Mordant. "The average person has three types of cones in his or her eyes. They're the basis for vision. Our friend here," he said, gesturing at me, "has four."

Mordant gazed at me with a terrifying intensity. "What does that mean?" he asked, his voice low.

"It means she sees a broader range of the color spectrum than the rest of us," Warren said. "That mug there is her cup. She uses it when she comes by. It's marked on the bottom so I'll always know which one it is. Party trick I like to play on visitors sometimes. We see that coffee cup, and it looks white, just like the others. She looks at it and sees . . ."

"What?" Mordant filled in, looking from the cup to me.

I shrug. "It still looks white. Just a different shade than the others," I said.

"Probably some defect during production," Warren said.

Mordant leaned back. "All right," he said, his voice slow and deliberate. "So that's the tetrachromatic part. But what is a—a . . ."

"A synesthete," Warren continued, "is a person who perceives his or her environment on more than one level. For example, if we look at the color of that cup, we process it as being white. But Abby not only sees it as white, and a different shade of white at that, she also experiences the color with one of her other senses. It might taste salty, for example, when she looks at it."

"Vanilla," I said, unable to remain silent. "White smells like vanilla."

"You should try wearing your favorite perfume while this girl puts her hands over her ears and complains about how loud it is," Miss Sunny said with a trace of annoyance.

"I'm also a supertaster," I whispered, hunching my shoulders as if, with a little more effort, I could disappear between the sofa cushions.

Mordant kept his gaze fixed on me, and it was as though I could read his mind. But he was wrong. My senses might be odd, and their combination unique, but they conferred no special advantages that would attract criminal attention. Lord knows I had spent a good bit of my life searching for any practical use for them, once Warren had figured out what was different about me. After all, I'd grown up thinking everyone could smell colors. They just didn't talk about it.

But as I watched Mordant's stare grow even more intense, I wondered if he knew something I didn't.

No one spoke for a while, then Miss Sunny broke the silence. "So you're telling us," she said to Mordant, "that someone—or some group—has an unpleasant interest in the names of the people on that list of yours. A list which includes a number of those in our little circle who are also, and I am guessing here, patrons of this Bloodlines group who, it would appear, are being targeted for kidnapping and/or murder. But why?"

Mordant frowned. "Do either of you know a man who calls himself Charles Jefferson?"

"Not I," Miss Sunny said. "Warren?"

My friend shook his head. "Don't recognize the name. Do you have a picture?"

"No," Mordant said, frowning. "I might be able to get one, though."

"And this list of yours, it belongs to this man?" Miss Sunny said.

Mordant opened his mouth, then closed it. "I found it among his possessions. I can't say for certain whether or not he created it, though. It might have been given to him. Perhaps by the people who hacked your husband's website," he finished, looking at me,

"And these people are . . . ?" Miss Sunny asked.

Mordant hesitated before shaking his head. "I can't say for certain. At least, not yet."

We discussed Hendrick's speculation that hate crimes might be at the bottom of everything, but the argument sounded weak now, after uncovering the connection with Bloodlines.

"So what now?" Warren said after the room had grown silent again.

Mordant looked at each of us in turn. "How uncomfortable does the idea of private security make you?" he asked Miss Sunny.

"As opposed to our own government's?" she asked.

"Money wouldn't be a concern," Mordant said. "I wouldn't want to see anything happen to any of you."

"This while you play *Columbo?*" Miss Sunny frowned. "And what, pray tell, makes you qualified for such a thing?"

Mordant shrugged. "You can trust me, or call the police."

"I might do that," she said, glancing at the phone again.

"Then decide for yourselves," Mordant said as he got up. "I'll be keeping an eye on Abby. You and your friends do as you wish." His tone wasn't impolite, despite the harshness of his words, but he'd clearly decided where his priorities were, and they centered on me, Christ only knew why.

"Here is my cell phone number," Mordant said, writing it down. "If you decide to take advantage of my offer, or if you think of anything else, please let me know. I'll do nothing unless or until I hear from you."

I embraced Miss Sunny, followed by Warren. The scent of his cologne vibrated harshly in my ears, alongside a less pleasant (though barely noticeable) undernote; unlike Miss Sunny's toilet water, its lilac fragrance suffusing the air around her with a gentle hum like that of a swarm of bees.

"Are you certain you'll be okay with him?" Warren whispered in my ear as I hugged him fiercely.

"I'll be fine," I whispered back.

I hope . . .

Mordant politely declined an offer from Warren to call us a cab. Before we left I promised my friend yet again that I would give Nancy a call the next day.

Mordant and I walked together in silence for half a dozen blocks. Finally I couldn't stand it any longer.

"What happens now?" I asked.

He took so long to reply, I'd almost decided he hadn't heard me. "Now we talk to your other friends. Not tonight, though, it's late. We'll wait until tomorrow." He looked at me. "It's a good distance back to the hotel. Not a problem for me, but what about you?"

The thought of walking all the way back to the Fairmont in Constance's Jimmy Choos made my thighs cramp. But after what had happened earlier, how much prolonged exposure could we risk? I had no doubt that Mordant's people would come for us if he called them, assuming he were to change his mind about that, which—based on what little I knew of him thus far—seemed problematic at best. But even if he did, how long would it take for them to find us, forcing us to remain in one spot until they arrived? "I'll let you know when I run out of gas," I said, putting on the bravest face my aching feet would allow.

He smiled without replying, and we continued on our way.

We traveled as before, avoiding people as much as possible, though at this hour the crowds had begun to thin out. As a conversationalist, Mordant made a fine cigar store Indian, which left me bucket loads of time to review our situation. "What do you think is going on? Exactly?" I asked.

He shook his head. "The less you know, the safer you'll be."

"Uh huh," I said. "Two kidnapping attempts—so far—and one attempted murder. What's left to say? Ignorance *is* bliss." I felt my lower lip push out petulantly. "If one of these times they manage to get it right, I'd like to have some idea what it is I'm dying for."

I watched as he wrestled with his thoughts.

"There may be no connection at all between what's been happening to you and my concerns," he said carefully. "If that's the case, I could be putting you at even greater risk by sharing them with you."

"Do you really believe that?"

A full minute must have passed before he replied, "No, not really."

"Okay then," I said. "Please tell me what's going on. Or at least what you *think* is going on."

Mordant looked around, as if checking for eavesdroppers. "Do you believe in possession?"

"What, you mean like in *The Exorcist*?" I asked.

He nodded slowly. "Perhaps. Or maybe something else. Say, some kind of intelligent parasite that can control a person."

I pursed my lips. "Like in that Heinlein novel, *The Puppet Masters*?"

"I've never read that book," he replied. "But let's pretend I have and say possibly, yes."

I almost asked if he was kidding, then remembered that I was walking down a public street with a fuck-all honest-to-god vampire. Or something so similar to one as to render any differences moot. "I've never heard of anything like that," I said. "The kind of church I grew up in, they'd have looked at you like you were crazy if you said you believed in demonic possession. You had to go over to East End or Five Points to find those kinds of folks." I looked at him. "Do *you* believe in it?"

Mordant looked uncertain. "I don't know what I believe," he finally said. "But I know what I saw."

The uneasiness in his voice disturbed me. "What was that?"

He paused before speaking. "I saw something staring at me out of another person's eyes," he said. "Something—different. From me, from you, from anything sane. People throw the word 'alien' around a lot, but that's the only word that makes sense to me. Alien. Something so—not human— that it hurts my brain just to think about it."

"And you believe . . . I mean, you can see these things?"

His jaw tightened. "Well, yes. And no."

"Now that's indecisive. So which is it?"

He began scanning the rooftops again, which reminded me of whatever it was he had been wrestling with after we'd left the lab. Another vampire? Maybe something worse? "I've seen them," he said, choosing his words with care. "But only when they were in control. I think the rest of the time they're quiet, maybe operating at a subconscious level."

While I didn't for a moment truly believe he had seen any such thing, my skin crawled at the possibility of such a horror movie coming to life. "Why not always be in charge?" I asked.

He shrugged. "Maybe it's a process that takes time. Or maybe the human mind can't handle being controlled past a certain point without damaging its ability to function properly."

I thought about what had become a staple of everyday news. Reports of murder/suicides, and worse. People committing horrible mass killings, then turning their weapons on themselves. The mentally ill, like the poor, would always be with us. But Mordant's tale had me wondering. Assuming he hadn't become a card-carrying member of the Tinfoil Hat Society, what if some of these acts of insanity weren't due to simple mental illness? What if someone—or some*thing*—else really was responsible?

If so, then who? And why?

Before meeting Mordant, before seeing for myself what he was, I would have pooh-poohed any such notion and kept my distance afterwards from the lunatic suggesting it. But now?

I smiled, and shook my head. *What do you know, Abby? Insanity* is *catching. Alien parasites? Demons possessing little girls who confuse crucifixes with dildos? Good grief.*

"What if . . . ?" Mordant said, before pausing.

"What?" I said, still smiling.

Mordant lifted his hand, as though reaching for words. "What if we have it wrong? About life after death and all that. What if there's nothing supernatural about any of it? We just think of it that way, the way the ancient Greeks believed lightning bolts sprang from the hands of Zeus, because they didn't understand the scientific basis for thunderstorms?"

"The way alchemy evolved into chemistry?" I said, then winced.

"Yes, like that." He gestured with his hands, as though literally building castles out of thin air. "What if all of existence is some multifaceted conglomeration of different realities that we can't normally perceive?" He looked over at me. "What if, when people die, they simply continue to exist in some other form? On some other level?"

I tried, and failed, to suppress a snort. He frowned, then faced front again. "Sounds crazy, I suppose."

"What it sounds like," I said, "are some of the conversations I used to have with the geek crowd in college after burning a fat one. Though, to be fair," I quickly added, "it does have the flavor of some of the wild physics stuff I've read about in magazines like *Discover*. Not that I could understand any of those speculations on things like string theory, or whether the universe is really a hologram or some such. I was a Liberal Arts major, which qualified me for two things: teaching or asking someone, 'Will that be for here or to go?'"

That pulled an unwilling smile out of Mordant, so I decided to cut my losses and kept quiet afterwards.

We exited Liberty Hill and trawled along the outer edges of the Mission District. Julius would have stared at me as though I'd lost my mind had I even suggested walking around here at this time of night. But traffic was light, and the few people out avoided us. *Those are some serious 'Do not fuck with me' vibes this man is putting out*, I thought.

"Did you say something?" Mordant asked.

"Huh? Oh, no, not me."

A delivery truck drove through a nearby puddle at a fast clip, spraying water in our general direction. Mordant grabbed me by the arm—reacting, not thinking—repositioning me with disquieting ease on the inside of the sidewalk as he studied, and subsequently dismissed, the vanishing truck.

"So damn much I don't know," he said, half to himself. "Even with all of my family's resources. Not much help to have a virtually unlimited supply of shovels when you've no idea where to dig."

"Maybe Jester's wrong," he continued, mumbling to himself. "Maybe the war has already begun. Maybe it started a long time ago."

I opened my mouth to ask *What war?* then jumped at a loud banging ahead of us. The delivery truck had double-parked with its rear hatch open, while a man with a clipboard pounded on the backdoor of what appeared to be a restaurant. When he saw us coming, he stepped forward, waving his clipboard in our direction, "Hey, I'm new to this route, can you tell me if I have the right address?"

Oh Christ, please do not be stupid enough to come any closer, I thought desperately. And just as if he'd somehow heard my thoughts, the driver paused, as though uncertain whether or not to approach us.

I took Mordant's arm and tugged. He flashed me a look, but I refused to let go, instead pulling him away from the building. After a moment he relaxed, allowing me to lead him past the truck's rear so we could cross the street.

When it happened, it happened very quickly.

Men poured out of the delivery truck's open hatch, like ants boiling out of a disturbed mound. One, a slim fellow as nimble as a monkey, leaped on Mordant's back and pulled a bag over my companion's head as two more men ran forward, desperately trying to tackle him. One wrapped his arms around Mordant's legs, while the other tried to pin his arms to his side.

I stepped back, mouth open to scream when—for the second time in as many days—an arm snaked around my neck and cut my breath off. I wheezed desperately, fighting for enough air to cry out, when my assailant's free hand shoved something metal-hard into my side.

"Understand something," a voice whispered harshly into my ear. "While we'd prefer to bring you in whole, that's not a requirement. And we don't need him alive either. So if it comes down to a choice between letting you yell or shooting you, I'm perfectly comfortable with option B. Do we understand each other?"

The man relaxed his grip long enough to allow me a wisp of precious air. "Okay!" I managed to squeeze out.

As soon as the word left my mouth, I saw Mordant freeze, his head tilting in our direction, though with the sack blinding him he could not possibly have seen either of us.

Then he leaped.

Since I was between Mordant and the man behind me, I caught the brunt of the impact, bouncing backwards as though I'd been hit by a car. Every molecule of air exploded out of my lungs with a tremendous *whoosh*. I hit the asphalt, scraping the skin off my arms and bare legs. A hand slid over my stomach and chest, and I felt points like daggers digging into my flesh, as if preparing to rip off my left breast like a drumstick from a turkey. "No!" I cried.

Then the hand disappeared, and I heard a scream.

The hold on my neck vanished, and I rolled over and up. A strange man—almost certainly the one who had been behind me—lay clutching his belly. A bloody mass of gray ropy sausages filled his hands as he stared at the gaping wound in his abdomen. "Christ! Fucking Christ! He ripped out my guts! Fucking Christ!" he squeaked.

"Hold him, goddammit!" Monkey Man said while fighting desperately to keep the sack over Mordant's head. And as I watched, I saw Mordant's movements slacken, growing more sluggish, and I caught the scent thick in the air between us, like the hiss of air brakes.

Garlic.

Then I looked down and saw it. A pistol, something modern, coated with chrome, probably the one which had been digging a hole in my side only moments before. I flashed back to earlier days spent in the fields of my grandfather's farm with my father as he taught me how to shoot tin cans off a log with his .38.

I stared back up at the three men as they struggled with Mordant, his movements growing weaker. Then the driver came into view from the other side, and I did the only thing I could possibly do.

I fled.

As I ran I heard a loud *pop* behind me, and the screaming from the man who had grabbed me suddenly ceased. A voice yelled. "What are you waiting for, an invitation? Go get her, you fucking chumlies!" Feet slapped against the pavement behind me as I dashed down a dark side street. Trash cans barred my way; I grabbed at them and pulled them down behind me, in the hope of delaying my pursuers.

Zigzagging between the shadows, I headed for the lively and (even at this time of night) still crowded inner section of the Mission District. Once in, I slipped past some revelers too drunk to notice (much less acknowledge) me, then crouched behind them.

I saw the truck driver arrive first. His head twisted furiously from side to side as he searched, face contorted with anger, his lips curled in what looked to be a vicious bout of cursing. He hesitated as he scanned the nearby celebrants, who had begun to stare at him. Glowering fiercely, he retreated and disappeared.

Heart pounding with a sickening ache, I noticed the revelers begin to drift away, exposing me. Terrified by the possibility the driver might return with his friends, I squeezed back in amongst them, smiling and nodding as they welcomed my presence and enthusiastically pulled me along, probably in search of yet another bar. Not the same group of folks Mordant and I had encountered earlier, thank God. That bunch might have recognized me and drawn away, leaving me exposed.

Okay, genius, what now?

More and more the thought of going to the police, of surrendering to them and their authority, appealed to me.

And what if they're *looking for you too? Not all of them, of course. But how many would it take to make sure you truly disappear, never to be found again?*

Christ, what was I going to do?

᠊ᢄᢄ᠊

I met Julius St. Claire at the tail end of one of the most depressing days of my life.

I had been on the phone with Bethany for the better part of an hour after a bad day of unruly and rude students, topped off by a visit to the principal's office to hear from the sheriff's wife how 'unfair and disrespectful' I had been to her son by giving him a D minus on his book report (instead of the F he truly deserved). Bethany's husband Otis had gotten a job as a youth pastor at a large church in Wake Forest the previous year, and my sister— still shy as a clam—had been having trouble coping with the politics of it all. So naturally she called me.

After listening with a sweaty ear for over an hour to her laments, I finally got her off the phone before the conversation segued into more conjugal complaints of marital bliss ("Is it normal to want it *every* day?"). If I, celibate as a nun for over a year, had to hear that complaint from her one more time, I was going to reach through the telephone and rip off that frustratingly perfect nose. Although even that was better than listening to her, weepy after half a glass of wine, go on about how she didn't deserve her husband, and that one day God was going to punish her for having 'impure thoughts'.

So when I got online, it was with an enormous sense of relief, which lasted only until I checked the room roster and saw Bluebeard's name. My finger hovered over the Enter key as I pondered whether or not spending time with my friends was worth hearing that jerk greet me with one of his choice nicknames ("Hey, Wideload! How are the tits hanging? Pavement level? Har har!").

Then, with a trill, Miss Sunny sent me an Instant Message.

DommeSunshine: Good evening, my dear. Do you have a minute?

I closed the room window with a sigh, grateful for the intervention.

PhedreFan: For you, Ma'am, always.
DommeSunshine: Good. I'm going to send you an invite to a private room.

I accepted the invitation when it came while mulling over the possibility that perhaps later I might create another disposable screen name and indulge in a bit of role playing. I hadn't done my 'up-and-coming actress who must remain anonymous' routine in a while, time to shake the mothballs out of it.

DommeSunshine: Thank you, dear.
PhedreFan: You're welcome, Ma'am. BTW, will you be needing the box? I know how hard it must be, trying to be all dominant and everything as you stand there staring up at my chin.
DommeSunshine: Then assume a respectful position, and neither of us will have to unduly exert ourselves, you while carrying your box, and me while tanning your sarcastic ass afterwards.
PhedreFan: ::sigh:: Yes, Ma'am. ::kneeling::
DommeSunshine: One day (and this is a promise), circumstances will allow me the opportunity to instruct you in proper decorum. Do keep that in mind.
PhedreFan: YES! Uh, I mean . . . PLEASE, NO! NOT THAT!
DommeSunshine: We'll see how cheeky you are after I give that tongue of yours some exercise.
PhedreFan: Begging your pardon, Ma'am, but we've had this conversation before. I'm so straight I make rulers look crooked. I could give you my sister's phone number, though . . .
DommeSunshine: I was referring to its use while screaming out your safeword.
PhedreFan: :shuddering deliciously:: Um, yes, Ma'am.
DommeSunshine: And in order to best expedite that glorious day, I have someone I'd like for you to meet.

I froze.

Cybering was one thing. I'd gotten quite good at it, to the point it was an almost tolerable substitute for what I truly craved. To be dominated. Controlled. Made helpless. And even darker fantasies . . .

The thought of which, their being made real and tangible, was terrifying. Not to mention exhilarating.

PhedreFan: Ma'am, you know I'm a cybersub. I've never so much as had my butt smacked. Not by anyone who knew what they were doing, that is.

DommeSunshine: That won't be a problem, my dear. You wouldn't be the first filly he's broken.

PhedreFan: You make it sound awfully . . . appealing.

DommeSunshine: I'm not selling you to him, my dear. Just introducing you. After all, it's not as though you might lose your head and do something precipitous and foolish, like that Bunny girl everyone was talking about last week. You have good sense. Usually. And anyway, Julius lives here in San Francisco, same as I do.

PhedreFan: Ah, I see. You're not fooling me, Ma'am. This is some clever ruse to lure me across the country so you can finally get me into a locked room and carry out some of those threats you keep making.

DommeSunshine: I do so enjoy a win-win scenario, my dear. But this is no ruse. My friend is quite real, just as I am. And there will be no reason for locks, of that I am certain. Not on the doors at least.

PhedreFan: You have more faith in me than I do, Ma'am. Don't you ever listen to Bluebeard? I'm a wannabe. A cyberslut. A gutless coward, as phony as a three dollar bill. I'd say two, but they actually made those once upon a time, didn't they?

DommeSunshine: You are not false, my dear, you are simply untried. Now, stop your shaking, I've sent the gentleman an invite. Here he is. Julius, may I introduce you to my dear friend, Abby.

LyonHeart: Good evening, Abby. :)

⚡

And while we chatted, the three of us, so far into the night that I could see through my bedroom window the atomic fireball sunrise peeking over the horizon, the prolonged conversation wasn't really necessary even then.

Because, just like in the movie, he'd had me at hello.

⌖

I followed my little crowd into yet another bar, filled almost to over-flowing, for which I was grateful. Every attack so far had been conducted in lonely spots with few if any witnesses. Not to mention that squatting amongst a horde of drunken revelers makes for great camouflage.

Okay, you're safe, at least temporarily. So what now?

What indeed? Since my immediate demise had grown a bit less prob-lematic, I found myself pondering over what had just happened.

How had—well, whoever these people were—known how to find Mordant and me? Their truck had appeared out of nowhere, long after we'd left Warren's. Which implied two possibilities:

(A)   Either Warren and/or Miss Sunny had contacted them, letting them know we had just left, or

(B)   Warren's home was bugged, like something out of an episode of *Revenge*.

I shook my head. I couldn't credit the former, which meant the latter was the more likely explanation. Which led me to wonder, were Warren and Miss Sunny in danger as well?

Maybe. But what if they were? What could *I* do about it?

If the house is bugged, then most likely the phone is too. Maybe even by police officers, tracing incoming and outgoing calls.

The more I thought about it, the more that made sense. After all, Mordant and I had been attacked twice, each time after leaving the home of one of the people on his list.

I thought about that. All those people, so many from our group.

But what if there was more to my paranoid suspicions than I wanted to admit to? What if Hendrick, or Miss Sunny, or someone else on that list was involved in these kidnapping attempts?

98

In the end, I realized, it didn't really matter. I had to concede the possibility, unbelievable though it might be, that one or more of my friends might have targeted me for God only knew what reason. In which case I couldn't go to any of them for help without knowing which of them it might be. Either that or they were targets themselves, and the people after me might trace me to the homes of my friends and kidnap them as well. Just as they had the now luckless Mordant.

The memory of his being taken, how he had fought in my defense even after my escape, shamed me. And while I knew nothing about what real vampires might be vulnerable to, I had seen with my own eyes how quickly they were able to subdue him by covering his head with a sack full of garlic. Though not quickly enough, I recalled, remembering the man Mordant had gutted.

He tried to save you. Did *save you. And you repaid him by running away like a coward. Bluebeard knew you so well.*

I felt hot tears trailing down my cheeks. Useless. I'd been useless. I couldn't help but remember some of my favorite female champions: Xena the Warrior Princess, or Buffy the Vampire Slayer. Even Veronica Mars could wield a Taser, and she had screamed like a girl more than once during that show's run when confronted with an attacker. Not to mention an endless host of similar heroines, none of whom would have abandoned a man who had saved their life. Twice.

This is real life. They're *not real. And if you had hesitated for just another few seconds,* you *might not have been real for long either.*

I wiped my soggy nose on my shirt sleeve. Okay, so I wasn't a hero. But that didn't mean I couldn't act like one. Those people at the Fairmont, Constance and the other two. They could help Mordant. I could go to them, tell them what had happened. They could do . . . well, something. I would go to them, turn myself over, and let them take care of everything; me included.

A painful cramp twisted inside my gut. Constance's Spanx. First thing I would do when I arrived at the hotel was cut that goddamned thing off.

If you make it.

I shook my head. I had to make it. And soon. Mordant might not even be alive. Or—well, whatever he was. But if he was alive, I knew the longer

I took, the less the likelihood he might continue that way. What did they call it on that HBO series? 'The True Death'?

I got up to leave.

"Hey!" said one of the young men to whose group I had attached my-self. "Where ya taking off to?"

"Have to get up early," I answered, forcing a smile. "Some people have to work tomorrow, you know."

"Huh? What time is it?" He checked his watch. "Jesus! Abe, look at the time! We got to get going, man, those guys are expecting us downtown at 9 a.m.! I'll call us some cabs, okay?"

The one he was talking to, who looked like a skateboarder (except for the gold Patek Phillipe on his wrist) waved him off, iPhone in hand. "No need for that, Jake. Just checked my app, there's a limo in between runs. We can crowd everybody in and head back to the hotel."

"Okay," Jake said, before gesturing in my direction. "Hey, we got room for one more?"

Abe downed the last third of his beer. "Don't see why not. Where you headed, sweetheart?"

My heart leaped. "The Fairmont?"

"That's on the way, right?" Jake slurred.

"Who gives a shit? But if there's not enough room, she sits in your lap," Abe said while pointing at the two of us.

Jake turned back to me. "You cool with that?"

"Sure!" I said, pasting a smile on my face.

"Ex-cell-ent! Let's do it, then!"

<hr />

I pressed close to Jake, hiding in his shadow as best I could while wait-ing for everyone to get into the limo, an enormous behemoth modified from some military-looking version of an SUV. I tried to appear noncha-lant, but couldn't help looking behind me every few seconds, fearful that the moment I ceased to be aware of my environment would be the moment I felt someone grab me from behind to pull me into a waiting vehicle, which would then vanish into the night, my disappearance a mystery which would turn into a cold case, never to be solved.

"You getting in, honey?" Abe yelled.

I started. "Coming!" I cried as I bent forward and squeezed into the already full vehicle, rotating so I could fit on Jake's lap. As I settled in, my eyes grew wide.

"Um, sorry," Jake mumbled, his embarrassment almost tangible.

"It's okay," I said, cheeks flaming, as I squirmed, shifting position.

"Um, could you please sit still?" he whispered, "Cuz you're just making it worse."

Freezing in place, I looked everywhere but at Jake as the limo pulled away.

The trip seemed to take forever. Everyone laughed uproariously as Abe raided the limo's mini-bar and began tossing miniature liquor bottles hither and yon. One couple initiated some major heavy petting, and at one point I felt someone's fingers casually sliding just under the hem of my (that is, Constance's) skirt. Clingy around the hips, while loose enough at the hemline to allow a spin showing some serious leg, it almost appeared designed to encourage such liberties. It was dark and so crowded I couldn't be sure who the hand they belonged to, so I simply took hold and removed the offending digits from my upper thigh without appearing to notice them.

Finally we pulled to the front of the Fairmont. I thanked everyone profusely, taking great care to examine my surroundings as I exited the vehicle while sliding off Jake's lap, the only one who appeared to notice my departure, then waved goodbye as the limo vanished into the night.

I got off the street and inside the hotel as quickly as I could without running, so scared was I of attracting curious eyes. I bore to the right, dodging the pillars and furniture like a pinball while crossing the baroque room with its opulent rug, bypassing the concierge station on my way to the reception desk. A man in horn-rimmed glasses, slim as a male model, looked free at the moment. I hastened in his direction.

"Pardon me," I said, gesturing in order to get his attention. "I'm staying in the Presidential Suite with some friends, and I don't have my room key. Could you give me one?"

His eyes narrowed to slits while he looked me up and down. "And you are?" he asked as he shifted to his computer.

The thought of giving anyone my name after all that had happened made my legs weak. "I'm not sure my name will show up on the guest list. Could you just give them a call and tell them that Abby is downstairs in the lobby?"

The clerk tapped on the hidden keyboard. "And your friend's name is . . . ?"

Christ, what *was* her name? "Bingham! Tracy Bingham. Or it might be under Arthur, I don't know which one of them actually reserved the suite."

He nodded as he tapped away. "I'm sorry, ma'am," he finally said, "But it appears your friends have checked out."

My stomach did a flip flop. "Checked out?"

"Yes. That would have been just before the start of my shift," he said.

Then I remembered Mordant's instructions. *I will call or text you every hour on the hour. If you don't hear from me, assume the worst and proceed accordingly.*

Had it been that long? I looked at a nearby clock. Later than I'd thought. Much later.

Now I really was alone. The three of them, after not hearing from Mordant in the allotted time, must have followed his orders and disappeared. Of course it was always possible that they had simply switched to another hotel, but if so, how would I find them? Much more likely they were all on a flight out of the city, on their way to god only knew where, fleeing for their lives.

So what now? Without Mordant's protection, I was now easy prey for whomever—or whatever—was trying to find and kill me.

Assuming that killing me was the actual goal, I thought, remembering the lab.

After asking the clerk every question I could think to ask ("No ma'am, no one left a message for you."), I found a chair and sat down to think.

I had no illusions. As previously noted, I was no hero. Whatever had happened to Mordant, there was nothing I could do about it. He was gone, unless his people could do something to help him. Either way, he wasn't my problem anymore. Yes, this made me an ungrateful bitch, considering that his actions had ensured my temporary freedom, but what could my worthless self do about that? I'd been *so* helpful during the attack, after all.

The question now was, what should *I* do?

The odds, as I saw them, were that whoever these people were, they *would* find me. And when they did, anyone with me at the time would also be in danger. Maybe I couldn't save myself, but I could at least keep someone else from getting hurt. Or worse.

The inevitable is coming. You know *this. Best thing to do? Go back to the Golden Gate Bridge and finish what you started.*

But what about my friends?

Hendrick and Miss Sunny know about the list, and which members of the group are on it. They may or may not believe something is really going on, but neither of them will keep this to themselves, word will *get around. Then everyone will just have to make up their own minds what to do about it.*

I swallowed past the lump in my throat. So this is it, I thought. This is how it ends. Either I kept running around as Grandma Pearl would say, 'like a chicken with its head cut off', waiting for these people to capture me and take me back to that miniature operating room, or I mustered half an ounce of courage and denied them their prize.

If only I had more frigging time, I thought. Then the choice would be taken completely out of my hands.

As I sat there mulling over my options, I experienced the prickly sensation on the back of my neck of being watched.

Trying to be casual, I turned my head slightly while shifting my eyes.

There, sitting at a ninety degree angle away from me. Slim, hair cut so close to the scalp you could see the white skin underneath. He wore a Schott's leather jacket, which looked too large on him, paired with brand new jeans and a heavy pair of black boots studded with metal. His elbow rested on the arm of his chair, his cheek on his fist, his eyes closed.

But I knew. I could tell. He was looking at me from underneath his eyelids while pretending to doze.

Now what?

I didn't think about it, because if I had, the insanity of my actions would have frozen me, like that woman in *Alien* who had just stood in place crying while the monster curled its tail around her, embracing her before it fed.

Standing quickly, I marched back to the front desk. The clerk with the glasses looked up at me as I came to a halt in front of him.

"That man is here to murder me!" I screamed, while pointing at Bald Guy, who wasn't pretending to sleep any longer. "He's here to kill me!" I jabbed my finger in his direction as the clerk's eyes widened, his head swiveling in the direction I was pointing.

Then I ran.

Avoiding the central revolving door, I flew to the side exit without looking back. My hope was that, with everyone staring at him, he wouldn't try to follow me—at least not right away—giving me time to build something of a lead.

I had made my decision. If I was going to die, it would be on my terms, my way. Then, if they somehow got hold of my body, they could do whatever the fuck they wanted with it, since I would no longer be alive to care.

I ran through the door, the glass emitting a loud *crack* as I shoved it open before hitting the outside air. In the distance I saw the upper stories of the Sunken Mansion looming over the block. I turned left, heading for the corner, then took another left. Fortunately the terrain sloped downward in that direction, as the Fairmont tops one of San Francisco's steeper hills. No longer running, I kept as brisk a pace as I could manage down the street, trying not to draw too much attention to myself while attempting to elude my pursuer.

And if I'd had a bit more time, maybe I would have succeeded.

I didn't see the hand that grabbed me by the arm. I only felt it, a grip that crushed muscle against underlying bone. Staggering, I fought for balance while being pulled into the shadows. A hand as broad as my face clamped down on my mouth as whoever, or whatever, had taken hold of me shoved me forward against the stone walls of a small alcove, crushing the air from my lungs as he pinned me in place like a bug in a science project.

"I ain't got no idea why you're doing your level best to get yourself killed," a deep voice rumbled into my left ear. "But I *like* living, so I'm telling you now to keep your damned mouth shut before you draw any more attention to us than you already have." The voice paused for a moment. "We clear, little lady?"

Terrified, I nodded. Or wiggled, I should say, since moving my head wasn't much of an option.

"Not sure I believe you," the voice said, sounding like Richard Roundtree after an hour spent yelling himself hoarse. "So before I remove my hand, we need to understand one another. My presence here is at the request of some friends of yours, who said I should pass along their names to you. The Binghams? You know who I'm talking about?"

Something like a squeak came out of my mouth and managed to slip between the sausage-sized fingers. The hand relaxed, along with the grip on my arm that I knew was going to leave bruises. Big, beautiful ones.

I twisted around, looking up. And if it hadn't been for the pressure of his body squeezing me against the stone, I might have dropped to the ground. Standing over me was quite possibly the largest man I had ever seen. White teeth flashed in a dark face. He looked as though he could have played front four for the 49ers. *All* front four.

"Why should I believe you?" I finally managed.

He shrugged. "Your call. I get paid either way."

I looked back toward the sidewalk and saw the bald man from the Fairmont approaching. My mouth opened again, but before I could cry out, the hand covered my face again.

"Bit of a screamer, isn't she?" the bald man said, an enormous grin on his face, in an accent that sounded Australian.

"Frightening clients leads to poor word-of-mouth advertising, Oscar," the big man said. "Didn't they teach you that during orientation?"

"Hey, I din't do nuthin. Just sat there minding my own business," Oscar said, pointing at me. "Then all of a sudden this one takes off like the devil's chasing her, screaming bloody murder all the while. Literally. By the time I dealt with the situation, she was gone like a fart in the wind."

"We'll talk later," the big man rumbled. "Right now we need to get the lady off the street and someplace safe." Once again he relaxed the hand over my mouth. "We all copacetic here now?"

I nodded as best I could. "So he's Oscar," I said, glancing at the bald man. "What's your name?"

"Leroy Brown," the giant said.

I blinked. "Seriously?"

"As far as you're concerned, it is," he said. "Now, I need for you to get your skinny butt over into that Cadillac Escalade currently double-parked. Oscar, get on your bike and follow us. But not too close. You see anything, buzz me."

"Roger that," Oscar said, twirling his index finger as he stepped briskly away.

I allowed 'Leroy' to guide me, his enormous hand resting in the small of my back. "What happens now?" I said as he opened the Cadillac's door for me.

He didn't speak, instead securing me inside the vehicle before circling it himself. He moved into the driver's seat with no wasted motion, and a moment later we merged into traffic and sped away.

"Where are the Binghams? And Constance?" I finally asked.

"They're safe, so far as I understand. And that's all either one of us needs to know about that," Leroy said as he checked the rearview mirror. I turned and saw what appeared to be Oscar's helmeted figure following us while perched atop one of those modern-looking motorcycles, what my grandfather would have referred to as a 'rice-burner'.

"And Mordant?" I said, unable to keep quiet.

Leroy looked over at me, confused. "Who?"

Need to know basis, huh? I slouched in my seat. "Never mind."

Leroy grunted. "Now, we were told to take you wherever you wanted to go, and to stay nearby until further notice."

I frowned. "What if I don't want you nearby?"

"Are you paying me?"

"No . . ."

"Answers that question then, don't it? Course, I suppose you could give the local constabulary a call. Should I drop you off? Tenderloin police station isn't too terribly far from here, as I recall."

I initiated and then maintained a sullen silence as Leroy drove, the enormous SUV's engine a barely audible thrum as we navigated the shadow-strewn streets. "Based on what we were told, it's considered advisable to avoid well-trafficked areas. Have any friends you can stay with?" Leroy finally said.

I crossed my arms petulantly. "I'd like to go home."

"Not recommended at this time."

"I need some of my things."

"Reach in the back floorboard."

I turned and looked. "My pocketbook?" I said as I pulled it into my lap. "How'd you get this?"

"Some of our people picked your car up the other day," Leroy said, eyeballing a sedan as it passed by.

I checked the contents of my purse. Driver's license, house keys, credit cards, a thick wad of cash in my billfold. "Where'd this come from?" I asked, waving it about.

"You should avoid paying with plastic. The cash was provided to minimize its use."

I'd noticed that Leroy sounded less 'street' than he had minutes earlier when we'd been standing next to one. "I can't stay with any of my friends," I said.

"The List?"

"You know about that?"

"What I know is that you and a select number of your acquaintances are apparently being targeted," Leroy said. "Are those the only people you know in the city? The ones on that List?"

"Pretty much," I said, sighing.

Then I remembered.

Nancy.

"I do know one person who's not on the List," I said slowly. "But what if I get her in trouble by going there?"

"I'm assuming if she's not on this List, then she's probably a safe bet. Or as safe as we're likely to get. What's her name?"

"Nancy."

"She have a last name? Or is she one of those one-name women, like Beyonce?"

"Campbell. Nancy Campbell."

Leroy nodded. "Well, it's your call. But I can't just continue to drive around the city, it's going to be light soon. You willing to listen to some advice?"

I shrugged.

"I'll take that as a yes. I was told that you're a real hot potato right now, and that the longer you're in San Francisco, the more likely it is that whoever's looking for you will eventually find you. Now, I'm paid to take a bullet for our clients, and I'm paid *very* well, but I'd prefer it didn't come to that. I say we get you out of town. Once we've put distance between you and whoever's after you, we can take some time to plan our next move."

My head had begun to hurt. "Where would you take me?"

"Let me worry about that. Problem is, it'll take me a day or so to set things up proper, and I can't do that chauffeuring you around. The longer we spend out in the open like this, the greater the odds you're going to be spotted. I need to park you someplace safe for the time being. Or as safe as reasonably possible."

I opened my mouth, then closed it. While the men who had tried to kidnap me had been human, whoever or whatever had given them their orders quite possibly *wasn't* human. Mordant had seemed certain that the man he'd wrestled with earlier hadn't been, that he was another vampire.

I wondered if I should mention that to Leroy, then discarded the notion. Either he knew as much as I did and was already as well-prepared as he could be, or else he knew nothing, in which case he probably wouldn't believe me in the first place.

"Okay, after giving the matter some thought, here's the plan," Leroy said. "We take you to this friend of yours. You hide out there for the day while I make my arrangements. Things like this can take time, but I'll see how many corners I can reasonably cut. Unless these folks are tracking you somehow, you being there shouldn't create any problems for your friend, and by the time they get a lead on you, we'll be long gone."

"You're going to leave me?" I said, my voice a high-pitched squeak that would have done the Chipmunks proud.

"Don't worry, Oscar will be nearby. He's very good at what he does, blending into the background. Usually, that is. Here," he said as he removed a mobile phone from his jacket. "Guaranteed to be untraceable. If you have any problems, just hit the first entry on the Contacts list. That's Oscar's. If for any reason he doesn't answer, call the second one. That's mine. Now, can you remember your friend's number? Or are you one of those people who loads everything into Contacts without giving it another thought?"

"I can dial from memory," I sniffed, not telling him that the only reason I could was because my husband had required me to memorize the numbers of all our family and friends. I vividly recalled him standing behind me, my legs separated by a spreader bar as he held Mr. Paddle in one hand and my phone in the other, while I recited each number as he scrolled through the listings, giving me a serious whack on the butt for each digit I missed. *Lose the phone, then where will you be?* he had said on more than one occasion.

It had never failed to irritate me over the years how often my husband had turned out to be right.

We pulled into Nancy's driveway just as dawn peered over the horizon. A perennial night owl, Nancy would often spent her evenings bouncing about the city like a pinball, clubbing and bar hopping into the early morning hours, coming to rest in her backyard barely dressed in a dental-floss bikini to 'take in the early morning rays'. Most of the redheads I've known either protected themselves from the sun with layers of oils and lotions or avoided it altogether, but Nancy reveled in its glow, nurturing a tan as minimal as her swimsuit while grumbling about how I turned brown as a berry in no time. "Bitch," she would mutter good-naturedly in that British accent of hers (with just a hint of the lower class in its vowels) whenever we sunbathed together, as she compared her pale, freckled leg to my own bronze thigh with a derisive sniff.

I had no idea what she did for a living. When I'd asked once, she'd smiled and squealed in an exaggerated Southern accent, "I have always relied upon the kindness of strangers." I decided she had a sugar daddy of some sort and didn't care to talk about it, so I left it alone. Even the home she currently lived in—her third since I'd known her—had been a gift of sorts. "I'm housesitting for a friend," she had told me dismissively as I'd gawked at the enormous Edwardian the first time I'd come by. She wasn't a member of our munch group, and had shown little interest in becoming one, but she was friendly with many of our members, particularly Miss Sunny, who had introduced us originally. A butterfly within the local BDSM scene, Nancy had a notorious reputation as a Holly Golightly, dallying for brief periods of time with one dominant after another—male and female alike—until inevitably she succeeded in 'wrapping them around my little finger', after which she quickly lost interest and moved on. Only Miss Sunny appeared to hold any sort of long term influence over her.

"I'm not careless enough or foolish enough to get caught up in her games," my one-time mentor had told me following that first meeting. "Don't get me wrong. Nancy possesses a rare combination of beauty and sex appeal—and is very much aware of it—which makes her a challenge. But she's a pain slut, and I'm a Domme, not a sadist."

When I'd later shared that exchange with Nancy, after an evening spent inflicting some serious damage on a one hundred and fifty year old bottle of Gran Marnier (gifted to her by some anonymous admirer), she had chuckled. "Sunny gets me, and refuses to take my shit," the petite redhead had slurred. "Which is why I let her top me. But she's right. I would never submit to her—or anyone else, for that matter—outside of scene."

"I don't really like pain," I had replied, equally inebriated. "Well, not all that much. No, really!" I'd argued as Nancy had practically guffawed at me. "It's the surrender. The loss of control. Knowing I have no say whatsoever."

"Is that why you let him . . . ?"

The heat of my flush had transcended that of the liquor. "We match well together," I'd said, a bit defensively.

She had shaken her head and smiled. "We're such opposites, you and I. Yes, I enjoy being beaten with a rubber hose; so long as I'm properly warmed up, that is. But what you do? Letting him drug you while he . . . ?"

"Please, don't!" I had told her, flesh crawling as I'd shuddered. "I hate, hate, HATE medical play! Letting him put me under is the only way I can handle it. It's all part of the fantasy anyway; me lying there unconscious, the helpless victim. And he always takes good care of me afterwards. I can barely see the cuts, and when he bandages me, he does an excellent job of it."

Nancy had shaken her head. "Mental," she'd said with a giggle. "Absolutely mental."

"Haven't you ever wanted to give yourself to someone like that?" I had asked, my voice barely a whisper. "Totally and completely, in every possible way, without reservation?"

And in what was for her a rare somber moment, she'd replied, "Once. Long ago," while taking a deep swig straight from the bottle. "Never again."

"Never?"

Then Nancy had smiled.

"I met someone, years ago who might possibly have made me reconsider," she'd said, the vanilla pallor of her skin floating in the air as she took another prolonged draught and changed the subject.

Leroy waited curbside while I walked up the driveway to the entrance. I knocked timidly, then banged harder when I got no answer.

I heard a muttered exclamation, then listened to the sound of chains rattling and locks being disengaged. Finally she opened the door to stare at me with bleary eyes, dressed solely in some Agent Provocateur ensemble that probably pushed four figures.

"What on earth are you doing here at this hour, banging on my door like a bloody census taker?" she said as she parted her thick mane to focus on me. "It's the freaking middle of the night!"

"Actually it's morning now," I replied, correcting her.

"Really?" She blinked, staring past me from the shadows of her foyer at the sunlight falling on her front yard. "So it is. Christ, what a night I've had."

"Are you alone?" I asked, checking her skin for marks, though it was almost a pointless exercise. Nancy's marble flesh rarely bruised, whereas I would bloom black and blue if you sneezed on me.

"Huh? Oh, yes, it's just me. You're wanting to come in, I'm guessing?"

"If you don't mind."

"No, no, that's fine. What about your friend?" she asked, looking past me at the Cadillac.

"Oh no, he's just dropping me off. So long as you're not slamming the door in my face, that is."

"Don't be daft, I wouldn't slam the door. At least not with this hangover. Oh, all right, get in here. Just step quietly, if you'd be so kind."

"Thank you," I said, waving a goodbye in Leroy's direction before following my friend into the house. She sashayed like a runway model over to a nearby sofa, then flopped down indelicately onto the cushions face first. "My poor head," she moaned, that heart-shaped rear perched up so enticingly even I was tempted to give it a swat. Except that I liked my hair where it was, attached to my scalp. Nancy entered into pre-scene negotiations with the careless élan of a dyspeptic contract lawyer, and woe betide anyone who took even the slightest of liberties.

I sat opposite her. The room reminded me of every other house she had ever occupied, as spotless as a showroom floor. "Sorry to put you out," I said, my voice barely audible even to myself.

"Huh? Oh, don't be ridiculous," she said, assuming a seated position. "I'm the one who should be apologizing to you, for missing the funeral. I, ah, had a family emergency of sorts. You know?"

I nodded, not really believing her. But that was Nancy. She was great fun, and wonderful company, but only when it was convenient for her. "I did get the card. Thank you."

"Oh, please don't. I'm a terrible friend, you should have disowned me long ago." She grabbed something that resembled a cigarette off the coffee table and lit it. "Are you sure you're okay? You're getting skinny as a rail."

"I'm fine."

"When's the last time you ate, Moppet?"

I tried to remember. "Sometime last night?"

"Well, there's nothing here. Might be some leftover tomato juice, we were knocking back Bloody Marys one after the other during the early evening. Just add terrible hostess to the list." She inhaled deeply, her head tilted back on the cushions. "My first cigarette in ages. I'd forgotten how good tobacco tastes."

I bent forward a bit and sniffed. "That's not marijuana?"

"Don't be ridiculous, I never touch the stuff."

"It looks hand-rolled," I said.

"It is. Learned how from my Da'. Always did his own. Kept a pouch of tobacco with him at all times, but couldn't roll a fag to save his life once he started drinking. So I'd do it for him." She took another deep draught, staring at me through a blue cloud of smoke that trilled like birdsong. "Why are you here, Moppet?"

I felt the anxiety as it swirled deep inside my belly, rising like a storm surge. I'd been carrying this burden alone for the past two weeks, and it weighed heavily on me. I'd been tempted so many times over the past evening to share it, first at Hendrick's, and then later with Warren and Miss Sunny. But Mordant had been there, locking the words inside me with his presence.

Now I was alone. Just me and one of my closest friends. And before I could stop myself, I looked down at my feet and listened as the words, slippery as raw oysters, escaped my lips. "I have leukemia."

Nancy sat up, mouth agape, looking for all the world like a red-haired guppy. "Wha . . . ?"

I closed my eyes. "It was my fault. I'd called Julius at his office after getting the diagnosis, asking him to come back to the house. I'd wanted to wait till he got home, but he was so upset, he knew something was seriously wrong. He wouldn't let it go, so I told him over the phone. He got all quiet, then said I should stay where I was, that he'd be right there.

"An hour later I got a phone call from the police. About the accident."

Nancy leaned back, as if pulling away from me. "Sweetie darling, it wasn't your fault," she said, refusing to meet my eyes.

I shook my head. She didn't understand. I wasn't blaming myself for Julius's absence, nor was I berating myself for creating the distraction that might possibly have caused his accident. Assuming, of course, it *had* been an accident.

I was angry.

No. Not angry. Enraged.

I was dying. Dr. Pestler had told me I had very little time, that he had never seen such an aggressive case as mine. I didn't have months. I had weeks, if that. And my husband, whom I had depended on for over a decade, had managed to absent himself from the unpleasant situation.

Or had he?

His name was on the List too.

I felt myself flush. I knew what I was doing, acting like an unconscionable brat, blaming my husband—however his death had occurred—for not being there, for not shoring me up with the strength I had come to depend on. His death almost certainly hadn't been his fault, I now realized. Which made me the worst kind of human being imaginable, a spoiled child who resented him for dying.

Not that the realization helped. Or diminished my rage.

You're a worthless cunt, you know that?

"Um, Earth to Abby?" Nancy said, snapping her fingers at me.

"Sorry," I replied, her words jerking me out of my reverie.

She curled her legs under her butt while folding her arms. "I'm not very good at this sort of thing," she eventually said. "In fact, I'm quite terrible at it. Meaningful empathy, that is. You should have gone to someone else. Warren. Or Miss Sunny."

I didn't argue with her. Because we both knew she was right.

"I need to lie down for a while, not have to think any more about it, about anything or anyone," I told her. "Any chance I could crash here? I just don't want to be alone right now. Come this time tomorrow, I'll be out of your hair. I promise."

"Of course, Moppet! Mi casa, su casa. You take the upstairs bedroom, and once you've had some genuine rest we can talk more. Okay?"

"Thank you."

"What are friends for? On second thought, don't answer that. Just—Oh, come here." She got up, opening her arms, and I walked into her embrace.

She held me tight, and when she released me I stepped away. "Sorry I'm such a mess," I said. "Would it offend you if I went outside for a minute, just to clear my lungs? I haven't been this close to cigarette smoke for a long time, not since moving here from North Carolina, and I was always sensitive to it even back then."

"Sweetie darling, you should have said something!" Nancy said, stabbing out the butt. "I'll open a few windows, let in some fresh air, and you come back in when you're feeling better."

"I won't be long." I made my way out the front door, closing it carefully behind me as I listened to her moving about.

Then I fled.

⚏

I didn't know what to do. How long did I have? I simply moved to the center of what was—for that neighborhood at this time of the morning—a very busy street, and just stood there.

The high-pitched ochre whine of a motorcycle reached my ears, and I watched the bike accelerate toward me. Tires screeched as it squealed to a halt. The driver flipped his visor, and I returned Oscar's wide-eyed gaze.

"You daft, girl?" he sputtered, head swiveling as he tried to look in every direction at once. "Or are you trying to get yourself killed?"

I lifted my skirt and mounted the seat behind him. "We have to get out of here," I said, forcing myself to speak slowly despite the painful pounding in my chest. "Now? Please?"

Oscar mumbled something unintelligible—probably some Australian version of 'stupid bitch'—then revved the bike and peeled out. I hadn't ridden on the back of a motorcycle since high school, but he didn't complain as I wrapped my arms around his chest and did my best not to unbalance him. As we accelerated, I looked back. Through parted curtains I saw Nancy's face, too small and distant for me to read its expression.

And then we were gone.

"Mind explaining that little bit of insanity?" Oscar said as we swayed into one turn after another.

"Her touch," I yelled, knowing how crazy I was going to sound, but beyond caring. "It tasted wrong!"

His head snapped around, then back as we shot through a stop sign. "You shitting me?"

I didn't reply. Instead I buried my face into his back as I remembered Nancy's arms circling my bare neck, the jalapeño flavor of her skin against mine.

Except Nancy's skin never tasted of peppers. It, like the pale fragrance of her epidermis, always tasted like vanilla, as did that of every other Caucasian I've ever known. With one exception. The hand of—whatever it had been—reaching inside Constance's car to grab me after shattering the window, its powerful fingers crushing my arm, the touch of its heated flesh as fiery as a habanero.

"*I saw something staring at me out of a person's eyes,*" Mordant had said. "*Something—different. From me, from you, from anything sane.*"

"Where the hell to now?" Oscar demanded.

I lifted my head. "Take me home."

⚏

It's one of my most vivid memories, the day I saw Julius's 'special girl' for the very first time.

He'd picked me up at the San Francisco airport in a rented limo. Once my luggage had been collected and we were on the road, he'd turned to me to say, "I've been waiting months for this."

Confused, not to mention horrendously nervous, my hands had slid protectively into the hollow of my lap. As ordered, I'd worn a dress for my flight. Also as ordered, I'd worn nothing underneath it. "Waiting for what?"

"To introduce you to my painted lady."

The words had rolled in my belly like jagged ice. Our Master/slave contract was a temporary one, subject to renegotiation or release when it expired sixty days after my arrival. I had requested that our little relationship test drive take place during the summer break from school, hedging my bets, but in all the time we'd spent getting to know one another— the online chats lasting for hours, the subsequent phone calls—I'd never thought to ask (or had even wondered) if Julius had other submissives. Stupidity? Blind fear? Cognitive dissonance? For the life of me, I couldn't have told you. True, the status on his AOL profile the day we first met had read 'single', but still . . .

I'd spent the rest of that trip into the city sitting quietly as I listened to my inner voice reassure me that, had there been another involvement, well, wouldn't he had mentioned it by now? Julius had never said a word about anyone else, even on his increasingly frequent business trips out east, made to accommodate both of our schedules as we'd continued to get to know one another. As a temporary Band-Aid, I'd decided that his 'painted lady' comment must have been a reference to his mother who, I'd been told, had a cosmetic penchant for thick foundation and excessive blush, fighting like a demon to hold on to a vanishing youth.

"There she is," he'd finally said as the limo slowed to a halt.

I'd looked around, confused. Then I saw it.

It was powder blue, or what we would have called back home 'Carolina Blue', with white trim and pastel pink accents. Three stories tall it stood, an elegant Edwardian with a peaked roof and a small round tower right out of a fairy tale. Not the bright garish colors of similar Victorians occupying the Haight-Ashbury district, but more subdued, more 'ladylike', its double doors fronting the facade like the cupid's bow of a scarlet mouth.

"Just a stone's throw from Barbary Lane," he'd said with a grin after opening my door. "Been in our family for generations. I loved my Boston brownstone, but I needed seed money for the company, so when it finally sold I gave the renters here notice and moved back in after they vacated. Cheryl stayed with me for a while after that, until it got to the point she needed twenty-four hour care."

During all the years we spent together, both before and during our marriage, I never could get used to the way Julius always called his mother by her first name. Had I even once dared to refer to mine as 'Mabel', the heat from her gaze would have scorched me to ash where I stood.

I held on tight to Oscar, replaying the smoky images of that day in my mind's eye, until the motorcycle turned into the driveway, forcing me to return regretfully to the present as he slowed to a halt. "What now?" he asked.

What now indeed?

I got off the back of the bike. "I don't know what to tell you," I said.

"*You* don't tell me anything," he said. "I was talking to the only person present here with any brains, myself. Believe me, if I had a better idea than bringing you here, I'd have mentioned it long before now. So hurry up and get yourself inside. I'll make it look like I'm hightailing it out of Dodge, then I'll sneak back around and find a place to hole up till I hear back from Leroy. In the meantime, if anything looks, smells, or even tastes wrong, you're to call me pronto. Understood?"

I gave him a nod. He returned it, then peeled out without so much as a backwards glance.

I watched Oscar's retreating form as he and the cycle vanished into the distance. It felt so strange. I was now alone, truly alone, for the first time in, what? Two days? Three?

I walked up the stairs to the front door, digging my keys out of the purse Leroy had returned to me. Then, feeling paranoid, I tested the knob first.

Locked. I relaxed a bit. But only a bit.

I unlatched the deadbolt. Julius had always been on me about that, telling me on multiple occasions that we got a break on our insurance by having the lock in the first place, so under no circumstances was I to leave the house without setting it. He was always worried that if we ever did have a break-in, and the police made note that the deadbolt hadn't been engaged at the time, the insurance company might deny our claim.

Of course, now he didn't worry about anything.

Sir Stephen looked up at me from his perch on top of the sofa just underneath the window, then dismissed me with a glance, reassuring me I was safe. At nineteen pounds, one would think he'd have been braver ("That's not a cat, that's a cougar," my future husband had told me when we'd first uncrated him), but Sir Stephen's was the picture next to the definition of 'Fraidy Cat' in the feline encyclopedia. Just the knock of a stranger on the door would transform him into a black and white blur as he scurried to conceal himself in one of his multiple hiding spots. It never ceased to amaze me how many tight spaces that little monster could manage to squeeze himself into. You'd think the animal had no bones whatsoever.

After kicking off Constance's pumps, with no small amount of relish, not to mention viciousness, I refilled the near empty food and water dishes, then pocketed the envelope I'd addressed to Warren and left on the marble countertop explaining my actions at greater length than the brief one in my car at the Warming Hut, which—thanks to Leroy and his people—hadn't been found. We'd had a longstanding agreement with my friend that should anything ever happen to both Julius and me, Warren would assume responsibility for Sir Stephen. In exchange, there existed a reciprocal arrangement for my friend's Russian Blue, Vlad.

"Hope you haven't outgrown your carrier," I told the beast, who blinked at me indifferently, then twitched an ear and went back to ignoring me.

Slipping into full autopilot, I made a circuit of the kitchen. Not that there was any real need, ever since the funeral my diet had consisted primarily of some form of take-out, and the kitchen remained spotless. The last meal I could clearly remember cooking had been the morning of the accident. Julius's favorite, nested eggs.

I walked over to our antique telephone table and checked the machine. No messages. Well, that wasn't particularly odd. Both my husband and I used our cell phones for family, business, and friends, relegating the landline to its perennial status as an emergency backup device, as well as a firewall against telephone solicitors and their ilk.

As I stared at the walls of what had been my home for close to a decade, it struck me that this could very well be the last day I spent here. I had no idea where Leroy and Oscar were planning to take me, of course, but it seemed wisest to assume the worst.

Are you serious? What's the point, you blithering imbecile? How much longer do you have, anyway? And what the fuck difference will it make if it's the cancer or one of those psychopaths that kills you? Either way, you know it's going to involve a literal shitload of pain, the kind you can't safeword your way out of, no matter how much you pray and plead for it to stop.

I stood there growing steadily more teary-eyed, a salty tide of self-pity sluicing over me. Despite my heart attack scare in high school, I'd never really thought much about death after reaching adulthood, not even when it got up close and personal; an elderly family member or onetime school classmate. Now here I was, marked for extermination one way or the other, but up until this point it still hadn't felt real. Yes, I'd taken a swan dive (well, more of a cannonball, really) off the Golden Gate Bridge, but that was the result of a week spent drowning in Julius's absence, not because of the leukemia. Following the visit from the two police officers, and their request for me to accompany them for identification purposes, the cancer had become almost meaningless. After all, what point had there been in circling a now-dead star?

But after the incident in the laboratory, when I had actively fought to resist death, something had awakened inside me, what I could only describe as the normative instinct for self-preservation. After Julius's death, my cancer had seemed almost incidental, just one more burden crushing both my body and my spirit. But then, while squatting in that panic room with Constance and the Binghams, I'd realized something startling. The fact was, I didn't want to die.

I wanted to live.

But now, standing in the center of the kitchen, I realized that that newfound desire was simply another form of denial. Soon, one way or the other, I *was* going to die. Nothing could stop it. That being the case, what possible sense did it make to prolong the inevitable?

No matter what my snotty inner voice insisted on repeating ad infinitum, I believed I wasn't a true coward, not where life was concerned, that is. Cowards don't take risks, after all. They don't face whom they know themselves to be and then act on that knowledge. I'd left my family and my friends, my job and my home, all for the opportunity to live my life under my own terms, exactly the way I wanted—no, not wanted, *needed*—to live it. How many others, their oxcart wheels caught in the ruts of familial and societal expectations, could say the same?

So prove you're not truly gutless, then. Spray some starch into that noodle you laughingly refer to as a spine, then 'git er done', before Leroy or Oscar come back. Those two men are risking their lives, and for what? A lost cause. Maybe your fate is set in stone, but does that give you the right to continue putting others' lives at risk? Just put your big girl panties on and do the deed.

Uh huh, right. And just how was I supposed to do 'the deed'? Neither Julius nor I had much in the house in the way of sleeping pills or the like. The oncologist had given me a prescription for pain meds, but I hadn't filled it yet. I could have stuck my head in the oven, but it was electric, not gas, and however dark my fantasies had gotten during my life, sati had never been one of them.

What about slitting your wrists? Just draw a warm bath, isn't that what they do in the movies? Two long gashes. Lengthwise, not straight across. Then just lie back in the water, close your eyes, and drift off. Who knows? Maybe there is an afterlife. You might wake up to Julius standing there on the other side, waiting for you, maybe even next to your dad.

I started to shake, and couldn't stop.

Ah, I see, Bluebeard was right after all. When it comes down to it, you really are nothing but a coward.

What's wrong with me?! I silently screamed. Long term there's no hope. After all, it's not a question of whether or not I'm going to die, it's a question of how much, or how little, time I have left. So why can't I find the strength to do what needs to be done?

Exactly! What are you still holding on for? You think Mordant is going to show up out of nowhere, thank you for abandoning him to the people who were, after all, looking for you, then subsequently offer you eternal life as a reward? Seriously?!

I took a deep breath and then, expelling it, made the decision.

This really is it, isn't it? I thought, almost calm now. And it's not as though I'll be going into the darkness with nothing. I've had a good life, all things considered. Lots of people have had it worse than me, far worse. Why not simply be grateful for all the good things I've had, and leave it at that? Not like there's anything I've left undone.

Then it hit me.

Yes, there was. One thing left undone, that is. Stupid, really. Not to mention an absurdity, a childish whim.

I stepped briskly down the hallway. If my husband had been here, there was no way on Earth I could have found the courage to do what I was about to do.

But he wasn't here. And I had to know.

Up the stairs, then down the hallway. Last room on the left, Julius's study. Never locked, but that didn't matter, since I was never allowed inside it without permission anyway.

I stepped into the office, then crossed over to the bookcase. Which, I had learned while snooping one day, wasn't a bookcase at all. It was a doorway, leading into my husband's private sanctuary. His 'secret room'.

Of course, that name was a bit of a misnomer, since Julius had never really made a secret of it. He'd told me all about the room, had even described its contents. Over the years, I'd decided that keeping this sanctuary—his miniature 'batcave'—private was his way of holding on to a piece of what had once belonged to him alone. After all, there would be no children to inherit. He had been upfront about his sterility right from the start, explaining that I shouldn't waste my time, nor his, if that was a deal breaker. And while a small part of me had always thought the need not to share that room had always been just a bit childish, it wasn't as though he had never indulged any of my own whims in turn.

I stood before the hidden entrance, the worn leather volumes and small carved figures crowding the bookshelves. There was, of course, no key. And had I not once peered through a crack in the door, my husband unaware that I was standing in the hallway just outside, holding my breath, I never would have known how to get in.

I reached behind the second and third shelves, slipping my fingers into the hidden sockets, then pulled outward, disengaging the locks. The weight of the bookcase opened it the barest sliver, and I stepped back to give myself sufficient room as I wrestled it open to stand at the threshold, taking it all in.

The room itself was surprisingly small. Wooden file cabinets crowded against one another along the rear wall, with an ancient rolltop desk made of oak on one side and a matching burgundy leather club chair and ottoman on the other.

I stepped in to look around, wondering which of many potential violations I should commit first prior to running my final bath. Then I saw it.

The briefcase rested on the floor, its scratched bulk leaning against the desk. Aged and worn, it bulged dangerously, as though it might split its seams at any moment. I removed a stack of binders and what appeared to be ledgers from the desk's matching chair, then sat down and lifted the case to my lap. Christ, it weighs a ton, I thought.

I thumbed open the brass lock, then looked inside. Unlike the rest of the room, its contents were neatly arranged in multiple pockets, along with one other item. Julius's laptop. Not the only one he owned, of course. Various electronic devices lay scattered all over our home, but this one was unique, because I had never once seen it outside of this room's walls.

I pressed the power button, but it didn't start. Most likely the battery was dead. I found the electrical cord in one of the smaller pockets, then attached it to the laptop and plugged it in.

"Seriously?" I muttered, watching Windows XP boot up. After what seemed like forever, I looked over the bare-bones desktop with its minimalist handful of icons. Nothing exceptional. The only really odd thing was a dual set of AOL shortcuts.

I played for a minute with the uncooperative touchpad, then gave it up. Searching the various desk drawers, I found an old serial port mouse. After taking some time to clean the lint off its inner wheels, I finally got cursor movement. Double-clicking the first AOL icon brought up a familiar sight, Julius's main account ID and a series of other screen names appearing below the drop-down menu, including two of my own: a vanilla one for family and such, and my more well used one, PhedreFan, which I'd transferred over to my husband's account after shutting down my own.

I closed that version of AOL down and opened the second, clicking on the arrow next to the main screen name, which lacked the ancillary bracketing characters of the other one, implying that this account was much older. And when the drop-down menu opened, I froze.

But no matter how long I stared at the familiar screen name, which had been burned into my brain so many years earlier, nothing changed. Instead it remained there, staring back at me, the only other user ID on that account.

Bluebeard.

＊＊＊

I sat in my husband's old oak chair, circa sometime around the Great Depression, unable to take my eyes off the ancient laptop's screen. I even consciously blinked. Several times.

Then I began ransacking everything in sight.

Most of what I came across was incomprehensible, so lacking in context that I had no idea what to make of it. Some simply stunned me, including, but not limited to, a statement from a bank I'd never heard of, covered with numbers so large they almost took my breath away.

Understand, the lifestyle we enjoyed could in no way be considered deprived. While our house, in terms of pure square footage, would be considered modest by the standards of the country at large (and dinky by those of my home state), this was San Francisco, and our quaint Victorian could easily have fetched millions on the open market, even prior to the current economic recovery.

These numbers, though? They defied my brain's ability to comprehend.

But perhaps the most disturbing find was the house title, accompanied by a large key, which I shoved into my pocket. When I saw the address and realized where it was, I almost broke down right then. At any moment I expected to find a second marriage license, with someone else's name next to my husband's.

Finally, exhausted, I made my way to the club chair against the far wall, shoved the boxes and stacks of papers covering it to the floor, then crawled into the empty space and slept.

⊰⊱

A persistent buzzing, flashing red like a turn signal, woke me. The doorbell.

I staggered upright, then made my way to the front entrance, only remembering to take security precautions as my hand touched the crystal knob. I put my eye to the peephole and saw the frustrated face of Oscar staring back at me, hands on his hips as his right leg jiggled fiercely.

"Goddammit, girl, do you have any idea what time it is?" he spat as he pushed by me after I'd opened the door. As I fought to focus, he stepped in front of me and shoved it closed, then locked the chain and deadbolt.

"I've been phoning you for hours!" he all but yelled, as he ran what looked for all the world like a perimeter check, peeking into rooms and cracking curtains, talking rapid fire all the while. "And I couldn't even phone the police, being under strict orders not to."

"I'm sorry," I said through the sludge currently acting as my thought processes. "I lay down, just for a minute." I rubbed my eyes as he opened yet another curtain. "What time is it?"

"Half past seven," he said after consulting his watch, a titanium Casio.

"Is everything all right?" I asked.

"So far as I know," he replied, finally relaxed after reassuring himself we were alone.

"Have you spoken to Leroy?"

"Not for a few hours. He said to sit tight. I told him I'd called your cell, but got no answer. He figured, like me, that you'd probably crashed for a while. You've looked like one of those zombies out of the Walking Dead since I first laid eyes on you. But when it started to get dark and I still couldn't get through to you, I got anxious, and . . ." He shrugged.

"Sorry," I mumbled.

"When did you lie down?"

I took a few deep breaths to clear my head. "Sometime around noon. I think."

"You sick or something?" he asked.

I almost answered truthfully, then thought better of it. "What happens now?"

"Leroy's just about got things set up," Oscar said. "The plan is, he'll be here sometime around midnight when traffic's light, then we caravan out. He got his hands on a van, armor-plated with bulletproof windows, made to look like a utility vehicle. I'll ride point. By this time tomorrow, no one is going to have any idea where you are."

I chewed my lower lip. Oscar wasn't going to like what I had to say next.

"I have to go someplace," I said.

He stared at me, dazed and confused. Not him, me. Dazed and confused, that is. "Excuse me?" he said. "Have you lost your mind?"

I shook my head. "No. I have to do this. Once we leave, I'll probably never get another chance."

"To do what?" he asked.

I squared my shoulders and did my best to look determined. "I have to have a talk with Mom."

The truth was that my mother-in-law didn't like being called 'Mom'. Not that she liked me much better; after all, I'd stolen her 'baby'. So, in a petulant display of passive aggression, I often referred to Cheryl as 'Mom' around our friends, which never failed to amuse my husband.

There were a few photos of her scattered around our house, mostly old black and whites of this gorgeous creature in elegant vintage clothes, with fashionably short hair and a facial structure as fine and delicate as the kind of china you could never imagine eating off of. "Vanity," Julius had told me that day, my first in his house, when I'd asked why there were no more recent pictures of her. "It got to the point she would vanish like a groundhog in February if anyone so much as mentioned taking her picture."

"What about your father?" I'd asked innocently.

Julius had gotten a strange look on his face. "He left when I was a baby," he replied dismissively. "At least, that's what Cheryl said. Or perhaps I should say that's what she told me," he'd said, looking thoughtful. "Truth is, I sometimes suspect she and my father were never actually married, which at the time—in our social circles—would have been much more of a scandal than nowadays."

I'd grinned at him. "I see nothing's changed," I had said, displaying the wicked streak I'd been careful to warn him about, long before we ever met real time. "You're still a bastard."

He had smiled, a dark curl of the lips. "You'll call me worse than that before the night is done."

And later that evening as I'd struggled, naked and bound to our canopy bed, cringing at the crack of my husband's favorite singletail, he proved himself a prophet yet again.

"I haven't seen my mother-in-law since . . . well, since my husband died," I told Oscar. "She doesn't even know."

His eyebrows rose. "She doesn't know her son is dead?"

"She lives at Stony Point Manor," I said, "You know where that is, right?"

He shook his head. "I'm not from here."

I headed for the bedroom, Oscar following close behind. "It's a very expensive and very exclusive retirement complex," I said as I began shuffling through my closet. "Cheryl's lived there ever since I've known her."

"She's not—er, you know," he said, tapping his temple.

I shrugged. "A touch of dementia, I think. She pretends otherwise, but there are times I'm convinced she doesn't really recognize me. She's elderly, not to mention frail. Requires round-the-clock care, and medical assistance close at hand." I pulled out an old pair of jeans, which I hadn't worn in, Christ, I couldn't remember how many years. The Master/slave contract I'd negotiated with Julius prior to his collaring of me required me to wear skirts and dresses only, sans undies, unless he gave permission otherwise. I wondered if the Levi's would still fit. "I'm lazy," my husband had said with one of his slow smiles as we'd reviewed the documentation of my voluntary servitude. "I like easy access." Which he demonstrated shortly after I put my name on the dotted line, bending me in half over the back of the couch without warning before yanking the hem of my dress over my head and taking me without foreplay, making explicit and highly-detailed comments about my nudity all the while.

I rummaged in the dresser until I found a sweater, then turned back to Oscar, holding it up as if he'd just walked in on me in changing. "Do you mind?"

"Hm, wha-? Oh, right!" he said as he gave the bedroom window a quick glance, as though half expecting to see a burglar climbing in. "I'll be right here outside the door," he said as he closed it.

I removed the blouse and skirt, followed by the Spanx, wincing all the while. By the time I was done, I could tell I'd need a few more of Constance's Little Helpers. The bruises from my fall into the bay had now bloomed across my right side like the scent of honeysuckle. The outfit came off with far less struggle than it had going on, which I was grateful for. Then I took a long awaited, and desperately needed, shower.

The jeans took more effort, as did the sweater. I eschewed a bra, my ribcage still throbbing relentlessly, reminding me to retrieve the Percocet from the pocket of her skirt. After a few jerks and tugs, I slipped on a pair of sandals, then stepped in front of the antique mirror next to the closet. "Oh my."

Don't get me wrong, I wouldn't be striding along the Victoria's Secret catwalk anytime soon. But the reflection revealed a 'me' I hadn't seen in quite some time. And though I knew why that was, I still couldn't help turning this way and that, examining myself from multiple angles.

"Say what you will about cancer," I muttered, "But with the right marketing, you could probably sell it as a weight loss program. Like those tapeworm diet clinics down in Mexico."

And though I felt all kinds of ridiculous for doing so, I spent some time in front of the bathroom mirror, just me and Lady L'Oreal, frosting the cake with some make-up, mascara, and a bit of lipstick in a shade my mother would charitably have referred to as 'whore red'.

When I exited the bedroom, Oscar did a double-take. "They spray paint those things on nowadays?" he said with a grin, nodding at my jeans.

The heat from my cheeks radiated down to my chest. "Can we go?" I said, fighting to include sufficient petulance in my voice to disguise an otherwise obvious pleasure.

He walked to the door and opened it with a theatrical flourish. "After you, M'Lady." And though I suspected he was making fun of me, I still felt the thrill any woman on the downhill side of her thirties would have in my place as I sashayed past him, allowing my hips a gentle bit of sway. He cleared his throat, then followed me.

⌘

Stony Point Manor nestles in what is, for San Francisco, a ridiculously large lot. More of a park, really, threaded by numerous pathways amidst a lush landscaping rumored to attract the fabled flocks of San Francisco parakeets which, after more than a decade in the city, I still had yet to see. The building itself is anchored by an original structure of faded brick (constructed just after the infamous 1906 earthquake) flanked by two more modern wings. Julius was monosyllabic about the place, but in a rare garrulous mood had once told me that Stony Point was financed privately, supported in part by endowments as massive and diversely invested as an Ivy League college's stock portfolio. I had no idea how they solicited customers, since they performed no marketing that I was aware of, and the minimalist website they did have was perfunctory at best. My base impression was that the management went to extraordinary lengths to cultivate a rarified air of social and economic exclusivity.

"You'll have to wait downstairs," I told Oscar as we entered the lobby. He didn't look happy about this, but finally nodded in acquiescence before taking a seat on a burgundy leather chesterfield sofa near the gas fireplace, allowing him to keep an eye on the people entering and exiting.

Various staff members, coddling their charges like spoiled children, smiled and nodded in my direction as I navigated the wainscoted hallways with their marble-tiled floors. I wondered how many knew about Julius. Not that my husband's death posed any risk of disturbing Cheryl's status. Julius's lawyers (Worthham, Howard, and Peele) had made it clear during the reading of the will that a trust had been established long ago for the St. Claire matron, ensuring that her residency at Stony Point stood no chance of being jeopardized.

"Well, hello there!"

I smiled and nodded at Claudia as the flaming redhead quick-stepped my way. She was my mother-in-law's personal caretaker, dividing her attention between Cheryl and another lady by the name of Allison Wainwright who was, as Claudia frequently put it, "A real pistol."

She hugged me. "I heard about the mister," she murmured into my ear, her warm breath as salty as an ocean breeze.

I expelled a prolonged sigh and relaxed, allowing myself a moment's luxury in the uncomplicated sympathy of her embrace. "Has anyone told her?" I husked.

"Heavens no!" Claudia said, matching my volume while doubling its intensity as she released me. "It would kill her. Truly it would."

It's killing me, I wanted to say, despite the recent revelations. I wondered what that said about the younger Ms. St. Claire. "Is she having a good day?"

"Very quiet," she said. "Which can turn good or bad in short order, but that's true for so many of the residents in this wing."

"Where is she now?"

"She just finished eating," Claudia said. "She told me she wanted to dine privately, so I brought her supper to her. When I left she was sitting by the window, staring out. You go on ahead, and if either of you need anything, just hit the buzzer."

I smiled, reliving (if only for a brief moment) the exquisite sensation of being thoroughly looked after and cared for. She rested her hand on my upper arm, gave it a squeeze, then hurried away.

I continued down the hallway to my mother-in-law's room. The thick wooden door was ajar, and I pushed it open. "Cheryl?"

As Claudia had said, the family matron was sitting in a wingback chair in front of her bedroom's bay window, which enjoyed a very pleasant view of the grounds. The setting sun cast a soft, pink glow like the scent of fresh baby powder over the flowering bushes and trees, all throbbing with the newborn Spring. "Who's there?" Cheryl called out without turning around.

I stepped inside. The room was more of a suite, with a sitting area separating the sleeping quarters from the outside hallway. White wainscoting bordered the walls in counterpoint to the trey ceiling overhead. Fresh roses in a large vase resting on a burled walnut end table suffused the air with a perfume like piano notes. The bed, larger than any single woman truly needed, had been turned down. "It's me, Abby," I said.

She turned in my direction, her face displayed in profile. While the years has taken a brutal toll on Cheryl, you could still see the remnants of what had once been a heart-stopping beauty, made all the sadder by the painful efforts to salvage what little was left: the heavy foundation and thick blush that did little to mask the sagging wrinkles of her face and neck, the eye shadow that might have been applied with a paint brush, her carefully maintained coif, dyed a rich chestnut brown, even a lipstick that almost matched my own. I fought to avoid a shudder.

"Have you two been quarreling?" she said in a cool, distant tone, still staring out the window.

Must be having a good day, I thought, *she recognizes me.* "Not at all. Why do you ask?" I replied, doing my best to keep my tone light as I took a seat opposite her.

"You never come together anymore," she said.

While I had few illusions regarding her feelings toward me, Cheryl's attitude had always trawled more along the lines of an exhausted acceptance rather than a malicious resentment, as though I were a necessary evil she had determined to make the best of. "Julius isn't here," I said, struggling to avoid an outright lie. "But he wanted me to check on you, make sure you were okay."

She wouldn't turn to look at me. "It wasn't necessary, you know," she said in a brisk, brusque tone. "I understood the necessity. I'm not a fool, after all. But he could have waited, before bringing you here."

When she didn't elaborate, I spoke up. "Waited for what?"

She sighed, a weary exhalation. "For me to die."

I bit my lip. "He loves you very much," I said, trying to comfort her, despite her words.

"Loves me? *Loves* me?" She turned, panic flowing like water over her face. "What's wrong?" she demanded.

Caught off guard by the intensity of her response, I stared at her. She couldn't possibly know. Could she?

"Nothing's wrong," I said, then added, "Should there be?"

Cheryl leaned forward, pinning me to my seat, her gaze laced with a raw combination of anger and fear. Her hands, wrinkled and covered with age spots, gripped the arms of her chair so tightly, her upper body almost seemed to vibrate. "Do they know? Did they find out?"

"They who? Find out what?" I said, struggling to keep my own voice calm in the wake of her obvious terror.

"I told him he had to be careful," she moaned, ignoring my question. "It's suspicious. People with that much money, they always have something to hide."

"You know about that?" I whispered.

"I always said the past would come back to haunt him," she mumbled, ignoring me. "Haunt us both. The truth comes out. It always comes out, no matter how smart you are, or believe yourself to be." She looked up at me, a suspicious glance. "What do you know?" she hissed, a mauve hostility in her voice. "What do you *think* you know?"

The growing aggression in Cheryl's tone frightened me. I gave the button next to her bed a side glance, while resisting the urge to reach for it. "I don't understand," I said. "Know about what?"

Slowly, as if rising out of a well, Cheryl leaned forward. I watched, confused, as she rose to step in front of me. "He promised me he would spare you the knowing. He promised he would never, ever share. Did he??" She bent forward, her breath a fetid cymbal clash in my face. Her hands gripped my forearms, the nails digging like claws into my skin with so much force that I cried out.

I twisted out of Cheryl's clasp and backed away, pounding on the buzzer as she stumbled after me, her face twisted with an ugly and terrifying hate.

"DID HE?!" she screamed as Claudia, along with another staff member, rushed in. "DID HE!?"

I watched the two staff members struggling with Cheryl, who suddenly collapsed into their arms, almost dragging them with her almost to the floor.

"IT'S NOT FAIR!" I heard her howl, an animalistic wail that pursued me as I fled the room. "IT'S NOT FAIIRRR!"

<hr/>

Shaking uncontrollably, I made my way back to the lobby. I'd never seen Julius's mother so distraught. Just before Claudia entered with her assistant, there had been a moment, as intense as the edge of a knife, when I was certain the woman was about to launch herself at me, consumed by a rage unlike anything I had witnessed from her before. Had she truly, finally, lost her mind?

Or did she know something I didn't?

"What's wrong?" Oscar asked as I walked briskly past him on my way out. He rushed to match my pace.

"You know, you could be a bit more helpful," he said as we made our way to his motorcycle. "After all, it's my job to keep you alive, and you're not making it easy."

What's the point? I opened my mouth to yell. But before I could get the words out, and thereby open up an entirely new can of worms, a blindingly sharp pain hit me in the left side of my abdomen. It hurt so bad it took my breath away. I couldn't even cry out, all I could do was hunch over, arms crossed over my belly.

"Christ, girl, what's wrong?" Oscar said as he grabbed me beneath the shoulders to keep me from collapsing.

Then, as suddenly as it had appeared, the pain was gone.

"What's wrong?" he repeated.

I maintained my position, terrified that any sudden motion might cause the pain to return, as I fought against the urge to vomit. "Cramp," I whimpered.

He nodded. "My sister gets 'em real bad during her time of the month. Or is this something else?" he added slowly, studying my face.

I shook my head. "I don't know," I lied.

"Want me to take you to the hospital?" he said.

I shook my head again. "It's gone now," I told him, standing straight again.

He eyed me suspiciously. "If you have one of those while on the back of my bike . . ."

"I'm okay. Really," I told him. "And I'm ready to go home now."

He looked around. Night had fallen. "It's not that far," he mumbled as though thinking aloud. "Getting a cab would probably keep you out in the open longer than if we just drove straight back to your place. Very well then, we ride. But if you get so much as a twinge . . ."

I nodded. "I'll let you know."

He gave me a grin with lots of teeth. "All I can ask. Okay, let's hit pavement. Once we get there, someone else will be taking over for me."

"Why's that?" I asked as we made our way across the parking lot, nervous at the prospect of being entrusted to a stranger.

"Leroy's been in touch with your friends, the Binghams. Seems there's another bloke they want found. Fellow by the name of Mordant Ember," Oscar said before revving his motorcycle, a sparkling orange racket that hurt my eyes and ears alike.

I grabbed Oscar's shoulder to get his full attention. "Do they know where he is?"

He stared down at my hand, then back up at me. "No clue. Leroy said he'd text me later with an update." Then he squinted at me. "Friend of yours?"

Good question. Wished I had an answer. "Is he all right?" I asked, folding my arms over my chest to conserve warmth against the vanishing day.

"Dunno. Soon as we get you home and my relief arrives, I'll head over that way and see what's what. You okay?"

I couldn't stop shivering. "Just cold."

"Here," he said, shrugging out of his leather jacket and handing it to me, along with his helmet.

Part of me wanted to gracefully refuse him; he'd be acting as a windbreaker while driving, after all, but the wimp inside me took over and accepted the heavy garment with a muttered "Thank you." Underneath the jacket he wore a long-sleeved Henley with the legend: "If You Can Read This, The Bitch Fell Off," stenciled on the back.

"No worries," Oscar said. "Now climb on and hold tight."

⚓

He took things slow, enough so that we received several angry honks from frustrated tailgaters. Then, as we approached a stoplight, I felt the beginnings of another cramp. "Oscar?"

He must have felt the jolt run through me, because he immediately kicked the bike into high gear, zipping through a sliver of a gap in traffic as he accelerated towards the nearest parking space.

That was when the car screeched to a halt directly in front of us.

There was no time to avoid it. Oscar twisted the handlebars, causing us to slide sideways into the vehicle, some sort of sedan. For a moment I had a glimpse of the driver, a fortyish man, head turned in our direction, face placid, as though all knowledge of the imminent crash was still swimming upstream inside his brain.

Then we slammed into him.

For a moment I was airborne. I bounced off something, maybe the roof or the hood. I couldn't tell for sure, half-blinded as I was by Oscar's helmet. Tucking myself into a ball, I rolled off the car, then hit the pavement, expecting at any moment to be crushed beneath the wheels of oncoming traffic. Finally I came to a halt against someone's tire while fighting for the air that had been knocked out of me. I opened my eyes and looked around.

Chaos. Cars were piled around me in a large circle, with me in the center. I searched for Oscar and saw him. At least, what was left of him.

"No . . ." I moaned.

The driver of the car that had caused the crash, a Toyota Camry, exited his vehicle and navigated the wreckage surrounding us. He glanced down at Oscar with a face devoid of expression, then turned toward me as he pulled something out of his jacket's right pocket. A pistol. Fighting desperately to force my limbs into something resembling motion, I watched him come for me.

Then he stumbled.

I looked down. Oscar had taken hold of the driver's ankle with his un-maimed left hand, struggling to maintain his grip.

Still expressionless, the driver aimed and fired once, then a second time. I watched Oscar's body jerk. Then he lay still.

Now unimpeded, the driver came for me again.

I couldn't stand, so I scrabbled backwards. The man, who looked like a high school principal, came for me calmly, his eyes as empty as a doll's.

"Nigger's dead too," he said as he finally caught up with me. "Your turn now." He moved to stand over me.

I bumped into something, another car, as I watched the driver point his weapon. People were yelling all around me. *I guess this is it,* I thought, before closing my eyes. As epitaphs go, it seemed lacking, but nothing else occurred to me. So I clenched my jaw, hugged myself, and waited.

I heard the firecracker pop, then a blow to the gut that knocked the wind out of me.

Kicking hard, sandals banging against the pavement, I shoved at the sudden weight pinning me to the ground. The driver rolled onto my legs, his expression dazed, his eyes blinking. Blood poured from his upper chest, saturating his shirt. And as I watched, the casual vacancy of his face melted like candlewax, replaced by a growing pain and horror, twisting his features into a lunatic's mask.

"No, no . . ." he said, his voice now animated. "Not like this! Please! You promised! Not like this . . . !"

I struggled, unsuccessfully, to free myself. The driver stared not at me, but through me, his eyes wild and terrified. He grabbed at my upper arms, his scent ringing in my ears like a muffled school bell.

"Please! Please help me!" he choked out as I lay there, terrified out of my wits yet unable to look away. He clutched at me as though I was a life-line against a sudden riptide.

"They eat away at you, till there's almost nothing left, like a wad of gum with no flavor," he moaned. "I kept praying to die, hoping that if I did, that would be the end . . ."

He pulled himself over me, until his face filled my world. I twisted, desperate to get away, to break his horrified gaze.

"But it doesn't matter!" he whimpered, a sound like the end of hope as he dug his nails into my flesh with the desperation of a drowning man. "Because when they leave, *they take what's left of you with them!*"

I heard someone screaming, a sound that seemed to go on forever, and it was only when I felt a pair of hands pull me away that I realized the screams were coming from me.

⛬

"Want a refill?"

I shook my head, cringing a bit when the officer stepped too close. She sighed, then moved away.

There had been so many questions.

Did he shoot you?

No.

Do you have any other injuries?

No.

Did you know the deceased?

I'd already told them all about Oscar, so I assumed they meant the driver of the Camry, who turned out to have been a shoe salesman. No previous arrests, one speeding violation. Not the sort of person you'd expect to crash into you, then shoot a man in the head, execution style.

And if hadn't been for that police officer blowing a hole in his chest, he'd have killed you too.

I watched as the detective stepped back to the coffeemaker for creamer. The faint scent of Cool Water (the female version) clicked in my ears like a playing card pinned to a bicycle wheel. No monotonous ringing, I reminded myself yet again with relief. Not from her, nor from anyone I'd encountered at the police station.

At least, not yet.

"When can I go home?" I asked her.

"Soon as we can scare up a driver," Winnie ("Short for Winifred.") said as she took a seat nearby. Though not too close. Even the possible hint of physical contact, after what had happened, was enough to make me flinch. Having seen multiple examples of this throughout my interview, Winnie now made a point of keeping a certain amount of distance between us.

"And you have no idea who that man was, or why he wanted to shoot you?" she asked in a calm, conversational tone for maybe the fifth time, as though we were discussing the likelihood of an evening fog.

For a moment, I wondered what her reaction would be if I told her what Mordant had told me. That there were possessed people out there with an unknown agenda, who appeared to want me dead.

Or did they?

The others, the two men in the medical lab, the ones from the van, followed by the ones from the Mission District who had taken Mordant, none of them had stunk with that same buzzing scent which had set my teeth on edge only hours ago.

They take what's left of you with them!

I had to consider the possibility that there was no connection between those others and the driver of the Camry. But if not, if these 'possessed' people represented a second group, then who—or what—was the first group? Did they want me dead for the same reasons, or different ones?

Assuming, of course, that they weren't all working together.

I considered telling the police about Mordant's list, and the other attempts to kidnap me. But those names, the ones belonging to police officers who had mysteriously disappeared, kept me silent.

I shut my eyes and rested my head on my arms, the strong smell of coffee tickling my ears like the sound of cicadas in the summertime.

"Okay, I can see you're pretty wiped, so we'll call it a night, finish this another time," Winnie said as she took a sip from a chipped mug that read 'World's Greatest Aunt'. "There anyone you can call for a lift home?"

I shook my head.

"Not a problem, we'll arrange a ride," she said, giving me an appraising look before crossing the room to murmur into a phone. I tried to listen without appearing to eavesdrop, but couldn't make out either half of the conversation.

Shortly thereafter, a knock rattled the glass of the door. "Somebody need a lift?" said a uniformed officer upon entry who was so old, he looked as though he should have been sitting in front of a house yelling at the neighborhood kids to get the hell off his lawn.

"This lady does," Winnie said, indicating me with a jerk of her thumb. "Who's the driver? Branson?"

"Nah, Epstein," the man grumbled.

Winnie smiled. "Thought he'd taken leave for his honeymoon."

"Too busy polishing the Captain's nuts. Bastard is deluded if he thinks anyone will give a shit, come evaluation time."

"You just wish you had something as cute as the newly minted Ms. Epstein to spoon with," Winnie said as she offered me her hand. After giving it a cautious glance, I took it while struggling to my feet, silently grateful for the support.

The old man, whom I'd nicknamed 'the Grouch' in my head, looked at me, then shrugged. "How the fuck you survived that crash," he said, shaking his head.

I almost told him that if he hurt as badly as I did, he wouldn't be making light of it. Pain like glue had fused my joints together, and it was only with Winnie's assistance that I could walk at all, as heavy as Oscar's jacket was. I remembered the Percocet in my pocket, then excused myself long enough to chase two down with a cup of water Winnie obligingly provided upon request.

Once I'd taken the pills, the detective escorted me down a long hallway, then out a side door, the Grouch close behind. A marked police car, engine running, rumbled next to the curb. A young officer, who didn't look as though he'd been shaving for very long, stood on the far side, his arms crossed.

"Married life treating you okay, Epstein?" Winnie called out as she led me to the rear door of the vehicle.

"I'll let you know when I get some married time in," the officer grumbled.

"Don't get your panties in a knot," Winnie said. "Anyway, the poor girl could probably use a break."

"Fuck you very much," Epstein said.

"Oh, stop sulking," Winnie said, barely suppressing a grin. "Lots of girls these days renew their virginity a year before the ceremony."

The young officer muttered something unprintable. Before she could move, I reached out to grab Winnie's arm. "Please don't go!" I said without thinking.

"Oh, don't you worry, I'm coming on this ride-along. Wouldn't trust a tamale like you all by your lonesome with Mr. Blue Balls here. Give him a couple of weeks with the new missus, and then maybe he'll be fit for female company again. Shotgun!" she called.

"After last week, you think I'd let you drive?" Epstein said with a snort as he got in behind the wheel.

Winnie opened the door for me. "Just you slide right in, honey."

I followed her orders, far more comfortable now that someone other than myself was in charge. Winnie slid into the front passenger seat, her profile a bit smudged due to the dirty plastic shield separating the front seat from the rear.

"Keep to the side streets, Epstein," Winnie said. "I don't have the first idea what's going on, but our passenger appears to be a very popular lady with some strange—and very homicidal—locals."

"Stalker?" Epstein said, giving me an intense look in the rearview mirror.

Exhausted, both physically and mentally, I simply shrugged. "Something like that," I said.

"Not hard to see why," he said with a grin. "You ever pose for Playboy? Cuz you look a lot like Miss January."

"Miss January was black," Winnie said.

Epstein shrugged. "Might have been Miss December."

"You really need that honeymoon," Winnie said, clucking her tongue.

We navigated the dark streets quickly as Epstein exceeded the posted speed limit by a considerable amount. Winnie showed no surprise over this, so neither did I. Ten minutes from the station I saw a man almost cross the street, before stepping back to walk away as we roared through an intersection.

"Whoa," Epstein said, his voice almost a whisper. "Detective Armstrong, are you still looking for that scuzbucket who shook his girlfriend's baby to death because the kid wouldn't stop crying?"

"You know I am," Winnie said, her voice now low and intense. "Why do you ask?"

Epstein tilted his head to the left in the direction of the man we'd just passed. "Because I thought I just saw him turn the corner behind us."

"You shitting me?" Winnie said, twisting in her seat. "Go!"

"You sure?" he said, giving me a glimpse over his shoulder.

"I lost that sonuvabitch after a six block run three nights ago. I'm not going to lose him again, not a second time. Turn this goddamned tugboat around!"

Epstein screeched to a halt, performed a quick three-point turn, then headed back in the direction we'd come from.

"Kill your lights, so we can get in as close as possible," Winnie said. "And if that *was* him, we've nailed his sorry ass. No other way out of that alley."

Slowing almost to a crawl, Epstein edged his way into the darkened street.

"To your right," Epstein whispered.

"Where?" Winnie asked.

"Just behind that dumpster."

Winnie craned her neck, turning her head so hard I could see the whites of her eyes.

That was when the gun went off.

Unlike the pop from earlier in the day, this was the roar of a much more powerful weapon. Winnie's head literally exploded. Blood, and what I could only assume were brains, splashed against the right window and the shield between us. The impact of the bullet had spider-webbed the plastic before punching a hole through it and the side window.

I froze, too terrified even to scream.

As I shrank back, Epstein turned in his seat, his eyes impossibly wide, head twisting on his neck as if he were a ventriloquist's dummy in a cheap horror flick. I caught the scent of him floating through the hole in the barrier separating us, his odor buzzing like a wind-up alarm clock.

Then he smiled, a grimace that pulled his lips an inch past his gums, before he spoke again.

"*We are Legion.*"

He lifted the gun and aimed it at me.

Screaming now, I ducked into the floorboard. Epstein (or whatever had control of his body) muttered a curse, soon followed by the sound of the door opening.

I scrabbled for the latch on the right passenger door, but no amount of fumbling with the handle did any good.

Of course you can't open it, you idiot! It's a police *car.*

There were a few steps, followed by the silvery metallic click of the far door handle. I saw Epstein's face in the window, twisted into an expression no human countenance had ever been designed to mimic.

Then, gun in hand, he started to open the door.

There was no time to think. After pulling my knees to my chest, I kicked out with both feet, slamming the door against him with the strength born of desperation—not to mention countless hours spent hiking the hilly streets of my adopted city.

His startled expression was comic, as well as insane. Arms pin-wheeling, he flew backwards, disappearing from sight with a teeth-jarring *thud*.

It took forever to clamber into an upright position. At least, it seemed like forever. I popped out of the door like a demented jack-in-the-box, knowing I shouldn't pause to look, that I should simply run. But I couldn't turn away.

There he lay on the sidewalk, flat on his back, head resting at an impossible angle against the base of a fire hydrant just behind him. Blood formed a growing pool on the filthy concrete sidewalk. He looked up at me without blinking, eyes fixed wide in a startled stare, and I knew he was dead.

My legs refused to support my weight any longer, and I slumped to the ground.

I can't say how long I sat there, staring at him. Voices alternated with bursts of static, like Fourth of July sparklers, from the police radio.

Then, just at that exact moment, the pain returned.

It hit me like the blow of a baseball bat, robbing me of breath. And as it did, I realized that this had nothing to do with my fall into the bay. Pestler had warned me about the symptoms of my disease, but I'd shut his words out at the time.

Pain in the right side. Can get quite brutal. Likely to come in waves, but eventually the intervals will diminish. We'll have to put you on a morphine drip at some point.

Oh God, I thought, while waiting for the agony to subside, it's going to get worse than this?

I sprawled on the sidewalk, twitching as the fire in my side faded to something almost manageable. At least for the moment.

Then I noticed the gun, still in Epstein's hand.

Why not use it? You're a cop killer now, after all. Think they're going to believe what really happened? Would you?

I took the gun from the officer's limp fingers, knowing as I did that I was covering it with my fingerprints, but long past caring.

How did the saying go? Eat a bullet?

Have to do it right. You don't want to miss, or you'll hit at an angle and end up disfigured in the hospital with the police asking you a ton of questions. Upper roof of the mouth, almost all soft tissue there. Will finish the job for sure.

Then my pocket vibrated.

Irritated by this latest distraction, I reached into the leather jacket and pulled out Oscar's smartphone. There was a text message.

"Mr. Monroe, we can't reach Leroy. Last we heard, he said he knew where they have Mordant. No police please! We've just had an incident. Time is of the essence! Sending link."

The name of the caller, according to the phone, was Constance Wingate.

I thumbed the link. It opened an app I wasn't familiar with, some sort of city map software. A blinking arrow showed my location, from which a thin blue line stretched in a northerly direction, according to the display's compass.

I pulled out the Percocet and dry-swallowed two more. At least, I think it was two, by that point things were a bit fuzzy. It took more time than it had previously, but eventually the claw in my abdomen relaxed its grip, allowing my abdominals to unclench. Still shaking, I clambered to my feet and took a few steps forward. The arrow moved with me.

Just after I noticed this, I glanced at the upper right hand corner of the screen. There it was, the almost empty battery symbol, flashing at me.

"So, contrary to my husband's frequent diatribes, it seems I am *not* the only person alive who forgets to charge her cell phone," I mumbled.

The sensible woman within (who rarely showed up when I needed her) opined that since the phone had been with me for a number of hours, it was quite understandable for it to be on its last legs. But I ignored the bitch.

Now, what to do?

On the one hand, I could simply continue with my plan to 'gargle lead' (a very Dashiell Hammett metaphor). That plan had the simplicity of expecting little from me, and demanding even less.

Option Two: I could phone Constance. The phone might die in the process, true. But it might not. And anything was better than Option Three.

So I reversed the call, and after a few rings got her voicemail. *Your call is being forwarded . . .*

Goddammit.

I left a message, keeping the explanation short as to why I was answering Oscar's phone, before telling her she should send in the cavalry ASAP. Then I hung up.

How long before she gets the call? Assuming, of course, she gets it at all.

I stood there in the darkness of the side street, a dead cop at my feet, and debated with myself, presenting every sound, reasonable argument as to why Option Three was insane.

You're one *person. What can* you *do?*

I can at least get there, see what's going on. Then when reinforcements arrive, I might have something useful to share that'll help keep Mordant alive. So to speak.

These are the same people who've been searching for you. *They want* you *dead too.*

So we all have that in common. Need a better counterargument than that.

They could draw that death out. Make it last considerably longer than you, or any sane person, would like.

Okay, a trenchant point.

After all, look at what they did to Julius.

Uh oh.

I felt the anger as soon as the idea occurred to me, though I can't say why it hadn't before. For the past week or so I had been suppressing fear, fear that the man to whom I had surrendered all power and authority in my life had, at the end, in an act of pure cowardice, committed suicide rather than face his wife's imminent and painful death.

I can't imagine life without you. How many times had he said that to me?

But what if it hadn't been his choice? What if he was also a victim, just like the others? What if his hideous and gruesome death, mangled almost beyond recognition by a subway train, had in fact been murder, by the same people who now held Mordant? Assuming, of course, that Mordant wasn't dead too. Or whatever passed for dead amongst his kind.

Which left me with two options. I could take Epstein's gun and finish what these people, who may very well have killed my husband, had started. Or . . .

I could chase the white rabbit into the hole and see how far it went.

⊰⊱

I removed my wallet from my purse, then crammed the oversized bag into a nearby trash can. It was heavy with female trifles, and I felt too weak to lug it around. All of the important stuff—money, my plastic, etc.—I had squeezed into the wallet, which I then shoved into the largest of the jacket's many pockets.

The smart phone rested heavy in my hand. No name on the graphic, and I didn't recognize the symbols on the display. The screen was enormous, and the casing appeared to be solid metal. I held it flat on my palm as I navigated the dark streets, following the blue arrow as it took point.

Odd how we cling to life, I thought, even while having a staring contest with Death.

Why the hell are you doing this, anyway? Revenge?

Not revenge, no. This wasn't a television show, and I was no Amanda Clark, honed to a razor's edge to purge a monstrous wrong with a frigid cocktail of justice and vengeance. I wasn't tempered for that, no matter how deluded my fantasies.

No, what motivated me, what kept me going despite a jaw clenched against the prospect of another tsunami of sheer agony, was a far simpler and more primal motivation. Survival. Because there, waiting at the terminus of the arrow's guidance, was my last opportunity to cheat death.

Mordant.

But then, isn't it all up to us in the end? Who and/or what we chose to be?

A-fucking-men.

Whatever had actually happened to him, whatever it was he had become, my imagination now teased me mercilessly with the possibility that some human spark might still burn inside him, a remnant of a former self not yet completely obliterated by his transformation into the creature which I had seen, on multiple occasions now, slaughter human beings with a feral and sadistic joy. A remnant with perhaps just enough room for one remaining human emotion.

Gratitude.

Then one day you find yourself in front of a mirror, staring at a complete stranger while asking, 'When did I lose myself?'"

I shook my head. Metaphors, nothing more.

Of course, the far greater likelihood was that I would make a mess of things, and succeed only in getting myself captured, before being killed.

And that would be different from the way things stand now how, exactly?

I stumbled, waking on my feet with a start. So damned late. My afternoon nap had kept me going, but now I was running on fumes. Not to mention the twinge which had started to radiate from my right side once again. I pulled the Percocet out of my pocket and dry-swallowed two more.

Go ahead, keep it up. At this rate, soon you'll be popping those things like Tic Tacs, then calling Rush Limbaugh for the name of his supplier.

There was a low tone from the phone. Glancing at the screen, I saw that the arrow had turned into a flashing dot. I looked up.

An older building, short and squat, composed of those uneven bricks that look handmade. It reminded me of the one which had housed the medical lab in the Tenderloin, only bigger. An almost complete wall of windows fronted the uppermost story, illuminated by the weak glow of a light just piercing the glass.

He's in there, somewhere. He has to be.

I stuck to the shadows as I crossed the street. There, a single door, just under an ancient awning. Locked, of course.

Now, according to the movies, this is where you shoot out the lock with Epstein's gun. Except that there's no visible lock. Not to mention the noise firing it would make, alerting everyone and everything on the block to your presence.

So now what?

I paced along the front of the building. Like most San Francisco structures, you could barely slip a sheet of paper between it and the walls of its neighbors. What few doors there were had either been bolted shut or boarded over.

Then I saw it at the end corner, as ancient and crumbling as the brick exterior. A fire escape, its ladder hanging just over my head.

Someone got here before me, I thought. Leroy, maybe?

I tested the rickety rungs, then made my way up to the first landing. It rocked in place, or perhaps that was just my imagination. No sane human being would have even considered using this borderline death trap, which certainly explained my presence. I clambered to the uppermost level and saw the bars covering the door which had, at one time, let out onto the landing.

The six foot windows began a good ten feet or more from where I stood, and were reachable only by a narrow brick ledge, its gaps visible and terrifying. Six inches wide, at best. It reminded me of that Stephen King short story, the one with the pigeon.

There, above, a pipe of some kind. Electrical most likely, running almost to the first of the line of windows which, unlike the rest of the building, appeared to have been recently cleaned.

I swung a leg over the landing's rail, then grabbed the pipe and shook it, hard. A bit of a wiggle, but not very much. Most likely it would hold.

And if not? Well, it was only a four story drop to the concrete sidewalk. Probably wouldn't even leave me enough time to choke out a scream on the way down.

I tested the brick ledge. No movement, but ahead looked dicier. Still, not as though I entertained a multitude of options.

The most terrifying moment came when I took my full weight off the landing, trusting only in the pipe and the ledge to support me. I clung to both, too frightened to move, then just hung there for a while.

Finally the fear subsided just enough to allow me to loosen my death grip, and I began making my way along the wall.

My life had been a horror story for almost two weeks now, but despite this my heart pounded like a kettle drum. I kept waiting for that cinematic moment, the one where the pipe comes partially loose, leaving me to dangle, barely holding on. Except that if the pipe gave, there would be no 'dangling'. Just a squeal of metal, followed by a horrifying *crack,* itself followed by the accompanying plunge.

For some bizarre reason, I flashed back to something my father, a one-time paratrooper in the 82nd Airborne, had told me. *If the chute fails, the fall doesn't kill you. It's that sudden stop once you reach the ground.*

I'd kept my eyes shut while inching along, so when the almost fall did come, it wasn't due to any support bolts giving way, but rather to a sudden grasp at empty air. Lost in the crawl, it had gone faster than I'd thought, and I had reached out for a nonexistent handhold, six inches short of where the pipe curved to disappear into the wall. For a moment all that supported me was my right hand and my feet on the ledge. I pulled myself flat against the bricks, scrabbling above my head with my left hand for a grip on the pipe, hyperventilating as my lungs fought desperately for air.

Eyes squeezed tight, I didn't move. Aside from my every muscle trembling, that is. If the pipe had chosen that moment to break away, there wouldn't have been enough air in my lungs to allow for a good squeak prior to my forty-foot high dive.

After a while, though how long I couldn't say, my racing heart slowed and my breathing stabilized. A few minutes after that, I could even crack open one of my eyelids.

That's when I saw him.

The angle was bad, and if it hadn't been for the clothing and his obvious height, I don't know that I would have recognized him. He slouched in place, manacled by two thick chains bolted above each of his shoulders into an exposed brick wall facing the windows. I couldn't see his face, as there was a clear plastic bag over his head obscuring his features, but I had no doubt; it was Mordant.

Now, how to get inside? The glass had to be shattered, and my precarious position made that difficult, if not impossible. Not to mention that, even after stretching, the closest window was just barely within reach of my fingertips

The pistol.

It would have to be removed slowly, being that it sat in the right hand pocket of Oscar's jacket. And in order to do that I was going to have to slide my left hand over my belly, while keeping a tight hold on the pipe overhead with my right.

It took forever, and I broke a serious sweat, not to mention almost dropping the gun when the barrel caught on a pocket flap. I felt the hollow rush in the pit of my stomach one gets when staring down from a great height as I maneuvered the pistol free. By that time every tendon in my body was vibrating like a plucked wire, and I knew that if I didn't hurry, I was going to lose my sweaty grip and fall.

Now there were two possibilities. I could use the gun as a makeshift hammer and smash it into the window, in the hopes of breaking it. Or I could fire it, shattering the glass that way.

Either way there was a risk of losing my grip. If I failed to break the glass by swinging the gun, my arm would fly backwards, possibly causing me to lose my balance and my footing. On the other hand, the same risk applied if I were to shoot the panes out, due to the recoil.

The safest thing, I realized, would be to loop my arm through the pipe for the additional leverage. Problem being, from that position I wouldn't be able to stretch out far enough to reach the window with the gun and hit it. Which reduced my options to just the one.

You do realize that if there are any guards around, they're going to hear the shot and come running.

"Right," I said, looking down. "Wouldn't want to do anything stupid now, would we?"

I had to put the pistol in my left pocket, allowing me to grab the pipe with my left hand long enough to hook my right arm through it. Feeling a bit more secure now, I retrieved the gun, then—pressing against the wall—I braced my left wrist against the edge where the sill lay, squeezed my eyes shut, then fired.

As I might have mentioned before, I used to shoot pistols with my Dad, small caliber ones with a *pop* like a firecracker. But the big Dirty Harry ones? They sound so loud in the movies, you think the bang must be exaggerated for effect. Take it from me, it's not. For a moment the world went quiet, as well as dark. Then I opened my eyes and saw it: a gaping hole in the glass. Large, but not quite big enough.

"In for a penny, out for a pound," I muttered, resetting myself and firing two more times, my face turned to protect it from flying shards.

Not quite so loud as the first time, and I wondered if I had damaged my eardrums. When the world finally stopped spinning, I turned to survey the damage.

Yes! The glass was almost completely gone, only a few slivers remained. True, they edged the window frame, but I believed I could avoid the worst of them. I shoved the gun back in my jacket pocket, yipping as the tender skin of my inner wrist came into contact with the overheated barrel. I fumbled, managed a grip just inside the window frame and then—heart in mouth—swung inside, losing my balance and falling into a heap on the floor.

I lay there for what seemed far too short a time, hyperventilating like there was no tomorrow. When the worst of the dizziness had passed, I got on my hands and knees, then began crawling in Mordant's direction. Grabbing the waist of his jeans, I pulled myself upright and shook him fiercely while screaming, "Wake up! Wake up, goddammit!"

Nothing. No movement at all. Then I saw them, multiple wounds. Not neat little holes in his flesh, but gaping slashes, as though someone had been hacking at him with a cleaver, or perhaps a machete. Some of the wounds were partially scabbed over, as if they'd tried to heal, only to surrender the effort as a lost cause.

He was dead.

Of course he's dead, you idiot. Have you forgotten what he is?

I shook my head. "No," I whispered, "Nothing human could survive injuries like this."

Repeat after me . . .

"Then why isn't he moving?" I cried.

As I stood there, shaking with fear and rage, I looked again at the clear plastic bag covering his head, tied off at the neck where they'd obviously tried to smother him when the gashes didn't do the job quickly enough.

Yes, because after all, if he can't breathe, then his heart would stop, right?

I took a closer look. There was something inside the bag, clustered around the bottom, held in place by the cord keeping it closed. I leaned in and caught the fragrant hiss of a pungent note.

Garlic.

I ripped the bag loose and threw it across the room. A few buds remained, caught in his shirt. I picked those out, then collected the entire mess and flung it out the woman-sized hole I had made in the window. I spotted a utility sink nearby, then washed my hands in it while scrubbing my flesh with one of the dirtiest bars of soap I'd ever seen. Just looking at it made my skin crawl.

Then I heard a moan.

I rushed back over to Mordant. He was moving, albeit as slowly as a ninety- year-old man who'd just run a marathon. But it was something.

The chains holding him in place were massive. Julius had used restraints on me before, but those had been delicate things a healthy Chihuahua, given time, might have snapped. These were massive links, like something you'd find attached to a forklift. I grabbed one and yanked. I'd have had better luck lifting the back end of a truck.

"Help me, for Christ's sake!" I cried, straining till my tendons creaked.

His tongue made a sluggish swipe over his cracked lips. Then he jerked forward, startling me, and for a moment I thought he might actually break free.

Then he slumped, exhausted by the effort. "Too—weak—from the healing," he murmured. "And not enough of that."

I tried to form a plan—maybe I could find some tools to break him free—then I noticed his eyes widen as he looked over my shoulder. "No," he whispered.

I turned my head, knowing as I did what it was he must have seen, while simultaneously hoping we were both wrong.

But we weren't.

Light.

Not much of it, not yet. A slim smear, setting the eastern clouds aflame with a talcum powder glow. I watched, frozen in place, as the rays of the morning sun sent questing fingers into the room.

Then I knew what I had to do.

You'll die.

I'm dying anyway! I snapped at the voice in my head. Six of one, half dozen of the other, as Daddy always used to say.

I pulled back the hair my husband had never allowed me to cut, exposing the left side of my neck. Standing on tiptoe, I shoved myself at Mordant. "Hurry!" I told him, "Before I lose my nerve!"

Something flared in his eyes, and for a moment I thought he was going to argue with me.

"There's no time!" I hissed as I looped my arms around his neck for support, pressing myself against him while gritting my teeth.

Then he bit me.

And I screamed.

I've been tortured before. Well, what normal people (whatever that means) would probably consider torture. As I've already said, I'm not a genuine pain slut. At least, that's what I've always told myself.

But this? This wasn't the loving caress of a deerskin flogger, or the bee sting of a whip's cracker. This was the brutal shearing of flesh, as though twin tines of a meat fork had been plunged into my neck. I screamed, barely managing to maintain my hold, helped in part by the clasp of his teeth in my exposed throat. My arms locked down in reaction, pulling me closer to his body, the flesh rigid and cold.

Then I felt it.

It began as a glowing warmth, deep and low, just below my navel. From there it spread, like the ripple of a stone dropped into water. My legs trembled, and if I hadn't had a death grip on Mordant, I would have slid to the floor. That or hung from his mouth like a kitten in its mother's jaws.

Soon the glow became a honeyed flame, filling spaces within me I'd never known were empty. My jaw muscles grew slack, my mouth fell open, and at any moment I expected to see my breath flowing through my lips like pure light. Tongues of cashmere flame licked at every soft and sensitive part of me, and I cried out with the wonder and the joy of it all.

"Don't stop!" I whispered, as I felt him swallowing. "Please don't stop . . ."

Then, so suddenly I could not catch myself, his jaw loosened and I fell.

"No!" I cried as I struggled to regain my feet, wanting nothing more than to pour whatever was left of me down his throat. "Not yet!"

Then sanity penetrated the chaos, like a bell's note in an orchestra, bringing me back.

I looked around. The sunlight had swallowed me. I lay in a yellow pool of it, watching in horror as it lapped past me toward Mordant.

"Oh God!" I cried out as I struggled, then failed, to stand. The edge of the light lay mere inches from his bare feet, and I realized that this had been their plan all along. Bound, paralyzed, helpless. This was how it had been intended he die.

"Pull!" I yelled, though there was no need. He strained, the tendons of his neck standing out in cords, the fluids of my body staining his chest like a crimson Rorschach blot. I heard something, a barely discernible crackle.

Then he slumped.

"No," I whispered in horror as I watched the waves of light lap at his feet, then flow up his legs and torso. "No . . ."

And as he screamed, I curled into a ball, covering my head with my arms, eyes firmly squeezed shut.

"No," I heard him gasp, a raw noise.

"I'm sorry!" I cried out through a throat salty with sobs. "I'm sorry!"

For a moment, there was complete silence. Then he spoke again.

"What have you done to me?"

For the longest time I couldn't move. Finally I lifted my face, and looked.

He stood there, bathed in golden light, his eyes wide, the pupils shrunken to pinpoints. I shook my head, unable to comprehend what I was seeing. Wasn't he supposed to be dead?

"What have you done to me?" he murmured again, as if waiting for the joke's punchline.

And of course I couldn't answer his question, since I had no idea what I'd done either.

"Is this why they want you dead?" he whispered while staring into the face of the morning sun.

Before I could say anything, a nearby door rattled. I fumbled desperately in the pocket of the jacket for Epstein's pistol, yanking it and a good part of the lining out as I aimed at the door just as it opened. A crowd of men, five that I could see, slipped into the room and immediately began to spread out.

"Don't move!" I cried out as I waved the gun, trying desperately to cover all of them.

The first three, their eyes as flat as mirrors, looked from me back to the last two who'd entered. The fourth one was dressed in a black military-style outfit with a patch on the sleeve, a bird's wing. The one who followed him didn't stand out in any particular way. In fact, he looked about as ordinary as it is possible to be. But I could tell, by the way the first three gave him space, by the way they regarded him, that he was somehow special.

Something about him drew my attention, and I met his gaze with my own. Mr. Ordinary's eyes were a soft brown, absorbing—rather than reflecting—the light. As I continued to stare at him, I found myself overwhelmed by a body-rattling fear, as though I stood at the precipice of a gigantic black hole, impossibly deep; this followed shortly thereafter by that sensation one sometimes gets while lying in bed, as if the ground had suddenly dropped out from beneath my feet. I bit my lip to keep from screaming.

A sudden noise from the right caught my attention, and I turned to see Mordant straining once more against the chains pinning him to the wall, his eyes brimming with a profound hatred. I waited for him to rip the links out of the brick, but finally he relaxed his efforts, staring at his still intact bonds with a dull combination of surprise and disbelief.

"Interesting," Mr. Ordinary muttered, before turning to face me. "Ms. St. Claire, while I am not a student of firearms, as is my associate here," he said, gesturing to the man in black, "I am well enough acquainted with them to know that revolvers have at best six chambers. Yours has already discharged at least three shots, and there are five of us."

"Won't be once I start shooting," I said as I kept the weapon trained on him, my false bravado at odds with my trembling hands.

Mr. Ordinary frowned. "We have here, it would seem, a delicate situation."

"See what comes from your 'no firearms' nonsense?" the Man in Black said, as he split his gaze between Mordant and me. "I could have gotten my gun from the car."

"Simply put, sir, I do not now, nor have I ever, trusted you," Mr. Ordinary replied. "At any rate, there was no time. Not to mention that there would be no situation at all had you simply followed my recommendations and dispensed with *it* right away," he said, indicating Mordant.

The Man in Black grunted. "She has questions. He has answers. We've used sunlight before. It's a very effective interrogation technique." He gave me a disgusted look. "Or was." He turned back to Mr. Ordinary. "So what do you suggest?"

Mr. Ordinary frowned. Both ignored me. "We cannot risk either one escaping. And these are now completely dominant," Mr. Ordinary said, indicating the remaining three. "Which means their host's minds are, in all likelihood, irreparably damaged, rendering any future use an impractical prospect at best."

"I haven't noticed that ever being a problem for you," the Man in Black drawled.

"Talent without discipline is a cliché," Mr. Ordinary said with a smile. "The human brain requires a delicate touch. Not unlike the juggling of eggs. Unless you prefer your eggs scrambled, that is. Believe me when I say that I understand your concerns, but rest assured that at a word from me, my compatriots are more than capable of quickly subduing the woman. Two might go down, but the remaining third should have no trouble flinging the lady through what remains of yon window there."

"After what we've just seen?" the Man in Black said incredulously. "Are you insane?"

Mr. Ordinary sighed. "I should have known it would come to this."

"We can't kill her! She must be taken alive! The Lady must be told!"

"That is *your* concern. It is not, however, mine," Mr. Ordinary said.

"Get out of here and leave us alone!" I yelled, continuing to train my gun on Mr. Ordinary, since (so far as I could tell) he seemed to be the one in charge. The other three had fixed their stares on me, appearing to wait only for the command to rush forward.

"You misunderstand, Ms. St. Claire," Mr. Ordinary said, his smile widening. "While death would be a significant inconvenience, for me as well as for my companions, it would be no great tragedy. And while I cannot say the same for my associate," and here he indicated the Man in Black, "I judge him to be enough of a fanatic for his cause that he will quite happily sacrifice himself for it, if need be."

As I maintained eye contact with Mr. Ordinary, I heard his scent buzzing in the air between us. Just like the driver, just like Epstein. And not only him, but the other three as well. The look in their eyes convinced me he was telling the truth, that each of them would walk into a hailstorm of bullets on command.

That being the case, there really was only one choice to be made.

So I turned toward Mordant, weapon extended, and fired.

The startled expressions on their faces paled in comparison to that of Mordant's, who stared at me, eyes wide with surprise, as brick chips flew from a spot inches to the right of his head. Nervous and shaky, I'd missed with the first shot.

But not the second.

The brick anchoring the right chain's bolt shattered, and as I ducked down Mordant snapped forward with a roar, ripping the bolt loose. The heavy links flew in a half circle, taking the top half of the Man in Black's head off, blood and brains splattering in every direction. The impact on the others, while it did not decapitate them, did knock them back, giving their one-time captive a precious moment of time.

But that was all he needed.

Using both hands now, he grabbed the remaining length of chain at its base and yanked, tearing the second bolt away.

Now he was free.

Two of them, including Mr. Ordinary, died quickly. The third made an effort, pulling out a knife I hadn't seen, but was no more successful than his fellows. And either the fourth wasn't quite so brave as we'd been led to believe, or perhaps he believed a witness was needed, because he tried to make a run for it.

He didn't get very far.

Then it was just the two of us.

Mordant stared at me, and for a moment I shrank from the heat in his gaze. Then he pulled me to my feet, speaking rapidly. "We're leaving. Now."

⋇

"How did you find me?" Mordant asked, leading me to the window I had shot out. As I tried to organize my scattered thoughts to answer his question, I looked down four stories to the sidewalk below, and then it hit me what he meant to do.

Before I could pull away he picked me up, as if to carry me like a bride over the threshold, then stepped off the edge. I choked back a cry as we dropped to the sidewalk.

The impact jarred me, and I bit my tongue when we hit. He stumbled as we landed, barely maintaining his balance as he grunted in pain.

"Are you all right?" I asked, once I could breathe again. He didn't answer at first, instead setting me on my feet before clutching at the wound in his side.

"I usually heal faster than this," he said in a low voice, his hand cupping the bloody slash.

"Do you need any help?" I asked.

He gave me an odd look, then shook his head. "I just need some recovery time." He looked around. "But not out here in the open." He took a step, then winced. "We need a safe place to hole up for a while." He smiled, despite his obvious pain. "Any suggestions?"

I pondered the question as we half-walked/half-ran away from the building. Soon there would be people out, and Mordant's obvious wounds would draw unwanted attention. "We could go to my house."

He gave me another one of his looks. "Is it safe?"

"Safer than the public streets."

"But for how long?" He crossed the sidewalk to lean against a nearby wall, appearing grateful for the support. "Do you have a phone?"

"I have this one," I replied, pulling out Oscar's.

Mordant took it from me. His arm shook as he fumbled with the device. "Questions," he muttered as he punched a number out. "So many questions."

He looked so pale, there in the morning sunlight. For a moment I thought his legs were going to give way beneath him. He listened to the phone, then hung up and dialed another number. "Voicemail on that one, too," he said with a sudden hiss as he clutched his side.

"You're going to collapse at this rate," I said, taking off Oscar's jacket and handing it to him.

"What's this for?"

"We need a cab, and no one is going to pick us up with you looking as though you've just come out on the losing end of a knife fight," I said as I helped him put the jacket on. "We're going to grab a taxi, no arguments. Follow me."

⊰⊱

The driver gave us the stink eye, but I simper disgustingly well. Soon we were pulling up outside my front door. I retrieved my wallet from Oscar's jacket, then shoved some money at the driver. Certainly too much, but I felt exposed and didn't want to take precious time calculating a tip. The cabbie didn't stick around either, pulling away quickly as soon as we both cleared the door.

Mordant resisted my initial attempt to help him up the stairway, only relenting on his second stumble. "Don't understand what's wrong with me," he mumbled as I got him inside.

"They worked you over pretty good, didn't they?" I said while guiding him to the sofa. "Give me a moment to put something over the cushions. Okay, there you go. Now just lie back, I'll see what we've got in the first aid pouch. Unless you'd rather go to the hospital?"

This earned me yet another look. I'd already locked the front door upon entry, now I dead-bolted it—just to be sure—then went searching for the kit. Julius had been a cautious player, so there was little doubt I would find just about anything I needed in it.

In order to get to the bedroom, though, I had to pass by the entrance to Julius's study. The door stood open, mocking me. I peered inside and saw it again, sitting atop the briefcase with all the paperwork I'd found. The house deed.

How long has he owned it, do you think?

I shut that part of my brain down, protecting what little was left of my composure.

After I found the medical kit, I stepped back into the living room. Mordant had gotten off the couch and was back on his feet. He stood over the coffee table, a framed photograph in his hand.

"You're going to open that wound again," I complained as I moved to his side.

"It's closing, finally," he said.

And though his voice was low, I could see the stress in his speech, a flicker like heat lightning in the spaces between the syllables.

"Do you know this person?" he asked.

The intensity underlying his words made me retreat half a step. It felt as though a tsunami of emotions now rolled beneath his forced casual tone, threatening to sweep away a brittle self-control. I peeked over his arm and saw the picture he held, taken a recent play party, of me sandwiched in between my husband and Miss Sunny, with Warren photobombing us over my left shoulder. "That's Julius," I said, my voice clotted with conflicting, and contradictory, emotions.

He shook his head. "Not him. The one standing just behind him, to the right."

I bent forward. I could feel my eyes burning. "That's Nancy," I finally managed.

Mordant shook his head. "No."

"Yes," I said, tapping the pixie's face with my fingertip. "Do you know her?"

He nodded, a glacially slow movement. "Yes. But not by that name."

I stared at the picture, a gossamer line of frost tracing the length of my spine. "So what name *do* you know her by?"

He inhaled, a prolonged process that seemed to go on forever, before he spoke again.

"Penelope Ember."

⊸⊟⊷

When we entered the garage, there it sat, my BMW. Three hundred series, of course. Leroy must have had it towed back from the Warming Hut. My husband had bought it for me less than six months prior, after I'd been rear-ended at a traffic light and my faithful Prius totaled out by our insurance company. The BMW was used, of course; I don't think my husband had ever purchased a new vehicle in his life. *Let someone else pay for the depreciation*, he'd always said.

I navigated the post morning rush-hour traffic while sneaking an occasional glance at Mordant. He stared, nervous as a cat, at the bars of sunlight crisscrossing the interior. I had the feeling he expected to burst into flames at any moment.

"How much further?" he asked.

"Another fifteen minutes or so," I said, pretending not to notice how the nails of his right hand rasped against the armrest.

He nodded. "Let me know when we get close."

"I will," I told him. The wheels inside my head spun, making me dizzy. "So she was the one who, um . . ."

"Penelope Ember murdered me," he said in a voice as cold as crushed ice.

"But you came back."

He turned in my direction, a slight movement. "Yes."

I adjusted my sunglasses, hoping that the shaded lenses masked my thoughts.

He could do the same for you.

But would he? Whatever it was about me, whatever property my blood had that now allowed him to walk in the day, would he willingly give that up?

If he doesn't, he'll lose you to the cancer anyway.

Maybe that was it. Perhaps the disease ravaging my system, for some bizarre reason, had conferred this property on my blood. Some weird side effect.

In which case, we were both royally fucked.

More than anything, I wanted to ask him if he would do it. Make me like him. The thought of death, once a welcoming image, now terrified me. And all the more so now, when it felt as though I had a lifeline dangling in front of my fingertips, just barely out of reach.

"Are you going to kill her?" I asked.

He jerked, a snap of a motion that made me flinch, then stared at me with a hellish intensity before collecting himself and—once again—feigning disinterest.

"I don't know what I'm going to do," he said as he stared ahead. "Something will occur to me, I'm sure."

We passed the rest of the trip in silence. And as we pulled into Nancy's driveway, Mordant didn't even wait for me to come to a complete halt, instead leaping out of the car. I was so surprised, I forgot to put the parking brake on.

He reached the entrance and stood there, studying it, as I approached. Then, without warning, he kicked it.

The thick door resisted the blow, which appeared to take him aback. It required two more kicks before the jamb cracked and broke, the door flying open. And before I could speak, he was inside.

I followed him.

Nothing unusual greeted us. I saw no one, heard no one. Mordant circled the front room twice, then took off down the hallway, with me close behind.

The search was made in silence. Given his rigid intensity, I'd half expected him to start yelling, demanding that Penelope/Nancy/who-the-fuck-ever show herself, but he never spoke, not once.

Nothing. No one appeared to be home.

Finally we'd explored almost all of the rooms, leaving only one, tucked away in the rear adjacent to the back door. Locked, of course. But not for long.

He smashed his way through it, staggering to maintain his balance. I entered afterwards, my head swiveling just as Epstein's had, as I took everything in.

Pictures. There were pictures everywhere. Sitting on the furniture, hanging from the walls.

And I recognized all of them.

Half were of me, or included me. There was one of me and my sister, curled on either side of my mother, whose body was cut off at the chest in order to focus on us children. And then there were the others. Me as a teenager. Me as a college student. Me graduating from UNC-Chapel Hill.

The bulk of the rest were of my sister, including a large portrait taken on her wedding day.

Then I saw it. And so did Mordant.

We stood next to one another, taking it in. There she stood. My friend Nancy, gorgeous (as usual) in a sparkly sheath dress, wearing a pair of New Year's Eve glasses formed into the digits '2009' as her hands rested on the arm of a man in a tuxedo, his features much younger than they should have been.

Mordant looked at the picture, then back as me. "Is that . . . ?"

I bit my fist. "Yes," I finally said, as I swallowed to keep from throwing up. "That's my father."

⚜

I couldn't look at the pictures any longer. I turned, hands over my face, and crossed the room.

"I don't understand," Mordant said, his expression a perfect mirror for the confusion I felt. I turned around before I reached the closet . . .

And heard the scent, a monotonous buzzing, now drilling its way into my head.

Mordant stared at me, his eyes asking the obvious question. *What's wrong?*

I wet my lips, then took in a deep breath and whispered, "Behind me."

The closet door slammed into my back, and I sprawled across the bed, barely catching a glimpse of the grey-haired man behind me. He had burst out of the closet, a pistol in his hand.

Mordant leaped. Before I could scream *No!*, the gun had been torn away and flung across the room. I watched in pure horror as the two of them fell behind the bed and below my line of sight as blood sprayed over everything; me, the wall, the bed's white, white duvet.

Then I heard it. The sound of what I can only describe as . . . feeding.

I grabbed the pistol from where it had fallen on the bed. God, it was so heavy. I lifted it and aimed as Mordant got to his feet.

"Goddamn you!" I screamed, my throat as raw as an oyster. "What have you done?"

His eyes narrowed. He reminded me for a moment of a dog with a bone, growling at an approaching human. "What are you talking about? He was about to shoot you."

I stepped forward, ready to open fire and fuck the consequences. "You just killed—" I said, pointing down at the gray haired figure sprawled on the floor, a man who . . .

Was not my father.

No! It had been him! I'd seen him!

Hadn't I?

Mordant looked at each of us in turn. Me, blubbering like a maniac. The bloody corpse on the floor, dressed like an 'urban camper'.

"I was so sure," I husked.

Mordant reached out and took the gun from my hand. "It wasn't the same man. I knew that," he said, his fingers brushing against mine.

And then I tasted it once again. The peppery burn of jalapeños at the touch of his skin on mine.

My sudden start surprised him. "What's wrong now?" he said.

My mind. I'm losing my mind.

Mordant grabbed me by the arm. "Let's go," he said, dragging me to the broken down door . . .

Before leaping back, almost flinging me to the floor. "Sonuvabitch!" he yelled.

I retreated. He released me without question, his focus on his right hand. He'd been crossing over a rectangle of sunlight shining through the hallway's rear window. I smelled a pungent odor, like cooked pork, a scent every good Southerner knows by heart. It twanged like a banjo as Mordant hissed in pain.

I shook my head. "I don't understand," I began.

Mordant cursed in a low voice. "I think I do," he finally said, looking over at me. "I adulterated it."

"You what?"

"Your blood," he replied as he clutched his hand close. "Whatever property it has that protected me from the sun earlier; I screwed it up when I drank from that—that other person."

The one from the closet. Whose scent buzzed like the bells I remembered from high school. Just like the driver who had shot Oscar. And the police officer who, or who had once been, Epstein. And just like those others, who had been holding Mordant prisoner, with the exception of the one who'd looked like a SWAT officer.

All of which had felt somehow familiar . . .

Then it came to me, and I finally remembered where I'd heard that scent before.

And as he stood there, cradling his burned hand, I told Mordant what I suspected.

⚍

We had to wait until sundown to leave Nancy's. I'd suggested the possibility to Mordant that he could renew his resistance to the sun by feeding on me again, but he squashed that idea in short order. "Too much, too soon," had been his only response. I'd nodded and fought against the impulse to pout, because there are literally no words to adequately describe the river-rush pleasure of his bite. I could literally have floated on that soft, pink cloud forever. Constance's Percocet were like baby aspirin by comparison.

Instead I made a tuna fish sandwich from what little remained in Nancy's sparse refrigerator, realizing as I did that the food it contained must have been used to feed my long-lost father. And I couldn't help but wonder, where was Dad was now? And why, over the years, hadn't he contacted me or my sister? Bethany and I had spent the better part of our lives wondering what had happened to him. Was he alive? Was he dead?

Well, now you know.

Did I?

And in that moment, I learned to hate Nancy.

Pardon me, not Nancy. Penelope Ember.

Finally the sun set in a raucous cacophony, like a flock of Canada geese in autumn. Time to go.

Neither Mordant nor I spoke much as I drove us to our destination. Instead he sat quietly, with only God knew what secret thoughts, whereas I felt like an open book after my former friend's betrayal, now on my way now to confront another.

I managed to find street parking not too far from Warren's house. The windows glowed, a cantata of light, and I wondered if she was with him.

"Just get us inside," Mordant said in a low voice as I rang the doorbell. "I'll take care of the rest."

I nodded while tugging at the scarf I'd appropriated from Nancy's closet to hide the marks on my throat. The wounds had scabbed over almost immediately, but the punctures themselves remained quite evident. Which made sense, I suppose. Nothing to be gained by having your food source bleed out on you.

It took another push of the doorbell to get an answer. Warren, bleary-eyed, cracked open the door to stare at us in confusion.

"Is Miss Sunny here?" I whispered, while standing on tiptoe to peer over Warren's shoulder.

"Huh?" he said through a yawn. "No, no, I haven't seen her all day. We were supposed to meet for coffee earlier, but she stood me up." He still looked out of sorts over it.

I nodded, relieved. "May we come in?"

"Oh, sure. Pardon me," he said, stifling a second yawn, "I'd lain down for a nap. That's why it took so long to answer the door."

We walked past him into the empty living room. "Warren, we need to warn you," I said over my shoulder, while looking around the room.

"Warn me about what?" Warren said, covering his mouth to hide yet another yawn.

Mordant stepped up to him. "About this," he said.

Then he reached around, pinning Warren's limbs with his left arm while covering my friend's mouth with his right.

"Mmph!" Warren said, his eyes now wide and terrified.

Mordant lifted him off the floor effortlessly, as though he were a child. I watched my friend as he struggled, knowing from personal experience the brutal strength Mordant could call upon.

"We know," he hissed in Warren's ear. "And now we're going to play a version of a game show I watched when I was a kid called 'Truth or Consequences'." Mordant tightened his grip, and Warren's muffled moans turned into screams. "How long?"

"Mmhmrrr?!" Warren cried, his panic-filled gaze rapidly switching from Mordant to me.

I took a step forward. Mordant warned me away with his eyes, but I couldn't stay away. I had to know for sure, beyond any reasonable doubt. And as I drew near, I caught scent of the noise again, barely noticeable beneath the cloying scent of Warren's otherwise overpowering cologne. A buzz, like a mechanical alarm clock. Just like Epstein, after he had shot his partner. And just like the driver, who had murdered Oscar at close range, before turning his weapon on me.

"What have you done to my friend, you goddamned son of a bitch!" I screamed.

"Put him down."

I spun around at the familiar voice, Mordant following my gaze. There she stood, at the kitchen door. Miss Sunny, a large pistol in her hand, the barrel as large as a pipe.

"This magazine is filled with silver bullets," she said, her glare focused on Mordant. "Yes, I know what you are. Which means we both know what happens when I start pulling this trigger. So I'll say it one last time. Put . . . him . . . down."

"You don't understand!" I yelled at Miss Sunny. "He's not what he appears to be!"

Miss Sunny refused to look at me, holding Mordant's eyes instead. "I'm well aware of that," she said. "And now you've ruined any chance for us to salvage anything from this debacle."

Her words confused me. "What?"

Miss Sunny angled her body in such a way that she could cover all three of us with her weapon. "I'd been given to understand you could spot them," she said, addressing Mordant.

"Only when they're in control," Mordant said, loosening his grip on Warren, though he didn't move away.

"I see," she said. "And exactly how do you know?"

Mordant shrugged. "I just do. But how could you . . . ?"

Then Miss Sunny smiled at him.

"My God," I whispered when I saw her teeth. "You're like him," I said, looking from her to Mordant. "But how . . . ?"

"What are you all talking about?" Warren said, his voice strained and panicky.

Mordant frowned. "Doesn't he know?"

"If I had to make a guess, I'd say he's in denial," Miss Sunny said.

Warren stared at her teeth, then began backing away. "You said it was a game," he accused. "Just another game. Are you seriously trying to tell me it's *real*? That *you're* really a, a—?"

"And what about you, Abby?" Miss Sunny said, ignoring Warren's rapidly escalating hysteria. "How did you know?"

Is his confusion real? I wondered, as Warren's terrified gaze moved to each of us in turn. "The sound of his scent," I told her.

She rolled her eyes, a familiar expression I'd long grown accustomed to. "Of course."

"He's a topovar?" Mordant said, shifting his gaze between Warren and Miss Sunny.

"Nothing of the kind," she replied contemptuously. "Feeding stock, nothing more."

"You're lying," he countered.

She frowned. "What did you just say to me?"

"I *know*," he hissed. "I know about *her*. And he smells just like her."

Miss Sunny stared at Mordant for a moment, then switched her focus to me, to the scarf circling my throat. I tugged at it self-consciously.

"I see," she said softly.

"Who else knows?" Mordant demanded.

Miss Sunny behaved as though she hadn't heard his last remark. "What to do?" she muttered. "Do I slay you, Sleeper? Risk whatever chaos that might bring in the times ahead? Or allow you to leave this house, privy to our greatest secret?"

Mordant looked at her, then back at me. I could see the hunger in his eyes. Feel it.

"Perhaps we could come to an understanding," he said, his voice low and intense.

Miss Sunny shuddered, as if waking. "Indeed we shall, though it will hardly be to your liking," she said, repositioning the pistol back in Mordant's direction.

He spared it one quick glance before meeting her eyes. "You wouldn't be the first to try killing me with silver," he said.

"So I've heard," Miss Sunny said. "Still, while far from convinced, I shan't press the matter. No, I had something a bit different in mind."

"And that would be?" Mordant said, his focus on the weapon.

Miss Sunny lined up the pistol's sight as she maintained her aim. "Winterfax has long arms," she murmured. "And they make a large circle. Such a large *protective* circle. She stared at Mordant without flinching. "But there are limits, even to the White Lady's reach."

His eyes narrowed. "What are you saying?"

"True," she continued, as though he hadn't spoken, "I'd not fancy testing that circle, as it currently stands. But how far does it extend? Your sister? Certainly. Her children? Without a doubt. But outside of those persons? Other relatives? Close friends? Their lovers?" She shrugged. "What is the circumference of Winterfax's embrace? No, here is what you are going to do. You will mind your thoughts, and share what you have learned here with no one. Not ever. Because, and believe me when I say this, even if something were to happen to me, then others, strangers to you and yours, would step forward to take my place. Strangers just as committed, and just as well-informed, as I."

Mordant's hands clenched into fists. "Are you declaring war, then?"

Miss Sunny shook her head. "So long as no one's secrets are shared, there should be no need for any further . . . unpleasantness."

He glared at her, his eyes aflame with an orange glow. "Touch any of my people," he hissed, "Harm one single hair on any of their heads, and I swear to you, I'll teach you more about war than you ever wished to know."

"Ah, then we *do* understand one another," Miss Sunny said. "Excellent. Now," she continued, gesturing with the pistol at the door, "feel free to excuse yourself."

Mordant's gaze switched from her to me, and for a moment I wasn't sure what he might do.

"She remains here," Miss Sunny said. "This is not negotiable."

I felt the longing in his stare, inspired by the blood in my veins. For a moment, I felt certain he was about to rush Miss Sunny, then strip her of her weapon, even kill her if he could, just to take me with him, consequences be damned.

And what would it mean if he did? How long did I have left anyway? Weeks? Maybe days? And what would he do if I told him the truth? Would he have mercy on me? Transform me into one of his kind to save my life?

Or would he sacrifice whatever days I had left to his hunger, so he could feel the sun on his face for whatever time I had left?

And as I watched, I saw his conflict resolve itself.

"I will not forget this," he growled, as he moved backwards toward the door, never taking his eyes off Miss Sunny's pistol.

"Remember whatever you wish," Miss Sunny said. "But speak of it, and you will endure the consequences."

He rested his hand on the doorknob. "This isn't over," he whispered.

Miss Sunny smiled. "My dear sir, it has not even yet begun."

He glared at her, a dangerous promise in his eyes.

Then he left.

Once he was gone, Miss Sunny slumped into her favorite chair, the gun hanging almost forgotten from her hand. "There will come a storm from this," she muttered to herself. "Penelope, ah Penelope! What have you wrought?"

Then her gaze switched to Warren.

"What's going on?" he said, white-faced.

Miss Sunny made her way over to him. "Still so much of you left," she said as she stroked his face. "Such a pity."

Warren shuddered at her touch, his eyes warm and moist. "It's real, isn't it?" he finally said.

"What's that, dear?" she replied as she continued to caress his cheek.

He swallowed. "The . . . episodes."

"Being out of control, you mean?"

He shuddered. "I thought it was like sleepwalking. Or some weird form of epilepsy." He began shivering uncontrollably. "Maybe a side effect of one of my medications . . ."

She drew him down to the sofa. "Do you hear it, when it speaks to you?" she said.

He released his breath, a long, drawn-out sigh. "I thought I was losing my mind."

"I hate to have to tell you this, sweet one, but you are," she said, coaxing his head onto her shoulder. "Though not in the way you mean." She rested one hand on Warren's lap, embracing him with the other. "It has too strong a hold on you now. There's nothing to be done for it."

He stiffened. "I can resist. I have before, you know. Refused to allow it control." He sobbed. I'd never heard such a lonely sound. "It just . . ."

"Keeps getting harder," she finished for him.

He didn't reply, nodding instead, a tear trickling down his cheek.

Miss Sunny touched his forehead with her own. "Have you seen what lies past it?"

Warren began shaking violently. "Please don't!" he whispered fiercely. "You don't *know* . . . !"

"I know what happens the longer we wait," she said. "Its hold on you might not yet be strong enough to carry away whatever is left of you, your essence, along with it when your body perishes. But if we allow it more time . . ."

Tears began flowing freely down his face. "Please," he choked. "I don't want to die."

"And I don't want to take your life," she said, her voice as cool and hard as fine porcelain. "But the longer we wait, the greater the risk. Even now . . ." She shook her head.

Warren swallowed a sob. "What are my choices? If any?"

Miss Sunny leaned back. "There are two. One, I remove you to a safe place where I can imprison you, and make open use of your blood for whatever time you have left, in which case that which remains of you will be taken when death forces the abomination to abandon your body." She stroked his hair. "You know your other choice."

Warren began crying openly. "I don't want to die!" he repeated, sobbing.

"And I don't want to kill you," she said softly.

We listened to him weep for a time, before he spoke again.

"Can you make it pretty?" he finally choked out. "Like before?

She slid her palm over his cheek, blotting the tears. "Oh, little one," she whispered, her voice a caress as light as silk, "I can make it beautiful."

And she did.

–⧉–

Fog had rolled in. I sat in the passenger's seat, Miss Sunny at the wheel as she slowly navigated the mist-strewn streets. As we crept along, I replayed Warren's last minutes in my mind. The slackening of breath and heartbeat as I held his hand (he'd pleaded for that much, until I'd finally relented). Then the sudden start, before both ceased forever.

"Do you think he made it?" I asked.

"Hmm?" she murmured. "Made what?"

I coughed nervously. "You know. To the other side. Tunnel of light and all that."

She shrugged. "If it makes you feel any better, yes."

I bit my tongue to avoid replying.

But I couldn't get that last spasm out of my mind, as though Warren had seen something terrifying, just before he died.

"What are you going to do with him? The body, I mean," I said.

"Not your concern."

I turned to look at her face, as expressionless as her voice.

"Where are we going?" I asked, not for the first time, or even the second.

Eventually she replied. "I think you know."

I didn't. Know, that is. But I suspected, and the knowledge flooded my lower belly with a warm, liquid fear, which only grew as the streets became steadily more familiar.

"Will I be going back with you?" I asked, amazed at how calm my voice sounded.

"No."

I swallowed the lump of growing panic. Could I jump out of the car? We weren't really going all that fast, after all.

"What's going to happen once we get there?" I asked.

"Not my decision to make."

And though I'd figured out our destination miles earlier, I still felt surprised when we arrived.

It solidified out of the mist like some medieval castle, a brick and stone structure as squat and unyielding as a granite hill. The Sunken Mansion.

We glided to a halt in front of the wrought iron gates. A moment later, before I had time to wonder what would happen next, they parted soundlessly. We drove through. I watched via the passenger mirror as they closed behind us.

Despite my terror, I could not help but stare about in curiosity as we made our way along the tree-lined driveway. I'd never been inside the grounds before.

Miss Sunny pulled around to park in front of a steep stairway leading to a columned porch. "Okay, Little One, this is where you get off," she quipped.

Despite the insanity of the situation, I still felt abandoned. "You're not coming?"

She shook her head. "Wasn't invited," she said. "Now, scoot."

A flicker of a thought flashed through my brain—*What happens if you say no?*—but I didn't entertain it for very long. "What if I run?" I husked, my fingers on the door latch.

"You won't," she said. "But if you do, well, I have one piece of advice."

"And that is?"

She smiled, a humorless grimace. "Run fast."

I got out and stood there, staring at the enormous structure as I listened to the sound Miss Sunny's car made before fading into the night.

Fine, I thought. *Let there be an ending.*

I made my way up the steps. Newer than the mansion itself, the stairway was an obvious afterthought; the bricks didn't even match those of the house. Their binding mortar had cracked over time, and I could feel movement beneath my feet as I made my way towards the manor proper. Testing each step before trusting my weight to it, I finally reached a pair of French doors. To my surprise, the panes were intact. This must have originally been the second, or possibly the third floor, fronted by a Juliette balcony, from which the foremost panel had been removed to allow access.

Then, as I stood there, pain hit me like a bullet, ripping a hole into my side. I gasped, leaning against the one-time balcony's wrought iron to avoid collapsing, then fumbled for what remained of Constance's Percocet. Eyes tearing, I couldn't see how many tablets were left. So I swallowed them all and sat down.

After a time the fire dampened to glowing embers and I pulled myself up by the door handle, its brass suffused with a green patina, preparing for the effort that would be required to force the doors open. To my surprise, they glided apart in effortless invitation. I swallowed, abdomen burning, and stepped forward into the darkness.

I won't elaborate on making my way through the upper floors. The initial entrance led into a large bedroom, possibly the Master. I noticed a soft glow from beneath the door facing me, just enough to illuminate a path across the room.

I can't say how long it took for me to cross that space, to place my hand on the doorknob. It felt like hours. And when I did open the door, I couldn't help but close my eyes, waiting for the unseen menace lurking on the other side to take hold of me.

But nothing did.

When I finally found the courage to do so, I opened my eyes. A hallway. And to my right a small table with an oil lamp, the source of the illumination.

I picked the lamp up and looked about. Doors lined the hallway, obviously I was expected. To the right a series of candles burned with a spearmint heat, leading to a wide stairway.

What was there left for me to do? I followed the flames.

It took some time to navigate the pathway which had been prearranged for me. I couldn't be certain how far down I traveled, but eventually I found myself in what could only have been the basement.

Less tidy than the upper floors (which weren't exactly what one would call clean), this level truly reflected the age and condition I would have expected from the house. But someone, or something, had obviously been this way recently, parting the cobwebs. To my growing disquiet, though, I could see no footprints in the dust on the floor.

After navigating a hallway formed from an endless supply of wooden boxes and crates, I reached the first anomaly.

The hallway ended in a wall. Stone, not brick, fronted by an enormous door of thick wood banded with iron which, I discovered when I placed my hand on the handle, had been locked. God Himself could not have forced his way past that portcullis.

Then I remembered where I had placed it, in my pocket.

The key was heavy. Old iron, like so much of the door itself. I anticipated a battle, but it turned in the lock's well-oiled tumblers with very little trouble. Only the slightest of efforts was required as the door opened with a gentle shove.

And as I stepped inside, my mouth fell open.

The room stretched out before me, a near endless corridor. The floor was set with paving stones, the walls a series of enormous shelves, accommodating large rectangular boxes.

No, not boxes.

Coffins.

I trod the length of the room, looking from side to side. So many of them, covered with a thick layer of undisturbed dust,

At the end of the room there stood a table filled with candles, almost like a shrine. And above the table, mounted on the rear wall, a coat-of-arms simple in its brevity; a golden orb on a blue background.

I halted, examining the nearest of the caskets. A smooth granite stone had been set in the shelf, with letters and numerals carved into its polished face. *Elizabeth Stewart. Beloved Wife. Born 1531. Died 1579.*

And as I stood there, I heard a voice in the distance behind me.

"Lifetimes tended to be briefer in those days."

I did not spin. Instead I turned, slowly, his name forming on my lips as I did.

"Julius . . ."

※

This is where I'm supposed to say he looked just as I remembered him. Except he didn't. He looked younger. Oh God, so much younger. The salt and pepper gray had vanished beneath a tide of chestnut brown curls, while the receding hairline receded no more. His belly had flattened to that of a youth who hasn't gotten his man body yet. He moved with a graceful, surreal ease, as if he were a teenager with boundless energy, just like . . .

Just like Mordant.

"I imagine you have a question or two," he said as he glided toward me, his broad form blocking the narrow space between the shelves and the desiccated husks of their contents. He dominated the airspace between us, like a snake hypnotizing a mouse, caressing one of the elegant sarcophagi as he moved closer.

He followed my glance. "I can't help myself," he said with a gesture, arms spread inclusively wide. "I can only be comfortable when I know they are nearby."

"Bluebeard," I said, retreating a step. "I get it now."

"You must have found my old laptop." He smiled. "Should have gotten rid of it, I suppose. Hindsight and all that. But I'm a bit of a hoarder. As you can see." He took another step toward me.

I shook my head as I continued to retreat. "I don't understand," I babbled. "What *are* you?"

He paused, the irises of his eyes subsumed in twin, coffee black pools. "Don't be obtuse, Abby."

I can't explain why it had taken so long to sink it, despite the evidence in front of me, surrounding me. "You're one of them," I whispered. "Like him. Like Mordant."

"Keep going," he said with an encouraging nod.

Swallowing, I shifted my gaze from one coffin to the next. "And them? They were . . . ?"

"Go on," he prompted, when I hesitated.

"Like me?" I finished lamely.

He smiled.

My knees buckled, and I started to collapse. He moved forward quickly, so very quickly, appearing next to me in an instant, grabbing me by the arms before leading me to a nearby stone bench. I sank down, limbs trembling uncontrollably.

"How many have there been?" I asked. "Like me?"

"How many wives?" He looked over my head, his smile redolent with memories. "Hard to say for sure. As the years pass, things tend to blur together. And sometimes one has to split the occasional hair as regards a working definition of the term 'wife'. Now me, I've always adopted the ceremonial customs of those with whom I've partnered, ranging from elaborate ceremonial engagements only finalized after a year or more, to something as simple as jumping over a broomstick together."

I shook my head. "That's not what I meant," I said, squeezing each word out like a forced tear. A pounding had settled behind my eyes. "That is, I can see that you've been—widowed—a number of times."

"What confuses you, then?"

I tried to find the words, but couldn't. Not with him staring at me so intensely. Then his eyes slid down to the scarf around my neck, and the realization hit him. You could see it, like a thunderhead passing over the sun.

"The Sleeper," he said, his voice thick with anger. "Mordant. He tasted you, didn't he?"

"It wasn't his fault," I whispered, knowing that by appearing to defend him I was almost certainly making things worse. "They had him chained in front of a wall of windows, waiting for the sun to come up and fry him. I was just trying to help him get loose. Break free."

It wasn't until I felt the pins and needles in my fingers that I realized Julius had squeezed the blood out of my hand, prior to releasing it. "I suppose, given the circumstances, your actions weren't beyond a certain degree of . . . rationalization," he said in a voice as thick as the rage glowering off him. "After all, I was dead. So far as you knew, that is."

"They probably would have killed me if I hadn't helped him," I offered.

He looked to one side, an old and familiar gesture. "So he knows," Julius murmured. "What makes you special. That's what you meant by 'those like me'."

I nodded. "How many have there been?"

"Far too precious few," he said, taking my hand again. His fingers stroked mine, their touch a spicy jalapeño flame. "The trait is recessive. And even worse, you—all of you—appear to be going extinct. Like redheads." He smiled again, though this one felt forced.

I stared down at the floor. "But . . ."

"What?" he prompted softly when I didn't continue.

I shook my head violently. "You were dead!"

"Not as you understand death."

I felt the beginnings of a hysterical scream crawl up my throat, like a small animal struggling to break out of its cage. "I can't take much more of this." Tugging in a useless attempt to free my hand, I finally gave up trying. "What *am* I?"

He pulled me close with his free arm. "You are a gift."

I tried to process his words. "Gift?"

"The stories were old, even when I was young, of those whose blood could allow us to walk during the day," he began, "But everyone, and I include myself in this, believed them to be nothing more than wishful legends. Claims that, supposedly, we had *all* been daywalkers, once upon a time. But something happened, an event long lost to history, and we . . . changed. There are those who claim that the White Lady of Winterfax actually remembers those days, even lived during them, walking in the unimpeded light of the sun. Personally I'm skeptical since, or so I've been told, she never speaks of that time.

"And then, one day, I found one of you."

"*You* did?" I said, curious despite myself. "How?"

He released my hand, then stroked my cheek. "You have to understand what our lives were like in those days. The Empire had fallen . . ."

"What empire?"

He raised an impatient eyebrow. "Which one do you think?"

It took a moment to comprehend what he'd implied, and even longer to accept it. "The Roman Empire?" I whispered, my voice barely audible even to myself. "You remember it? Lived during it?" I shook my head to clear it. "My God. How old *are* you?"

"Not old enough to remember the days of the true Empire," Julius said, a corner of his mouth twisting, "I came long after, reborn into my House during those centuries when the northern barbarians swept regularly through a Europe ruled by kings too weak to protect their countrymen. Our House had long abandoned what we all knew as the Eternal City, removing ourselves to lands we owned far to the west, near the coast. Those who served us provided for our needs, and we in turn protected them. That is, until the invaders discovered us. Visigoths, I think. They raped the women and slaughtered the men, sparing only those they intended to sell as slaves, while relishing what no doubt had appeared an easy victory.

"But only until night fell . . .

"After we emerged from the basements beneath our villas and dealt with the invaders, a quick accounting revealed that much of our feeding stock had been decimated. We could never have survived on what the barbarians had left us, and in our rage we had slain the invaders to a man. So some of us remained, to guard what was left of our flock, freeing myself and a few others to go out into the countryside to seek replacements. Understand that, in those days, raiding to replenish a *hashna* depleted by war or plague was far more common than it is in these modern times. I found the first one, a female by a riverbank, all but insensate. From the state of her body and clothing, it was obvious she and her people had been found by the same barbarians who had come for our own. She appeared to be in shock. But I was hungry after our battle, not to mention desperate. After the feeding I remained with her as she lay nearly unconscious in the throes of *Som na Idilque.*"

"What's that?" I asked cautiously.

Julius smiled. "The literal translation would be almost meaningless to you, but most refer to it as 'The Ecstasy'."

Aptly named, I thought silently, remembering what had happened with Mordant.

"After the feeding I felt weak, causing me to wonder if the girl was somehow diseased, despite her obvious youth," Julius continued. "Then I remembered nothing. Until I woke from a deep sleep, my skin warm, the sun just overhead.

"Understand, Abby, I hadn't known sleep for decades, and after so many years retained no more memory of it than a man recalls his mother's nipple. So when I woke to the sun on my face, I shut my eyes and waited for the pain, followed by the end.

"But there was no pain. And I didn't die.

"I won't bore you with unnecessary details, but once I realized what had happened, I carried the girl with me as I made my way back to my people, returning later for the rest of her family. Cautious experimentation revealed that she was not the only one of her kind. Two more, a brother and a female cousin, shared her unique gift. All grey-eyed, just as the old stories claimed."

Julius sighed. "Since that day, Bremen has sifted through the mud of humanity in search of what precious few like them—like you—we could find. The gift is incredibly rare, and has grown more so with each passing century. Being a small House, we have long isolated ourselves, to keep your existence a secret from all others of our kind; our sole advantage over the larger rival Houses, who would not so much as hesitate to take all of you from us, if they were to learn about your gift."

"Houses?" I asked.

The corner of his mouth twitched. "Mordant told you nothing, I see. Our kind divided itself into twelve clans long ago, an event we call *Coloque.* Since those days the various Houses have had little to do with one another. All the more so as humanity has extended itself to the far corners of the globe," he said reflectively.

I struggled to collect my thoughts. "But you're not like Mordant," I said. "You're warm. You eat regular food. Your heart . . ."

"Yes," he replied. "Our hearts do beat, albeit sluggishly. When feeding on those like yourself, whom we call the *lediquire,* the favored, we are virtually indistinguishable from normal humans. We eat human food, drink human drink. We even sleep. But all of this comes with a price. For while the blood of the favored cloaks us in human flesh, it also weakens us, sapping much of our strength and vitality. Which means we heal less quickly than is normal for our kind. We also age."

I stared closely at him. "But you . . ."

Julius studied the back of his hand, the one with a death grip on my own. "The effect of *lediquire* blood fades the longer one goes without. Even more quickly when one mixes it with the blood of; well, shall we say, the less favored."

"But you were dead," I said stupidly. "I saw your body at the hospital. They didn't want me to, and Warren tried to talk me out of it. But I insisted." I shook my head, trying—and failing—to clear it. "Nothing could have survived those injuries," I whispered.

He nodded. "I almost didn't. My body was damaged so severely that I lay in the grave for days, as if truly dead. And might not have recovered at all, if not for Sunny and Hendrick."

It took a moment for me to absorb what he'd said. "Hendrick too?"

"Yes," he said with a nod. "If not for them, I might be under the earth still."

It took time to comprehend what he was saying. "They dug up your corpse," I whispered.

"Actually, they paid someone else to do it," Julius said. "I would have preferred not being interred in the first place, but the 'accident' drew too much attention." He paused before speaking again. "Fortunately, the manner of my death made an autopsy redundant."

"Was it really an accident?" I asked.

Julius shook his head. "No. I was pushed."

How could you have ever believed otherwise? "Did you see who did it?"

Another shake of the head. "No. It happened very quickly. I was unconscious for some time, then woke inside that coffin." He grimaced. "That was a terrifying moment. My body had consumed all of its resources repairing the damage done to it, leaving me too weak to free myself.

"After a brief but understandable emotional outburst, I discovered a small flashlight lying in my hand, with a note wrapped around it. Hendrick had placed it there before the casket was sealed, the message reassuring me that my situation was only temporary, and that they would see to my freedom as soon as time and opportunity allowed."

I heard what he had not said. "Did the digger have time to realize what he'd done?" I said bitterly. "In the end?"

Julius stiffened. "It was quick. Not to mention necessary. *Lediquire* blood could not have healed such extensive damage so quickly. It had to be *topovar.* The less favored." He waved his hand. "He suffered little. And even then, it was insufficient. It took days for what remained of my face to heal."

His face? "That was you, wasn't it? The one who attacked us in the Tenderloin? You were wearing a mask."

Julius shook his head yet again. "I did not 'attack' you. On the contrary, I thought I was rescuing you. And yes, it was necessary to hide my face, since no one could have looked at me at the time without screaming. We were all scattered across the city, searching for you, after I went home and discovered you were missing. Our sources had given us several leads, but Mordant found you first. At the time I thought he was one of your captors. So we struggled. Strong, that one. The Sleeper." He flexed his fingers, a strange expression on his face. "Is it true that he once fasted for a month's time without losing his mind?"

I shook my head. "I don't know anything about that."

"Of course not. Such a ridiculous story." Julius snorted dismissively. "Soon they will claim he can fly." He trailed his fingers down the length of my throat, tugging at the scarf around my neck, his eyes opaque and unreadable.

I remembered Mordant's teeth in my flesh. The sensations unequaled by any liquor or drug I had ever consumed. The 'Ecstasy' indeed. "You never did that to me, did you? That way?"

He shook his head. "I could never have hidden what I was from you had you ever been allowed to experience *Som na Idilque.*" His nails trailed down the length of my arm, raising thin white lines. "It was different in the past. Easier to keep things under control. But now? In these modern times? The risks of exposure have grown exponentially over the last hundred years or so. A crisis point approaches. Something must be done. Things cannot continue as they have. The old ways are no longer sufficient. In your case, I decided it would be best if you knew nothing. Even the risks of playing off the pretense of a vampire fetish were too great."

"Which is why you drugged me," I murmured. "So you could pass off your feeding as medical play."

He patted my hand. "Such a bright girl," he said. "I chose so well."

Then it hit me, like an open-handed slap. "Bloodlines . . ."

He nodded. "That is how we found you," he said with a nod. "And Warren. And the others."

"The medical surveys."

"Stroke of genius, that. If only I could take credit for the idea. While the rise of science and technology has become a bane for our kind, they do offer a few advantages, for those with the wit to exploit them." He frowned. "Losing the database has slowed our plans, but hasn't disrupted them entirely. We still have the hardcopies, after all."

The pounding in my temple had turned into a drill bit boring its way into my brain. "Why us?" I lifted my head to meet his eyes. "What makes us so damned special?"

Julius shrugged. "I can't say. Some subtle factor we have yet to isolate. Damn losing Warren. He could have helped so much."

As I sat listening to him, a sudden understanding came over me, and I felt my blood run cold. "Oh, my God. Cheryl!"

For the first time, Julius looked uncomfortable. "What about her?"

I looked at him. "She's not your mother, is she? Jesus fucking Christ!" I jumped up and moved away, his hand finally releasing mine. "She's your *wife!*"

Julius nodded. "Yes."

And as I digested this, I recalled the puzzling conversation Cheryl and I had had earlier. "She knows, doesn't she? What you are, I mean."

"As I said," he repeated. "Those were simpler times. And before she could be allowed to die, another had to be found to replace her, before my advancing years risked my own death. It was necessary." He drew himself up. "She has no reason for complaint. I took care of her, gave her a good life, a far better one than she'd had before I came into it, of that I can assure you." He gestured at the coffins around us. "And when her last day comes, she will be brought here, to join her sisters."

I took a step back. Wrapped my arms around myself, my brain spinning.

"I need to know something," I said.

"What?"

For the first time, I met his gaze squarely. "Where is my father?"

He shrugged. "With her," he said insouciantly.

"Penelope?"

For the first time, I had surprised Julius. "You know?" Then it hit him. "Ah. The Sleeper again."

"Why do you all call him that?"

Julius's nose wrinkled. "An ancient prophecy. 'But when the walls grow thin, the Sleeper shall dream no more.'"

I raised my hands, then lowered them. "What the hell does that mean?"

"I've no idea," Julius said with a shrug. "And neither apparently does she who said it, since the price of that vision was her sanity."

I forced my mind back on track. "I want to see him. My father. Before . . ."

And at that moment, the pain returned.

I cried out, clutching uselessly at my belly. At first I thought the pain might fade, that I could wait it out. But it didn't. It continued, growing worse and worse. I bent over, pressing my hands to my stomach.

"Help me," I gasped.

Julius didn't move. Instead he watched me with a clinical detachment, as though I were a moth trapped in a spider's web, fluttering desperately to escape.

In that moment, I hated him.

"I'm dying," I whispered. "The cancer—"

He nodded. "I know."

What? "You know?" I somehow managed to choke out.

He nodded. "The good doctor briefed me on every aspect of your condition. How serious it is. How little time you have left." He rose from the bench. "I can smell the sickness in you."

Anger rose with the agony, I forced both down. This was no time to be disrespectful. Not if I wanted to live.

"You know how to take the pain away," I pleaded, tears flowing. "Will you?"

He stared at me, his face as unreadable as a mask. "No," he said.

What? No?

That can't be true. Please, God, don't let that be true.

"You're going to make me beg. The way you always have," I said as I fought to force a smile. "Aren't you?"

And just when I thought it couldn't get any worse, the pain redoubled, slicing into my insides like a jagged knife. I sank in a heap to a stone floor as cold as my husband's eyes.

"Please!" I said, when the talons curling around my intestines relaxed a bit and I could breathe again. "For the love of God! Do something!"

Yet another burst of pain, as though someone had heated a poker cherry red before shoving it through my navel to swirl around my intestines. I hyperventilated, trying to draw in enough breath to scream.

"Please!" I begged. Yes, begged. I was now past anger, past even fear. There was nothing left but a coruscating agony, a fountain of molten lead scouring my insides hollow.

Blinded by the pain, I heard his footsteps as he moved to stand over me. "It shouldn't be much longer now," he said quietly. "No need to worry. I've taken care of everything."

Oh, Jesus, no. Not like this. Not like this . . .

He's going to put you in one of those empty spaces along the wall. Probably won't even bother with a coffin like the others. You'll just lie there, cold as stone, while the rats and the roaches crawl over you. Nibble on you.

"PLEASE!!" I begged, now weeping uncontrollably. "It's killing me!"

He didn't speak, not for the longest time.

"Yes," he finally said. "I know."

And then I died.

⌖

I watched the light approach, a distant smear, fuzzy around the edges. Shouldn't there be voices too? I thought. Family and friends, here to welcome me to the other side?

Maybe that's not how it truly is, I thought with a sudden surge of terror. *Who really knows, after all? Maybe what comes afterwards is a horror show to make the* Walking Dead *look like a Hallmark movie by comparison.*

"Abby?"

I heard the voice. Recognized it. But what was he doing *here*?

"Abby?"

I licked my lips. Dry. So dry.

Then I opened my eyes and there he was, bent over me, his face mere inches from my own.

"Julius?"

He didn't reply. We were both sprawled on the floor, Julius cradling my head in his lap. He stroked my hair for some time before he spoke again.

"It's over now," he said.

For a moment I felt lightheaded, as though I was about to faint. "What's over?" I finally managed.

His hands came to rest on my temples, the pressure of his fingers uncomfortably tight. "Everything." He smiled. "And nothing."

I took a breath. And when I did, I realized I hadn't been breathing until that exact moment. "I don't understand."

Julius left off stroking my hair to embrace me, "You have completed *Daylaire*," he said softly. "You have been Elevated."

I relaxed into his arms, my head a whirlpool of swirling thoughts and emotions. He held me close to his chest.

"What are you saying?" I asked, too weak to move. "I had cancer."

"Yes," Julius agreed.

"I was dying."

"You were." My husband rested his chin atop my head. "And you should have told me what was going on. About the appointment. The tests." I heard a sullen anger in his voice. "There was so little time."

"Time? Time for what?"

"To initiate the change." Julius shifted beneath my head. "*Daylaire* is a temperamental beast, even at the best of times, particularly where the *lediquire* are concerned. Your physician required a bit of encouragement, but eventually he revealed all. I had known something was wrong, you see. I had smelled it in you.

"So later that evening, after my conversation with Pestler, I placed it in your wine. A few drops of my blood. You might say I 'threw the dice'. Was there enough time? *Daylaire* typically takes a full month. It was a gamble. Which would win out? I considered telling you the truth, about everything, about what I had done, but what if the disease took you first? I didn't want to build your hopes, only to watch them crushed. And while there *are* stories . . . well, let me just say that, within our House, we do not believe in fairy tales about the dead rising from the grave."

"But *I* just died," I protested. "Didn't I?"

"Not true death," he said, kissing me on my brow. "A momentary transition. Nothing more."

I lay there, my brain too full to comprehend my situation. "What happens now?"

He rested his chin on my head. "This will be a difficult time. For both of us, but only for a short while. Our family—now your family—will see to our needs while I educate you and prepare you for your new life. We will make do."

As he spoke, I felt it uncoil inside me, a wave of need as overwhelming as the tide. It submerged me, permeated me.

I turned my face up, looking deeply into Julius's eyes.

Then slapped him. Hard.

And as I watched, the startled expression on his face morphed into something dark. Primeval.

Familiar.

Then, with an almost hysterical laugh, I ran.

But I didn't get very far.

There was a small room, not very far away. He dragged me, his fist in my hair, over its threshold.

And as the door slammed shut, I screamed.

Until he silenced me . . .

<hr />

The passing days blended one into the other. I was allowed no freedom. Though, as Julius had promised, we did not lack for sustenance.

But the less said about that, the better.

He had to secure me, of course. No fur-lined cuffs, or soft nylon ropes. I was far too strong now for such fragile bonds. Once he even nailed me into place.

He pushed me, as he never had before, with horrors unlike any I had ever known. A wire coat hanger, heated a glowing red. Thick jumper cables that sparked with a blue soprano light. A whip threaded with wire.

And knives. So many knives . . .

Then one night, surrounded by oil lamps as pungent as nutmeg, it happened.

I will never forget that moment. Body still torn, lips wet with healing life, I found myself straining against my bonds in a new and different way. And when my husband approached me, some unspeakable object in hand, I spoke the word I had never dreamed would pass my lips.

"*Hyacinth*."

There was nothing left to be said. He looked down on me where I lay, his expression unreadable.

Then he loosened my bonds.

Even as he did, I wanted to scream, to cry out *No!* This was who I was. Was . . .

Things are different now. Not long ago I paused in front of a mirror and, much to my disquiet, saw an unrecognizable figure with her thin limbs, the scar from her heart surgery now long gone, her sapphire eyes staring out of the cold glass as if in contempt for the dim shade in front of her.

My relationship with Julius is different now too. In the days following the first time I had ever made use of my safeword, I was inconsolable and beyond comfort. To pass the time, I found a private place and holed up there with my laptop, which Julius had fetched for me. To divert myself, I went to a place I had not set foot in for many years; *La Chateau.* To mark the occasion I created a new screen name, something innocuous, designed not to draw attention.

At first I simply monitored the chat, speaking with no one. I even blocked my Instant Message capability and ignored comments about the 'lurker'.

So when I saw the name, and experienced the initial unfamiliar sensations, they confused me.

But they didn't stop me.

There were misspelt words in his profile, but the overall intent couldn't have been clearer. "Are you woman enough to control me?"

And I remembered, so very long ago, composing a similarly boisterous challenge of my own.

Even then I couldn't be sure it was the same person, until I checked his profile. Sneadsville, North Carolina. And then there was the screen name.

Freight Train.

So, as I unblocked Instant Messenger, a narrow strip of wood peeling from the wood beneath my nail, I argued with him, the unseen Mordant.

This is a natural progression. Just like Hendrick's stories about the Old Guard. You apprentice yourself for the time when you will no longer bow your head to another, when the roles are switched.

Mordant was wrong. I am not a stranger to the woman in the mirror. And I'm certainly not like those others. The Driver. Mr. Average. Warren.

Warren . . .

No one, and nothing, is taking control of me, control of who and what I am. My memories remain completely intact. I am the same person I have always been. I am not disappearing. I am simply—growing. Changing. Evolving.

It is a completely natural thing.

I am not becoming a stranger to the woman in the mirror. I'm *not*!

I'm not . . .

Epilogue

She drove through cones of cold light falling like cobwebs from the streetlamps overhead, slowing only when she could finally make out the outer edges of Golden Gate Park. Driving past the conservatory, she made her way to the de Young museum, its massive bulk a sullen dreadnaught blocking out a large portion of the sky. Slowing to a walking pace, she scanned the benches.

There.

Maneuvering into an empty parking space, Sunny (whose House name was Sunestra which, in her mother's tongue, meant 'moonless night') got out of her car and crossed over, glancing from side to side to ensure the two of them were alone.

Her target sat erect, knees pressed primly together, a scarlet Hermes pocketbook in her lap. The woman lowered her head briefly in acknowledgment. "Sunny."

She hesitated before sitting down. "Penelope."

Each avoided the eyes of the other, staring instead into the surrounding darkness, alert for movement of any kind.

"I take it," Sunny said, after clearing her throat, "that since you made a point of excluding the 'Mistress' honorific, this is your way of informing me that you will not be welcoming the lash again anytime soon?"

Penelope smiled. "I'm sated for the moment," she said. "But look me up again in another century or two. Of course," she continued, "by that time I may well have flipped my tail yet again, and choose to call in that favor you owe me, that I might educate you in turn."

Sunny's shoulders tightened, then relaxed. "We can speak more of that day when it arrives. Should it ever come."

"You think it shan't?"

"What I *think*," Sunny said, enunciating each word carefully, "is that such hopes might well prove academic long before then."

"Oh ye of little faith," Penelope tossed off. "Mordant came, didn't he?" She smiled again, a tooth-filled motion.

"He might have killed me," Sunny murmured. "And taken the girl for himself, costs be damned."

"But he chose not to. Not if it meant putting the lives of those he cares for at risk," Penelope said, her voice airy with confidence. "As I said before, I know him well."

"Then tell me this," Sunny replied. "What would you have done, had he chosen differently, all those years ago?"

Penelope's smile faded. "Sacrificed his sister, you mean, to save himself?"

"Yes."

The redhead's gaze grew thoughtful. "Then he would have been of no use to us, and I would have slain him on the spot."

"And what would we have done then?"

A shade of the smile returned. "Reconvened the Twelve," Penelope said. "After asking Him where we should go from there."

"You have spoken to Him, then?"

Penelope shook her head. "Not since that last day."

"Has He spoken to you?"

The slim redhead closed her eyes. "Several times."

"And said what?"

"What He always says," Penelope said, brushing a minute speck of dust from her dress. "'Have faith.'"

Sunny made a noise. "I'm sick of hearing about faith."

"Which may be why He speaks to me, and not to you."

"I would rather listen to the *Ylydrim*."

Her companion's hands tightened on the handles of her bag. "So said Argenta," Penelope reminded her companion. "And look what happened to her."

Sunny stared into the lamp overhead, watching the moths as they danced. "I hate fumbling through the darkness, knowing not what I might stumble over next."

Penelope briefly touched her arm. "Your work is done for now."

"That's what I meant," Sunny hissed.

The two sat in silence for several minutes.

"You are confident, then? What he will do next?" Sunny finally said.

A smile returned to Penelope's lips. "Mordant will seek me out to the end of Earth and time," she sang. "I am certain of this." After a pause, she spoke again. "What of Abby?"

"The sickness and the change wrestled one another almost to a standstill," Sunny said with a frown. "*Daylaire* won out in the end. Though it was a close race, to hear Julius tell it."

Penelope nodded. "Good. We will need her in the days to come."

Sunny spoke carefully. "If I did not know better, I would say you had a soft spot for that one."

"Then you do not know me at all," Penelope replied stiffly. "Say rather that she reminds me of—someone I once knew. A long time ago."

"At least there is another who can sense the presence of the *Golgorhim*," Sunny said after a prolonged pause. "Should we lose Mordant in the end."

"That was never his true purpose."

"Oh?" Sunny said. "What, then?"

Penelope tilted her head as an owl hooted in the distance. "I'm not certain. Not yet. *He* says nothing on this matter," Penelope mused. "But in the end, perhaps it is best none of us knows. We are only Twelve, out of all the Houses. Yet even that stretches the boundaries of His comfort. The enemy must suspect nothing, not until it is too late."

"Have you taken precautions?"

Penelope nodded again. "Jester has chosen a second to take his place, should it prove necessary, now that he has seen the truth of things. And after what almost happened, he keeps an even closer eye now on Argenta, though sometimes I wonder . . . ."

"What?" Sunny finally asked.

"Nothing," the pale redhead said, emerging from her contemplation. "What she saw, so long ago—"

"Is what waits for us all," Sunny stated emphatically, "Should Mordant not play his part. Whatever that part is. By the way, what of Abby's father?"

Penelope squared her shoulders. "I shall keep him with me. There is no choice in this. I must always be free to walk through night or day." She turned back to Sunny. "What will House Bremen do now, Visconté?"

The dark woman's brow furrowed. "Go to ground, I think. We were too exposed, even before. Now things are worse. Though in the end there will be nowhere for any of us to hide, should we fail to prevent the coming of Shi'Naith."

"'And after this, the Harvest'," Penelope quoted somberly.

Sunny studied the clouds scuttling overhead. "I still wish we knew more,"

"The more we know, the greater the danger we might reveal some crucial information unwittingly. Stick to your task, and distract yourself with other matters. Time grows short." Penelope stood. "Let me know how to communicate with you, after you and yours have found new lodgings," she said as she walked away.

As Penelope disappeared into the fog-strewn gloom, Sunny stared after her retreating form.

"And what will you do, my friend," she murmured, "if, while leading our young Mordant on a merry chase, you should turn a corner to unexpectedly find him there, waiting for you?"

Rising, she walked back to her car, wondering over the question that for many years had given her no relief. For Argenta had been the strongest of their small circle, a woman who from childhood had conversed on a daily basis with the dead. What unimaginable horror could have devastated such a mind?

Shuddering, the Visconté suppressed her concerns, then got into her vehicle and drove away into the night.

A Dalavar Glossary

Chantsary: The right hand of the Visconti.

Coffeyar: Literally, the walls. A term used to denote the protective secrecy relieved only when solely within the presence of House members.

Coloque: The Separation, the splitting of the Breed into separate clans, which ultimately became the twelve Houses.

Dalavar: The language of the Breed.

Dashlas: New Breed, less than a year old, who are not yet allowed to feed in private.

Golgorhim: Literally, 'Bloodless'.

Hashna: A blood harem of a member of a particular House.

Hashnaid: A female member of a hashna.

Horshno: A male member of a hashna.

Khompah: The informal term for the Lord of a Hashna, as opposed to the more formal Tenegar. Khompah would only be used by a member of one's own Hashna, all others would refer to him or her as Tenegar.

Lediquire: Literally, would refe

Livoire se Andoln: The capital of Andol, a small country on the western-most border of Russia.

Rhejmar: Literally, the Hunger, though it is more commonly used to refer to the potential loss of control due to the Hunger.

Sinégar Ink: An ink effectively invisible to human eyes, but visible to the Breed.

Sireling: A newly created member of the Breed.

Som na Idilque: The Ecstasy. The altered state of mind of a human which occurs during a feeding, marked by heightened euphoria and a willingness to allow one's self to be literally drained of blood during the process.

Topovar: A collective noun used to refer to those who both serve the Breed and who act as sources of blood. But while all Hashnas are Topovar, not all Topovar are members of a Hashna. A Hashna lives under the same roof as its Khompah.

Tenegar: The formal term for the Lord of a Hashna.

Usoleta: A term used to refer collectively to the various member's of a House member's followers. Not the equivalent of family, yet more intimate than 'servants'.

Valyar: One of the twin rulers of a particular House. As opposed to the Visconté, who is the final arbiter over internal House matters, the Valyar is charged with the responsibility of dealing with all external matters, particularly threats to the House. The position has fallen out of favor over time since the Great Reconciliation. Typically, though not always, a male role.

Visconté: One of the twin rulers of a particular House. The Visconté rules the Hearth, and is the final word on all matters dealing with House traditions and etiquette. While the Visconté may not always deal with House business matters, she will always appoint and oversee those who do. Typically, though not always, a female role.

Ylydrim: Literally, 'Outsiders'.

Fourteen Months Later . . .

The first thing you need to understand is that I'm the villain of this tale.

Am I its worst villain?

Tell you what, I'll let you judge that for yourself.

Bud Lancaster and I were sitting around the fire in our canvas chairs, splitting a six pack while slapping at mosquitos. The flames gave the night a lick and a promise, hardly enough to lift the shadows. He finished his beer, then crushed the can before tossing it over his head. "Hand me another, would you Jake?" he said.

I pulled a cold one out of the cooler, a Pabst Blue Ribbon, and pretended to shake it before handing it to him. He'd been drinking that brand ever since I'd known him, back in the days when we warmed a bench together, playing football for the Sneadsville High Vikings while watching 'Freight Train' Collins punch through offensive lines like a nailgun. Me? Well, in my early years I used to drink Guinness, back when I was searching for an identity to hold on to. Supposedly my dad's dad was Irish, and for a while there I bought into the whole culture thing. Now I just drink whatever's on sale. Beer's beer, nothing more to be said, unless you're one of those prissy microbrewery types who thinks you're supposed to like the taste. You don't. That's the point. Or else you'd do nothing but stay drunk.

One of the burning logs let out a loud *pop*, causing Mike to jump. Bud told him to calm the fuck down. Nobody likes a jumpy redneck, especially when he's shouldering an M16.

"They're late," Bud said to me after taking a pull.

I leaned back to look up at the stars. This far out from town, you can sometimes get a nice view, though nothing like what I recall growing up. I remembered the time I saw what had to have been the Milky Way, a streak of stars as thick as dust stretching across the sky. I grabbed a bottle out of the cooler, whatever my fingers touched on first, then rubbed the melting ice off on the grass. "You remember what it's like to be young, don't you Bud?" I drawled. "Those two probably pulled off somewhere to spend a few minutes necking. Or maybe Gypsy's giving Jacob's knob a good polishing."

Bud didn't say anything, just grunted. He and Donna had split up not all that long ago after fifteen years together, so it made sense he was unlikely to be all that sympathetic regarding the fires of young love.

Fifteen years. You'd think after putting that much time in, it wouldn't be worth the effort of starting all over again.

Bud looked over to watch me watching Mike. "You worried?" he asked.

I popped the tab on whatever I was holding in my hand. "What have I got to be worried about?" I drawled.

Bud nodded. "You know, same as I do," he said. "Now Mike, he's an idealist. Which means he actually believes what we're about to do is going to change something in the end."

"And you don't?" I said, taking a cautious sip. Can't be too careful with some of these off brands. You never know what might be floating around inside them.

"No, I don't," Bud said, blowing out a sigh so heavy, he made a motorboat sound with his lips. "It's like this episode of Married With Children I once saw, the one where Al goes looking for some guru and finds Waylon Jennings, who tells Al that they're both dinosaurs, and all there is left for them to do is leave big footprints."

"That's the plan, isn't it?" I said, keeping an eye on Mike while searching for Harvey with my peripheral vision. "Leave a big footprint? So to speak?"

"Yup," Bud said agreeably. "You see, Mike there, he thinks that once the bomb goes off and the shooting starts, folks are gonna rise up to join us."

"Could still happen," I said, peering down the nearby dirt road, a hump of grass and weeds running down its spine

Bud shook his head. "Nuh huh. Pulling a tour of duty apiece in both Gulf wars taught me something." He dipped a pinch of snuff, placing it behind his lower lip. "Them sand niggers have one thing to recommend them which can't be denied, and that is this; they have the courage of their convictions. Those folks live in garbage heaps, so when it comes time to strap a bomb to their chests and take out the enemy—whether it's their own people or our soldiers—they'll do it without hesitation."

"I always heard it's because none of them are getting laid," I commented amiably.

"But here, in this country?" Bud continued, ignoring me. "Conservatives live too high on the hog. Gotten too soft. They don't understand sacrifice." He spit on the ground. "Now Timothy McVeigh, he understood. He knew there was an excellent chance of him getting caught and dying for the cause. But he did it anyway." Bud spit again. "Which is why he's a hero, even though he must have known he'd never be acknowledged as one. At least, not openly.

"But the rest of us? You, me, them boys? We honor his memory," he said, gesturing in Mike's direction. "We keep the faith."

"I heard that."

Bud took another swallow of his beer, then squinted down the road. "That Harvey?"

I followed his stare. The gangly teenager was two-stepping it, his shoulders bouncing with every stride. "Headlights coming," the boy called out.

"Must be them," Bud mused. "Mike, step out of the road, numb nuts, before you getcher ass run over,"

We watched as the distant gleam swelled into a pair of headlights, drawing to a stop nearby. Harvey circled the car while Mike stepped up to the passenger's door to open it for the lady.

Gypsy popped out like a jack-in-the-box, her short bob of hair streaked with a rainbow of colors, her arms sticking straight up over her head, the fingers on both hands shaped into devil horns.

"Woohoo!" she howled as she slipped between Mike and the car, pressing noticeably close to her doorman as she made to head our way. On the other side Jacob got out, nodding politely to Harvey as he started in our direction.

"Let's blow some shit the fuck UP!" Gypsy continued with a grin, arms still in the air.

Bud nodded. "Couldn't agree more," he said with a wink as he formed a pistol with his finger and aimed it her way.

And as he did, Mike pulled his Browning out of its holster, then aimed it at the back of Gypsy's head and fired.

I've seen folks shot before. I've spent a lot of time with the Nightwings overseas, after all. But I'd never seen someone plugged like that, execution style, unless they had a bag over their head. A fountain of blood spurted out of her mouth, like she was vomiting, and I clearly saw one of her teeth fly into the fire.

Jacob turned his head at the sound. "What the fuck . . . ?" he said, just before Harvey wrestled his .32 out of his rear waistband to open up on the base of Jacob's skull. I think he missed the first and third time, but not the second. And that was all it took, really.

I remained in my seat, studying everything as it happened. And when it was all over, I turned to face Bud, who had remained in his chair while staring at me like a hawk.

"How come I didn't know about any of this?" I asked him, fingers resting on the butt of my Glock.

He shrugged. "Was on a strictly need to know basis," he said, getting up to stand over what was left of Gypsy. I joined him.

"Why?" I asked.

He gave a wave that included both of the bodies on the ground. "I've got a cousin who works for the Social Security office. She's a true believer, though, just like us. So when I got suspicious of Miss Hippy Chick here," he said, toeing what was left of Gypsy, "I asked Mabel to do some checking. Neither one of the names these two gave us checked out. Now, that don't necessarily mean they're Feds or Homeland Security or whatnot, but they knew the rules." He spat on the ground again, before turning back to the fire.

I stepped forward, feeling an itch between my shoulders as I did, while looking down at what remained of Gypsy's head.

Then, as I looked down, it moved.

I stood in place, watching her body animate just like one of those zombies in that TV show. She put her hands underneath her chest, then struggled to her knees.

I stepped back. "Um, Bud?"

He turned my way and I could see it by the light of the fire, the way the blood just drained out of his face, as if someone had opened a spigot below his neck.

Mike stood frozen as the girl, her hair clotted with blood and brains, clambered to her feet before turning around. Her face was a crimson mask, and she smiled with the shattered ruins of her mouth.

"BOO!" she said through a rictus grin.

Then, before Mike could move, she swung at him like a kitten batting at a strand of yarn and ripped his throat out.

I kept moving back. And as I stepped behind Bud, I saw him reach down for his shotgun.

Then, just as he locked hands on it, I pulled my Glock out and shoved the barrel against the back of his head. "That's far enough. You just set that ten gauge down now, real gentle like."

He turned his head slightly, looking up at me over the pistol's barrel, gaping at me like he was a goldfish. "Jake? What the fuck are you doing?"

"My job," I said. "Now, you've got a choice. Either you hang on to that fowling piece, in which case I'll be forced to start emptying this clip into the back of your head, or else you put that bad boy down and maybe, just maybe, you'll live to see another sunrise."

He looked at me, then back at Mike and Harvey, still twitching where Gypsy and Jacob were worrying over them like two dogs with a pair of rats. "Maybe?" he choked out.

"Yep. Course now, that depends."

"On what"?

I took a good look at the six inches of belly hanging over his rodeo buckle and shrugged.

"On just how fast you can run."

From the Author

I hope you've enjoyed *The Secret Room*. If you'd like to read more about my thoughts on this book, what's come before, what comes next, you can do so in the Afterword which follows this section.

If you'd like to be kept current on new books in the universe of the Breed Wars, as well as related titles, you can do so by subscribing to my mailing list over at walterspence.com.

We independent authors lack the resources of traditional publishers, so if you like what you've just read and want to spread the word, you can do so by leaving a review at places such as Amazon, Goodreads, etc. And if you chose to do so, thank you so very much. It's readers like yourself who give writers like us the opportunity to expand our readership.

If this is the first novel in the Breed Wars series you've read, you can find the first book in the series, *House of Shadows*, at Amazon.com.

And if you have any questions, or would simply like to share your thoughts, you can email me at walterleespence@yahoo.com.

Afterword

This one came hard.

They say that about sophomore efforts of all kinds. Books, albums, etc. A lifetime's worth of thought and energy often goes into that first effort, leaving comparatively far less time for the second. Not sure that's why this one came tough, though. Maybe because the protagonist was female, and a very unique female at that?

Could be.

But enough of that. Let's talk instead about what comes next.

When I first began the Breed Wars series, I had in mind a background tapestry, each with its own individual panel. A universe, if you will. Think of the parable of the blind men and the elephant, with each person feeling a different part (a leg, an ear, the trunk) and all they know about the elephant is what lies within their grasp.

This universe, the one of The Breed Wars, is like that. There is a background story going on behind the scenes, and each person whose tale is being told is only aware of how their own individual lives are being affected. But with the epilogue of this novel you, the reader, get a backstage glimpse (so to speak) of those folks behind the curtain, allowing you the opportunity denied to the principals, to learn a bit more about what is truly going on.

I've always loved episodic tales. Series like *Lost*, for example, where individual events are spun into the fabric of a much larger story. And like most writers, I enjoy sharing what I enjoy consuming. So here we are.

Fair warning, the next book to come out will not be in the Breed Wars series. The good news? That book already exists in its first draft, so it shouldn't take too terribly long for it to make its way to you. It's titled *The Caballa*, and while not a Breed Wars novel, it takes place (at least partly) in the same universe and is a part of the same overall story. You'll even see a familiar face or two, and meet some you'll likely encounter later on. Following that will be book two of *The Chronicles of Mordant Ember*.

One final note. As a present to my readers, I've begun a serial titled *The Diaries of Penelope Ember*, which I am posting to my website at walterspence. com. These episodes take place during the thirty year period from *House of Shadows* and will be posted once a month or so, with episodes first going out to my newsletter subscribers, and then posted to the website approximately three weeks later.

I want to assure you, my readers, that I will always do my level best to make each of these novels a satisfying experience in and of itself. There is, in my mind, a fine balance to be maintained between teasing the reader with the question of what comes next while simultaneously ending each tale with a satisfying catharsis. Even though such things are rarely the full and complete end of the story . . .

One last thing. Lacking the resources of traditional publishing, we independent authors depend heavily upon our readership. A review of our novels, even if it's just a couple of sentences, means a great deal. I hope you will consider reviewing *The Secret Room* on your favorite site, as well as its predecessor, whether that site be Amazon, Goodreads, or elsewhere.

Thanks for keeping me company on this journey.

Sincerely,
Walter Spence

Acknowledgements

First, I would like to thank the members of the online book club Horror Readers for their constant support and encouragement during the writing of this book. Yes, it took much longer than any of us would have preferred, but the most important thing for me was to produce the best possible work I was capable of. It is my sincere hope that the final product resting in your hands justifies the time it took to get here.

I would especially like to thank those persons who took time out of their busy schedules to act as beta readers: Charlene Cocrane, Shanta Krinsky the Zombie Kitten, Ted Nolan, Ashley Pack, Matthew Pontiff and Kimberly Yerina. Your feedback and encouragement meant a great deal to me.

I'd also like to acknowledge my editor, C. J. Pinard, for her work on the final draft.

In addition, I would like to offer a special thanks to those folks who enjoyed and took the time to rate and/or review this book's predecessor, *House of Shadows*. Reviewing a novel can be intimidating; this I know from personal experience. We authors are typically discouraged from personally responding to reviewers as a rule, so I wanted to take this opportunity to acknowledge you here. As readers we often hear about sophomore novels not living up to their predecessors, so it is my deepest hope this novel has not only met, but exceeded, your expectations.

And lastly, I'd like to give special thanks my wife Debbie who (as I have already noted) has never stopped believing.

Biography

From an early age Walter Spence channeled his fascination with life, the universe and everything into an obsession with the literary and dramatic arts. After years of splitting his attention between writing and acting, he realized a choice had to be made. You are reading the results of that decision now.

After collaborating with fantasy author and Compton Crook Award winner Holly Lisle on *The Devil & Dan Cooley* (book two of the Devil's Point trilogy) he began working on various projects, including a novel called *The Caballa*, which he describes as "*The Lion, the Witch and the Wardrobe*, as written by Stephen King." During this time he was "sideswiped" by the idea for a multi-volume tale of humans and vampires joining in common cause against a mutual enemy, a series he titled *The Breed Wars*. *The Secret Room*, book two in the series, continues this tale.

If you'd like to keep current on future book releases and other noteworthy events, you can sign up for his newsletter at walterspence.com.

And if you have yet to read this novel's predecessor, it can be found at Amazon under the title *House of Shadows*.